CW01658636

THE WOVEN LIE

LIZ HARRIS

HEYWOOD PRESS

Copyright © 2024 by Liz Harris

All rights reserved.

No part of this book may be reproduced in any form or by any electronic or mechanical means, including information storage and retrieval systems, without written permission from the author, except for the use of brief quotations in a book review.

This is a work of fiction.

Cover design by JD Smith Design

1

July 1948

K*entish Town, London*
Late evening

In a cold panic, Violet Hammond stood at her bedroom window and stared out at the darkening night. Had she just made the worst mistake of her life?

As a newly qualified teacher, she'd been looking for a position in a school when she'd come across an advertisement for someone to run a small museum. It had instantly caught her imagination. As she'd read through the details a second time, excitement surged through her at the thought of doing something she'd never previously considered, and she'd promptly resolved to apply for the job.

Before writing her letter of application, she'd managed to get to the museum. It had been well worth the effort as it had given her ideas for what she could put in the letter. To her amazement, she'd been given an interview, and at the end of it, to her even greater amazement, Dr Russell and the two trustees who'd interviewed her had offered her the position.

But now that she was back at home, thinking about the events of the day, had it been rash to accept the responsibility for something she knew nothing about?

What's more, the museum was in a village called Harton, which was in Suffolk. It was some distance from London, so she'd have to leave the home she'd known all twenty-five years of her life and find somewhere to live in Harton.

And she'd be going there on her own!

When her sister Rose had gone to live in Jersey, she'd done so with her husband, Tom. And when her younger sister Iris had gone to live in France, it had been with her husband, Pierre. They'd each had someone with them.

But she wouldn't have anyone at her side.

There'd be no one with whom she could sit and talk at the end of the day, with whom she could share the good moments and the bad, with whom she could discuss any anxieties she might have, like she'd always been used to doing with her parents.

So was she making a gigantic mistake?

She leaned against the cool windowpane and stared across the road at the terraces of three-storey yellow-brick houses, each of them topped by a steeply pitched slate roof, and each with a small front garden, all of them identical to the houses on her side of the road.

It was a view that had come to represent her security.

Years ago she'd taken the view for granted, having seen it almost every night as she was growing up. But after the blackout years, and the many frightening nights when she, Iris and her parents had sought refuge from bombs in the

Anderson shelter that her father had erected in their back garden, she now took note of her surroundings in a way that she'd never done before.

Being able to look nightly through a blackout-free window at the houses opposite had come to be a comforting reminder that the terrible times were past, and that it was safe to look forward to the future.

But had she that day opened the door to a different sort of danger—a danger that could lurk in the unknown?

In two weeks' time she'd have to say goodbye to the view and to Kentish Town, the part of London in which she'd been born, the only place she'd known as home. And she'd be saying goodbye to the parents she loved.

Should she be doing this, she thought in sudden anguish, and turned back to the lamplit room.

Her eyes moved from her iron bed with its floral eiderdown to her oak chest of drawers, on top of which were three neat piles of her college files, to her dressing table where her hairbrush, comb and hand mirror were arranged in front of the swing mirror. Both the hand mirror and hairbrush were backed by an embroidered flower that was protected by glass, a present from her younger sister, Iris, who was a better needlewoman than both her and her sister Rose.

And the most imaginative.

It was Iris who during the war years had introduced a new way of displaying the items for sale in their father's haberdashery shops. It was what Iris had done at that time that had given her ideas for how to encourage more visitors to Harton Museum, and that inspiration had obviously been what got her the job.

She switched her gaze to the bookcases standing against the wall, their shelves filled with books she'd read for pleasure and books she'd needed for her course. Several framed photographs were lined up on one of the bookcases, and she went across to them, picked up the photograph closest to her and stared at it.

Her haberdasher father stood rigidly next to the chair on which her mother sat, both of them unsmiling. It didn't do them justice, she thought, putting the photograph back in its place. No one could have had two kinder parents, and the photographer had completely failed to capture that quality.

The next two photographs were of Rose and Iris with their families. Unlike her parents, they were all smiling broadly at the camera.

She took a step back and looked thoughtfully at the faces of her sisters.

They, too, had taken a giant leap into the unknown. When Rose had gone to Jersey and Iris to France, both of them with a husband they hardly knew, they'd taken a risk on everything working out well with their husbands and that they'd enjoy living elsewhere.

Their courage had paid off, and both seemed happy in their new, very different lives.

And now she, too, was about to do something different with her life.

It had worked out well for them, so why wouldn't it work out for her?

Of course it would!

It was time she stopped agonising about the decision she'd made, she scolded herself, and started to see it for the adventure it was.

For that's what it was going to be—a very exciting adventure!

Enthusiasm stirred within her, just as it had done when

she'd first seen the advertisement. Yes, she was about to take a very different path from the one she'd been working towards for so many years, but that was because it was the right thing for her to do at that time.

If she'd become a history teacher immediately after leaving college, she'd have ended up spending her whole life in a school, first as a pupil, then as a wartime replacement for teachers who'd gone off to fight, then in the teacher's training college and finally as a teacher herself.

From the moment she'd seen the Harton advertisement, she'd known that she wanted to experience something different. But it had to be something that would give her a real challenge, and she'd instantly realised that the museum would offer her that.

As for going to Suffolk alone, she was unlikely to be without someone to talk to for long. She was sure to make new friends there. For a start, the people she'd met after her interview had gone out of their way to be welcoming and had seemed really pleasant.

Dr Russell, the man who'd had to step down from running the museum, couldn't have been more helpful. Apparently, he'd had to give up his position because his workload as a GP had become enormous. The new free health service had taken over all the hospital beds, nurses and consultants, and much of the work involved in putting everything under one umbrella for the first time had fallen on to the shoulders of GPs, he'd told her as he'd driven her to the station after the interview, which had been held at the museum.

But busy though he was, he'd suggested that if she was prepared for the amount of travel she'd again have to do, she could go to Harton the following Monday and take a closer look at the museum with him. He'd said that he would then show her the office, and after that take her to see a small house she could rent for a modest sum. No one could have been more welcoming.

And nor could the woman she'd met after the interview.

She hadn't yet met the girl who did any typing there and helped in the galleries and on the reception desk, but she'd met the main assistant, an older woman called Gladys Wilson. Apparently, Gladys had worked there for years. She'd come across as extremely pleasant, and had insisted that Violet ask her for help if she got stuck.

No one could have had a better introduction to a job than the welcome given her by both Dr Russell and Gladys Wilson.

And another reason why she shouldn't worry was that she'd been given a six-month probation period. If she didn't like the job, or they didn't think her work satisfactory, or if she didn't like living in a small village despite its proximity to the town of Bury St Edmunds, she could always leave the museum and go into teaching.

So, all in all, she was confident she'd made the right decision, and smiling to herself, she went across to her bed, climbed under the eiderdown, and secure in the warmth of the welcome shown to her by Dr Russell and Gladys Wilson, she drifted into sleep.

Bury St Edmunds, earlier that day

Bending over the small oak table in front of him, Stanley Patterson stopped what he was doing and glanced up at Gladys Wilson, who was pacing up and down the middle of the shop.

'Do sit down, Gladys,' he said. 'You're making me nervous.'

He resumed applying a light coat of beeswax to the surface of the oak table.

Gladys went and sat on the wheelback chair closest to her.

'I'm so angry, Stan!' she exclaimed.

'I rather gathered that,' he said mildly, and continued polishing the table.

'That job should've been mine. I've been there for years. Who runs the museum every time Edward gets delayed in his surgery, or is too busy to stop what he's doing? Me. And that's all the thanks I get!'

He made an indistinguishable sound.

'To overlook me like that, it's unforgivable!' she raged. 'And to appoint a chit of a girl who's no experience at all! They'll expect me to tell her what to do, I suppose. Well, I won't. Let Miss Violet—' she said the name with venom, 'find her own way through the maze.'

Shaking with anger, she glared at him.

He straightened up, put the rag and beeswax in a box on the shelf behind him and went and sat opposite her in an armchair upholstered in needlepoint fabric.

'If that's how you want to play it,' he said, folding his arms and stretching out his legs.

'How else can I play it?' she retorted bitterly.

Stanley shrugged his shoulders. 'She's inexperienced, you say?'

'Apparently she came and had a look at the museum before applying for the job, but she's never run one.'

'That means she's unlikely to pick up on anything she shouldn't,' he remarked. 'And she'll be too busy, anyway, beavering away at an unfamiliar job to notice anything untoward going on.'

'Don't you believe it!' Gladys snapped. 'Edward couldn't stress her energy enough. He went on and on about her ideas for displays, how she planned to give the museum a new look, and how she was going to bring in groups of schoolchildren. Changes cause disruption, and they make people look closely at things they've never looked at before. I don't think either of us would like to see that happen.'

'So, what d'you want to do, then?' he asked. 'D'you want to shut down our business? We could, you know. Patterson's Antiques is strong at the moment, so what we make is an extra for me, and as we've already done pretty well for ourselves, it's been a very good extra. But if you feel you've had sufficient, we don't have to continue.'

'Of course I don't want to stop,' she said icily.

He grinned at her. 'I rather thought you might say that.'

'The museum's only unwittingly giving me what I'm due. They don't come close to paying me what I deserve. And also there's Eric to consider. I don't think either of us would want to incur his wrath. Yes, I remove the artefacts and you find the buyer for the original, but it's Eric who makes the copy. He's made a lot out of this, and he has a mean temper.'

'But only one of us is in a position to make the perceived threat go away,' Stanley said smoothly.

'What *are* you talking about?' she asked irritably.

'It's very simple, Gladys. If you don't want the new woman there, get rid of her. You're perfectly placed to make that happen. After all, who will Miss Violet turn to when she doesn't know what to do? Why you, of course.'

Frowning, she stared intently at him. Then her brow cleared and her thin lips curved into a smile.

'You're absolutely right, Stan. She will.'

2

H*arton, Suffolk*
The following afternoon

HAVING LOOSENED his tie and removed his suit jacket as he left the museum, Dr Edward Russell slung the jacket over his shoulder, turned left into the high street and started walking slowly past Museum Road, the narrow road that led up from the high street into the marketplace.

Pausing on the other side of Museum Road, he stood for a moment looking at the ivy-covered stone cottage that stood on the corner of Museum Road and High Street, the cottage that was to be Violet Hammond's home.

Then he continued up the high street, past the bus stop from Bury St Edmunds and past the cluster of ash trees and sycamores on the other side of the road, where their leaves were catching the last rays of the late afternoon sun.

A little way ahead of him, High Street curved to the left

and became Church Road. The village hall stood on the opposite side of the road at the curve, its windows reflecting the sun, its grey stone walls tinged with honey.

The sight of the village hall always filled him with pleasure as it meant that he was almost home, his house being only a short distance up Church Road from his surgery.

But not today.

A gnawing sense of worry was outweighing any feeling of pleasure.

His anxiety wasn't about any of his patients. Martin was going to do any house calls that came in, so there was no need for him to do any home visits that evening. And it wasn't just that he'd had a bad night's sleep, followed by a tiring day in which he'd done his morning and afternoon surgeries and had then gone to the museum to sort out some of his files.

It was more than that.

He reached the curve in the road, crossed over and went up to the noticeboard at the foot of the drive that led to the village hall. Seeing that there were no new notices, he strolled up the drive towards the hall and turned into the large garden to the left of the building.

Lengthening shadows were reaching out from the corners of the garden but they had yet to consume all the vivid green of the grass. And the flowers in the central plot that had been lovingly cultivated by the gardening committee were still a radiant mass of violet, pale blue and lilac-tinged pink.

He went and sat on the nearest wooden bench, leaned back, closed his eyes and for a moment or two let the birdsong that soared from the thicket of horse chestnut trees at the back of the garden wash over him.

Had he done the right thing, he wondered.

He opened his eyes and straightened up.

It had certainly seemed the correct decision the day before when, carried away on a wave of excitement, he hadn't hesitated to suggest to his fellow trustees that they appoint Violet Hammond to take over the running of the museum. But now he wasn't so sure. Should he perhaps have slept on it, and in the clear light of a new day, confirmed to himself that in appointing her they'd be doing the best thing for the museum?

It wasn't that she wouldn't have the ability to do the job —she'd got a Teacher's Certificate validated by the University of London, so she'd be eminently capable. It was that despite her being completely inexperienced in running a museum, he had chosen Violet Hammond over Gladys, who'd worked in the museum for years, and whose work was faultless.

It was the minute he'd seen the surprise in Gladys's eyes when he'd taken her aside and told her that they were giving the job to Violet Hammond, surprise swiftly followed by acute misery, and then a fleeting touch of alarm, fuelled no doubt by concern for the future of the museum, that in a sudden chill moment, the knowledge that he'd made a decision based purely on instinct had sent a wave of alarm through him.

Now it was too late to do anything about it.

All he could hope for was that, if he'd made a mistake, Gladys would be on hand to prevent anything dire from happening. But as he was the one who'd taken a chance in giving Violet Hammond the position, he, too, must be equally alert.

He would just have to go into the museum more

frequently than he'd intended, he decided. He hadn't wanted to do that, being inundated with work for the new health scheme, but he owed it to the museum to ensure that his impetuous decision didn't result in any damage. It was his responsibility so he couldn't in all fairness stand back and leave everything to Gladys.

And furthermore, if employing Violet Hammond *did* turn out to be a mistake, and he wanted to terminate her appointment ahead of her six months' probation, they were both civilised people and they could talk about it and hopefully come to an equitable agreement about her leaving.

He got up from the bench.

He'd done sufficient worrying for one day. As there was nothing he could do about the decision that had been made, there was nothing to be gained by getting into a state about what might or might not happen, and he'd do well to get back home.

What he badly needed now was to empty his mind over a quiet drink in the peace of his house.

He picked up his jacket, went down the drive, turned right and walked up Church Road, past the surgery, up to the next road on the right, on the corner of which stood his house.

Closing the front door behind him, he hung his jacket on the mahogany coat stand just inside the wood-panelled entrance hall, crossed over to the sitting room, opened the door and went into the room.

He stopped abruptly.

His fiancée Jean Forbes was sitting in one of the armchairs, her district nurse cap on the table next to her.

His heart sank.

She looked up from the book she was reading and smiled at him.

'Mavis let me in and suggested I wait for you in here,' she said brightly. 'You don't mind, do you?'

'Of course not,' he said, swallowing his disappointment at not having the solitary evening he'd wanted. 'It'll save me from walking up to you later to tell you what happened,' he added, feeling obliged to embellish his first lie with a second.

'That's good because I'm dying to hear how the interviews went yesterday. Not that they won't have gone well.' Jean closed the book, placed it on the occasional table next to her and looked at him expectantly.

'I think we made a good appointment,' he said, sitting down on the sofa opposite her.

'I'm sure you did, darling.' She got up, went across to the sofa, sat down next to him and rested her head against his shoulder. 'Gladys knows the place inside out, so you can now forget about the museum and get on with your practice. She's an excellent administrator. Nothing will change.'

'That's exactly the problem, and that's why we didn't appoint her.'

'You didn't?' she exclaimed. Sitting upright, she turned and stared at him in surprise. 'Why not?'

He gave a slight shrug. 'It's hard to say. When I set off yesterday morning, I thought we'd appoint Gladys. As you said, I knew the museum would be in safe hands. And then we didn't appoint her. I almost don't know why,' he said, shaking his head, 'but we ended up giving the job to the youngest candidate, the young woman Violet Hammond.'

'You must know why,' Jean said with a trace of irritation.

He shrugged. 'All I can say is, she seemed very pleasant and very capable.'

'So's Gladys very capable. It's a fact. She doesn't just seem it. She's run the place by herself often enough and there isn't a thing she doesn't know about the management of the museum. She won't be pleased,' Jean said. 'She was certain you'd appoint her.'

'That's true,' he admitted. 'And even though I felt excited when I read Violet Hammond's letter of application, as I told you at the time, I still thought it most likely that Gladys would take over from me.'

'So what happened?'

'When I interviewed Violet, and heard her plans for the museum, I glimpsed the life she could breathe into it, and I suddenly questioned whether we *should* be continuing as we've always done, or if we should aim to be more adventurous than that. And on the spur of the moment I suggested to the others that we expand our horizons, and there and then we appointed Violet Hammond.'

'Has she any experience of working in a museum?' Jean asked.

'Not really,' he said ruefully. 'She trained to be a teacher, and she's got an interest in history. But with that background she'll have a natural interest in the museum, and I'm sure she'll soon pick up what she needs to know. After all, I'm a doctor. I got the job of running the museum on the strength of my position in the community alone, not on any actual experience, and I managed.'

Jean frowned. 'But you'd known the museum all your life. Your father was a keen collector and had always taken an interest in the place, and indeed had run it for a time. So you weren't the complete novice that Violet Hammond sounds. How does she or you know whether the ideas she's come up with will work in practice? Why would you risk being stuck with an inexperienced manager rather than the able Gladys Wilson?'

'That's what I've been asking myself all afternoon. I just hope I'm not expecting too much from Miss Hammond.'

She hesitated. 'Is she very pretty?'

He glanced at her, annoyed. 'I suppose you could say she is. But this isn't about the way she looks, it's about the way she thinks. And it's about what the museum needs. It needs a good shake-up, and that's what Violet Hammond will bring to it.'

Her smile didn't quite reach her eyes. 'You didn't say that the museum needed a good shake-up when I saw you two nights ago. On the contrary, you were anxious for things to run as smoothly as possible in the future as you're going to be pretty busy.'

'When I said that,' he said, trying to hide his irritation at having his anxiety reopened and deepened, 'I was thinking about what was best for me, not for the museum. I've made an appointment in the interests of the museum, which will move it forward. I'm sure that's what the trustees expected me to do when they asked me to take the lead in finding my replacement.'

'Well, you know what you're doing, darling,' she said. 'And of course, Gladys will still be there, and she'll help Miss Hammond.'

'That's right,' he said. 'And Miss Hammond's on probation,' he added.

'That could prove fortunate.' She put her head on his shoulder again. 'Since we're talking about moving things forward,' she murmured, 'perhaps we should set a date for our wedding? After all, we've been engaged for a year and a half.'

'And we will.' He slid his arm around her shoulders. 'I know that the extra work caused by the health service arrangements has rather dominated the past few months, and I'm sorry about that. As soon as things have settled down, we'll fix a date. I won't leave it much longer. For the moment, though, shall I make us a gin and tonic? I don't know about you, but I could certainly use one.'

'Good idea, darling,' she said. 'I feel like something a little stronger than Mavis's tea.'

3

H*arton,*
The following Monday

VIOLET LEANED BACK, tilted her face to the sun and sighed with pleasure. Then she straightened up and glanced at the countryside that lay to the right of the worn wooden table at which she and Dr Edward Russell were sitting.

Cotton-wool clouds were drifting across the clear blue sky and the late morning sunshine was sheening an undulating patchwork of fields in various hues of green and yellow, all of them bordered by a thin dark line of green, that gently rolled away from the pub into the distance.

'This is blissful,' she said contentedly, and she looked back at Edward.

He smiled at the obvious happiness of the pretty woman opposite him, her shoulder-length chestnut hair shining in the sun and her large hazel eyes framed by long dark lashes.

He ran his fingers through his dark brown hair and

cleared his throat. 'It's often quite blowy up here,' he said, 'but today it's quite still.'

'Then it's my lucky day,' she said with a laugh. 'I left my hair loose, and it would've gone mad if there'd been any wind.'

She glanced to her left at the warm grey stone façade of the inn, then her gaze moved down to the sign that hung from a post at the corner of the small garden in front of the pub.

'Is this called the Brown Hare Inn because of the number of hares in the area, Dr Russell?' she asked, turning back to the food that had just been put on their table. 'Mind you, I'm not sure I'd know a hare from a rabbit,' she added, breaking off a piece of the bread on her plate and balancing a chunk of cheese on it.

'I think we can drop the Dr Russell—Edward will do,' he said with a smile. 'And perhaps you wouldn't mind me calling you Violet on occasions that are more social than work.'

She blushed. 'Of course not.'

'The difference between the two is quite easy,' he continued. 'A hare's golden brown, with a pale belly and white tail. It's bigger than a rabbit and has longer legs. Its ears, too, are longer, and they've got distinctive black tips. This is the sort of area hares like—open farmland, grass and hedgerows. Particularly hedgerows. You've probably noticed that fields in Suffolk tend to be separated by hedgerows.'

'Yes, I have. But why not have a fence or a stone wall? That's what I've seen in most of the places I've been to. Admittedly I've not been to many, but I've seen pictures.'

'Perhaps the best reason is that hedgerows look so lovely, and they give off a wonderful aroma. If you look closely at them, you'll see that they're full of hawthorn and wild roses, and crab apples and wild plums, not to mention holly, which is used for Christmas decorations. With so many flowers in the hedgerows, the fields are surrounded by lovely blossom in spring.'

'I'm looking forward to the spring, then.'

'But it's not just their appearance. Hedgerows are good for cattle. They provide shade in summer, and protect them against the cold wind in winter. Also they give a home to birds, and help them survive the winter. That's because hedgerows are full of the sorts of things that birds live on, such as hips, haws, seeds and berries.'

'That's so interesting,' she said.

'As for the name of the inn, yes, there are lots of brown hares in the area. Admittedly, there are plenty of other mammals, too, but there's another possible reason behind the name.'

'What's that?' she asked, cutting another piece of cheese.

'It's said that many years ago, just after the owner bought the pub, a local farmer rolled up and gave him a newborn hare to look after. The farmer had accidentally killed the mother with his tractor. The pub owner took in the hare and called it Harry.'

'Harry!' she exclaimed, and burst out laughing.

Edward grinned. 'That's right. The owner gave Harry a large wooden beer crate to sleep in. But hares are nocturnal, and as Harry got bigger, the noise he made at night started keeping the family awake. In the end, the man decided to free Harry, and he took him and left him in a distant field. But he swore afterwards that Harry used to return in the evenings, sit in the field and stare towards the pub. Harry never forgot him, the pub owner said, and he would never forget Harry. Hence the name.'

She stared at him, then laughed.

Two clear blue eyes looked back at her in amusement.

'I can't imagine a better reason for giving a pub a name,' she said lightly. 'I shall always think of it as Harry's Inn.'

'It's such an unusual story that it just might be true,' Edward said, smiling. 'But another possible reason is that Harton, the name of the village, comes from the Anglo-Saxon words for hare, which is *hara*, and farm, which is *ton*.'

'So we live in hare's farm!' she exclaimed, and she laughed again.

He nodded. 'That's right.' He helped himself to a pickled onion from the bowl in the middle of the table. 'It's a real treat to be able to relax with a bit of bread. What good luck that bread rationing ended today,' he said. 'It's felt a long two years since the rain destroyed the wheat crop and they started rationing bread and flour again.'

'It's been good for the waistline, though,' Violet said.

'I don't think you need to worry about that.'

She blushed again, and he quickly took a second pickled onion.

'So what d'you think of the area so far?' he asked after a minute or two. 'This isn't considered the prettiest part of Suffolk. Bury St Edmunds is a lovely market town, of course—or Beodricsworth as it was known in Saxon times—but as for the surrounding countryside, although the land isn't completely flat, it doesn't have the sweeping hills of further south, or the wonderful heathland near the coast.'

'I can't compare this with anywhere else in Suffolk as I don't know the rest of the county, but I think it's lovely round here.' She indicated the fields behind her. 'I come from Kentish Town, which I like very much, but it couldn't be called pretty by even the most enthusiastic resident. It has life and vibrancy, but it's bustling with people and traffic and shops and dust and it's far from peaceful. I love the peace and quiet around here.'

'But will it be too quiet for you, do you think? Except for the start and end of the school day, and the market on Saturdays, the village is fairly tranquil,' he went on. 'You're young, and young people require life and activity, if my aged mind recalls correctly what I felt at your age.'

'You're not that old,' she said hastily.

'Ouch!' he said in amusement. 'The implication in those few words is depressing.'

She smiled at him across the table. 'I don't think I'll find it too quiet,' she said. 'It's going to be wonderful living in a lovely place that doesn't hold any associations of war for me. Now that the war's behind us, I don't want to be reminded of it. I know people are now talking of a Cold War, but that isn't as chilling.' She burst out laughing. 'I'd like to say that was a deliberate pun, but I can't.'

He grinned at her. 'I did wonder.'

'I meant there's no large-scale fighting directly between the two big powers, and I doubt there ever will be. As a country we've a lot to be grateful for, and on a personal level, getting this job is what I'm grateful for.'

'I'm glad you feel that way.' He hesitated. 'I'm still mildly concerned that you might get bored here, though. There's not a lot of the sort of activity I imagine you'll want.'

'Then you imagine incorrectly. As you'll have heard me say at my interview, I'm a serious sort of person. I enjoy quiet evenings with a book. Historical stories are my favourite. Working in a museum surrounded by daily reminders of our past is the answer to a dream I didn't know I had.'

'I'm somewhat relieved to hear that. It's what came across in your letter of application and also in your interview. I just hoped you hadn't changed your mind, having had time to think about it and having seen the village.'

'I haven't,' she said firmly.

'And of course, it's always possible that I've made living in Harton sound duller than it is. We're only three miles from Bury, after all, and there's a cinema there and theatre, and also dances. There's a good bus service to take you there. Lucy will tell you that. She lives in Bury and comes in by bus every day. Also, there are dances in places other than Bury. The villages round here put on dances every so often and people from the neighbouring villages go to them.'

He stopped talking and gave an awkward laugh. 'I'm afraid I must sound like a schoolteacher to you, the way I'm going on.'

'Not at all,' she said. 'It's all really interesting. I'm sure I'm going to enjoy living here. For a start, I love the house I'll be renting. I can't believe how lucky I've been. It's got character, but it's also got hot and cold running water in both the kitchen and the bathroom. And the bathroom's inside! Not all old houses offer that.'

'I know the house is small, but are you sure there's nothing you'd like to see in it that wasn't there?'

She shook her head. 'Not a thing. It seems to have everything.'

'Well, when you've started living there, if you find you're missing anything, just let me know.'

'Thank you. Everyone's been very kind. When I spoke to Miss Wilson again this morning, she couldn't have been more helpful. She said I must call on her if I have any problems. And Lucy seems really pleasant.'

She took a sip of her beer and pulled a face.

'I take it you're not a beer drinker,' he said, amused.

'Leave it if you want. I'm curious, though, as to why you asked for one.'

'Because you did,' she said, and gave an awkward laugh. 'I didn't know what to order so I copied you. At college, I had a beer on occasions when the others did. I didn't really like it but I thought I might've got used to it by now. Also, I've read about Greene King and their brewery in the town, and how popular beer is here. I wanted to fit in now that I'll be living here.'

'You'll fit in, I'm sure, and you won't need beer to make that happen.'

'I hope you're right,' she said, sliding the glass further away from her. 'D'you live in Harton or Bury?'

'In Harton. I live very close to the surgery. My partner, Martin Lloyd, lives above the surgery. It's just as well we don't have far to travel as we're both going to be even busier than usual in the coming months. With the Bury hospital signed up to the National Health Service, and with people choosing their own GP and signing up to the practice they want, we'll have our work cut out. We'll now be the ones who access hospitals, specialist care and sickness benefit. Checking the applications for health care alone is going to take up a huge amount of time.'

'It'll be more difficult, won't it, as there's a shortage of nurses and district nurses, isn't there? I read that in the newspaper.'

He shook his head. 'That was certainly true a short time ago, but the recent hike in wages has had the desired effect. I fear there'll still be a degree of chaos for a while, though. It was difficult enough in the past to give sufficient time to the museum so I've always had to lean heavily on Gladys's goodwill. But now it'll be completely impossible to do anything outside my practice.'

'It must be exciting, though, to be part of such a change,' Violet said. 'It's hard to believe that people won't have to pay for their medical care or dentistry any longer.'

He nodded. 'That's right. I always look forward to hearing what Jean has to say about how things are going in the hospital.'

'Is Jean a nurse?'

He hesitated a moment.

'She's the district nurse attached to our surgery,' he replied. 'She trained as a nurse at the Queen's Nursing Institute, then got a midwifery qualification so she can provide the expectant mother with personal service, a home delivery and continuous care. But her range of services, too, are now expanding. It's no longer just care in the home, but also in the wider community, which means school nursing, health visiting and health education. She's also got to keep tabs on our patients who end up in hospital.'

'That does sound a lot to do.'

'It is, but fortunately she loves the work. As for now, though,' he said briskly, 'if you've had enough to eat, I suggest I get you back to the station.'

Bury St Edmunds

Frowning, Edward walked slowly away from the station that lay on the outskirts of Bury St Edmunds and wondered why he hadn't told Violet that Jean was not only his and Martin's district nurse, but also his fiancée.

It must be that he hadn't wanted to exchange personal details with her, he decided. Something within him must have realised that it would be better to keep things on a purely business level. Violet didn't need to know he was engaged, any more than he needed to know if she had a fiancé or was walking out with someone.

After all, they weren't even work colleagues.

Her inexperience meant that he'd have to pop into the museum more frequently than he'd intended, which would be a kindness to her, but it didn't necessitate him knowing whether or not she had a man in her life.

Not that she did, he was pretty sure. The things she'd said that day had made that clear.

He reached his Austin Sixteen and got in. For a few minutes he stared back at the station, then with a sigh he inserted the ignition key and started the car.

As she sat in the train staring through a grubby window at the fields and towns they were racing past, she wondered if Dr Russell was married—or rather, if Edward was married, as he'd suggested she call him.

When she'd asked about the woman he'd mentioned, Jean, she'd assumed that Jean was Edward's fiancée, and she'd been astounded by how much she already disliked her, even though she'd never met her.

Her instant aversion to Jean, and the fact that she'd found herself holding her breath as she'd waited for Edward's reply, had taken her quite by surprise.

When she'd heard that Jean was his district nurse, she'd been able to breathe again. If Jean had been anything more to him than that, he would have described her differently.

He was sure to be with someone else, although he hadn't mentioned it.

Someone like Edward, who was really good-looking, who was tall and broad-shouldered, comfortably off, with a good career, who was interesting and seemed very pleasant

—the ideal man, in fact—was bound to have been captured long ago. If he wasn't already married, he'd be engaged.

But there'd have been no reason for him to volunteer information about his private life, and she didn't even know why she was thinking about it. She wasn't looking for a husband. It was the job she was interested in, not a man.

The train slowed.

Leaning against the window to look ahead, she saw that they were approaching a station. Glancing to her right she saw a field of cows grazing in the sun. To her a cow was a cow, but she was sure that Edward would know one kind of cow from another.

Not that she would ask him.

She must be wary of thinking about him in any way at all.

By the time she moved into her little house a week on Sunday, ready to start the job on the Monday, she must have emptied her head of all thoughts of Edward, and when she met him, she must keep solely to topics relating to the job. If she wanted to know about the different kinds of cows there were, she'd look it up in an encyclopaedia. She wasn't going to give Edward another thought.

She looked at her watch, and wondered what he'd be doing that evening. Then she mentally kicked herself at feeling so excited at the thought of seeing him again in less than two weeks' time.

4

H*arton,*
Later that evening

Martin Lloyd put a snifter of brandy on the occasional table next to Edward, and then sat down on the other side of the fireplace.

Leaning back in his armchair, Edward took a sip of his brandy, stretched out his legs and smiled broadly at Martin. 'I hope you don't mind me stopping by like this, Martin,' he said, 'but I wanted to tell you that after I'd taken Miss Hammond back to the station, I called in on Mrs Waters.'

'So she's back from the sanatorium, is she?' Martin remarked in surprise.

'Indeed she is. They thought her well enough to complete her recovery at home and she returned yesterday. I thought I'd better check that she was comfortable and had everything she needed. In future, of course, it'll be Jean who visits her, and Jean who arranges her appointments at the chest clinic.'

'Lucky for Mrs Waters that they caught the tuberculosis early and didn't have to remove her lung or part of it.'

Edward nodded. 'Absolutely. Anyway, I was pretty sure you'd have finished any house calls by now, so I thought I'd come up and let you know I'd seen her.'

'I'm glad you did,' Martin said. 'We've not really seen each other in the past week, and I've been keen to hear how the last few days have gone. I'm not referring to the riveting news about Mrs Waters, you understand,' he added with amusement.

'They've gone very well, I'd say,' Edward said with an air of satisfaction.

'Which bit?' Martin asked drily. 'Facing the formidable Gladys after the interviews and having to endure her silent reproach, or your tasks for today, namely showing Miss Hammond around the house that'll be hers while she's here, and being obliged to lunch with her afterwards?'

Edward laughed. 'Yes, Gladys wasn't the happiest of people. I stood before her with my head bowed, like a recalcitrant schoolboy. The right words came out of her mouth, and she assured me she wouldn't hesitate to help Miss Hammond find her way round the museum and become familiar with its daily routine and so on, but whenever I dared to raise my eyes to her face, I saw great hurt and disappointment.'

'Gladys wasn't the only person who thought she'd get the job—everyone else in the village did, too. She's not going to like being the object of their unspoken pity.'

Edward shrugged. 'I realise that. But keeping a person happy shouldn't be top of the list of considerations when making an appointment. While it's true that she knows everything there is to know about the museum, it's also true that she's not the warmest of people. If I'm honest, I respect her ability, but I don't much like her as a person.'

Martin nodded. 'I'm with you there. I don't think many people do. But as you say, she's efficient and her work is always satisfactory.'

'Well, now we have a chance to do better than that,' Edward said. 'Miss Hammond, or Violet, which she said I can use, seems very intelligent, and with her enthusiasm for the museum and her ideas, and her very pleasant manner, I'm confident things will move up from merely being satisfactory into something very much better.' He finished his brandy and sat back, smiling to himself.

Martin picked up the bottle of brandy from the table next to him, got up, went across to Edward and filled his glass. Returning to his chair, he poured himself a little more brandy, and sat back down.

'Your air of contentment suggests that you enjoyed your lunch with Miss Hammond,' he remarked as he settled himself comfortably again. 'I imagine she's quite pretty as well as being both intelligent and amiable.'

Edward took a sip of his drink. 'You and Jean must have been reading the same book,' he remarked, returning his glass to the table. 'She, too, asked about Violet's looks. She *is* good-looking, I admit, very much so. But my satisfaction with her appointment is solely because I think she'll be excellent for the museum.'

'I'm sure it is,' Martin said, exaggerating a soothing tone of voice. 'But perhaps you should be careful to tone down your enthusiasm when mentioning her to Jean,' he added. 'The way you spoke about Miss Hammond just now could give Jean some cause for alarm.'

'Jean's no reason to worry,' Edward said dismissively.

'She knows that all I care about is the museum. Apart from her, that is.' He frowned thoughtfully. 'But I'll admit you've made me think, Martin. Maybe I *have* been a little too fulsome in my praise of Violet,' he said slowly. 'Although Jean couldn't possibly have any reason to worry—for a start, Violet's ten years younger than I am—it would explain her sudden desire for us to fix a date for our wedding.'

'It's not that surprising, is it, or even that sudden? You've been engaged for almost two years!'

'It's even longer than that if you count our engagement from when, aged seven, I proposed to Jean in the school playground and she accepted.'

Both laughed.

'In normal circumstances, I'd agree that we'd been officially engaged for long enough and should set a date for the wedding,' Edward continued. 'But look at the past few years! The circumstances in which we found ourselves were hardly normal.'

'That's true. We're obviously still feeling the effects of the second great war.'

'But it's not just the war, is it?' Edward retorted. 'Labour's landslide victory in 1945 meant that it was only a matter of time before we had a health service that was free to everyone at the point of delivery. So although it may not have been a surprise when we got the National Health Service Act in 1946, the past two years, getting everything into place before the Act took effect, haven't been easy.'

Martin nodded. 'I agree. Obviously, such a massive change created a lot of work, especially for GPs like us, but it hasn't stopped other people from getting married, has it? There was a wedding in Harton only last week. We were there, if you recall.'

'Ah, but the groom wasn't a doctor! I can't imagine any

doctor being able to find the time to think about a wedding at the moment. Jean understands that.'

'If she's asked you to fix a date, it suggests that her understanding is running out,' Martin said warmly. 'I suspect your fulsome praise of Miss Hammond might partly be responsible for that.' He paused to take a sip of his drink. 'But whatever the reason, I assume you're now thumbing the pages of your diary, searching for a suitable date. Am I correct?'

'You're not, I'm afraid.'

Martin raised his eyebrows in surprise. 'Why not? You love Jean, so why the reticence to do as she's asked? It isn't unreasonable, after all. If you're waiting for a lengthy space in your diary, you'll have a long wait. We're going to have even more work in the future, not less.'

Edward looked up at the ceiling, then back at Martin. 'Reticence is the wrong word. It implies that I've reservations about marrying Jean, and I haven't. I've known her virtually all my life and we've been the best of friends since the day we met at school. She's a lovely person, and I can't imagine not being with her for the rest of my life.'

'And not only is she really pleasant, but she's beautiful, too, which makes you a very lucky man,' Martin said. 'Some people might think that no matter how busy you are you now owe it to Jean to set a date and thereby give her peace of mind.'

He picked up his glass and looked at Edward, his expression serious. 'It's easy to be dazzled by something new, Edward. If Jean's pushing for a wedding date, that's what she'll fear could happen. And if, despite her request, you're still hesitating to come up with some suggestions, she could feel that, even after so short a time, you're already in Miss

Hammond's thrall. After all, you speak so warmly about her, and Jean's only human.'

'My reluctance to fix a date has nothing to do with Violet,' Edward said firmly. 'It's because so much has been happening, and still is. Like everything else, weddings demand time and work. As soon as you've set the date, you're involved in making decisions about goodness knows what. I'm afraid Jean will have to be patient for a little longer.'

He took a sip of his drink.

'Don't think I don't feel badly about postponing the decision, because I do,' he added. 'I hate upsetting Jean.'

'Then perhaps you should've appointed Gladys in your place, or at the very least, been more restrained in your comments about Miss Hammond,' Martin said drily. 'You've only got yourself to blame for the position you're now in.'

Edward gave a loud sigh. 'I hate to say it, but you're absolutely right. We'll fix a date the next time I see her. But the wedding will have to take place next year. This year's too busy.'

Martin smiled. 'I'm sure just having a date will make her extremely happy. Apart from anything else, she's bound to feel very ready to leave her parents, who are still somewhat stuck in the past, in a time when men retired to their library at the end of the meal and left the women alone. Jean must be looking forward to running a home of her own.'

Edward gave Martin a wry smile. 'To turn the conversation to you, Martin, and move it away from me, as I'm now feeling somewhat guilty, what about *your* future plans? With Florence so sadly dying like that, you obviously didn't feel like going ahead with the purchase of the house you'd been on the point of buying. But that was three years ago. Are you still happy to carry on as you've been doing?'

Martin leaned forward and made as if to speak.

'You're welcome to stay here as long as you want, of course,' Edward added quickly. 'I love having you here, and I really appreciate being able to come up for a chat at the end of our surgeries. If you weren't up here, we'd only have to get in someone else, which wouldn't be as pleasant for me. But wouldn't you prefer to live in a house that didn't have a medical practice on the ground floor?'

Martin shrugged. 'Not really. This house is full of my memories of Florence. She's in every room, so it's like she's still with me. If I moved away, she wouldn't be in my new house in the same way, and those memories might grow dim. I'd hate that.'

'I can understand that,' Edward said quietly.

'And as I've got my own entrance through the side door, I don't need to come into contact with any patients when I'm not on duty, which works very well. Plus, the redoubtable Hilda occasionally goes beyond the call of a receptionist's duty and comes in with a stew that she's cooked for me. If I were somewhere else, that might not happen.'

Edward grinned. 'I'm sure you're right about that. I certainly never get fed by her fair hand, and I live by myself, too.'

'She'll assume that Jean and Mavis are making sure you don't waste away. After all, Jean looks after our patients so brilliantly that Hilda will assume she's looking after you, too.'

'You're right about Jean being a good district nurse. The practice couldn't have a better one. All the patients love her.'

'And so do you, Edward. Setting a date will remind her of that. I hope you don't backtrack on your resolution this evening.'

Edward shook his head. 'I won't. You're right. It's time I

stopped thinking about what I want and started to think about what Jean wants. And as she's made it pretty clear what that is, you can be sure I'll have my diary with me next time I see her. And I'll go one step further,' he said. 'I won't go into the museum unless it's absolutely necessary.'

He smiled at Martin and picked up his glass. 'Let's toast the future. After that, I must get off home.' He raised his glass. 'To the museum and its new boss, and to Jean, the best district nurse a GP could have.'

Martin raised his glass. 'To Jean,' he said, 'your future wife.'

5

I*n the museum,*
The following Monday

'THE MUSEUM'S overseen by a board of trustees and supported by the local authority,' Gladys Wilson told Violet as they sat in the small staffroom at the back of the museum, facing each other across a Formica-topped table.

'Over the years,' she went on, 'it's been developed by donations from the collections of private benefactors such as Dr Russell, Edward's father. The late Dr Russell was an enthusiastic gatherer of interesting artefacts.'

'I assume he was interested in paintings, too,' Violet said, 'as there are quite a few paintings around the museum.'

'That's right. But relics from the past were his particular interest, which isn't surprising as this is an area of great archaeological interest. Dr Russell was keen to see the number of artefacts in the museum increase, and being a man of great force and determination, he encouraged his friends who were similarly minded to donate from their private collections.'

'Did they agree?'

'They did indeed. All of them strongly believed that everyone, not just a wealthy man's family and friends, should be given the chance to see items that throw a light on the way people lived in the past and on major events in the region. To further this, they also left sums of money to the museum to help with the running costs, with the result that there's an impressive number of exhibits for a museum located in a small village. In fact, there are now too many items for them all to be displayed at any one time.'

'How generous of Dr Russell and his friends,' Violet said in wonder.

Gladys nodded. The pale-coloured Yardley face powder trapped between her nose and her cheek cracked.

'It was,' Gladys said. 'It means that the museum's able to fund the purchase of any items of local interest. That'll be something that falls to you.'

Violet pulled a face. 'That sounds scary. How will I know what to buy?'

Gladys smiled. 'Don't worry, I'll help you.'

'That's a relief,' Violet said gratefully. 'Was the late Dr Russell a trustee of the museum like Edward?'

'That's right. Edward was appointed to the board when he reached a suitable age, and he took over the running of the museum when his father retired. Although he's had to step down from the job, he's remaining a trustee. Like his father, he has a real love of history and a desire to preserve anything that tells us more about the past.'

'I love history, too,' Violet said. 'I trained to be a history teacher.'

Gladys looked at her in surprise. 'Why did you change

your mind? I would've thought that an interesting career for a woman.'

'It's difficult to say. One of my sisters married someone from Jersey and lives there now, looking out at the sea. She was there throughout the German Occupation, which was very difficult for all of the people on the island. My other sister's married a French man and lives next to a river in a beautiful little town in Brittany.'

'What interesting lives they must have,' Gladys said pleasantly.

Violet nodded. That's just it,' she said. 'All I've ever done was go to one sort of school or another, and I began to feel that I wanted to experience something different, like my sisters have done, but I didn't know what. The minute I saw Dr Russell's advertisement, I thought that's it. I instantly knew I'd love such a job.'

'But surely working in a museum's not so very different from teaching in a school.' She smiled questioningly at Violet.

Violet frowned thoughtfully. 'I can see why you'd say that,' she said at last, 'and even more so as I'm hoping to bring children into the museum. But it's not like teaching the same groups of pupils week in, week out, and preparing lessons, marking exercise books and writing reports, so there's quite a difference.'

'But you'll have plenty of forms to fill in here, and there'll be regular reports to write for the trustees. Just not on children's attainments,' Gladys said with a smile. 'They're detailed reports, nevertheless. And you'll be surrounded by four walls, just as you would've been in a school,' she persisted. 'One of the purposes of a museum is to teach people about the past, so you'll be teaching within these four walls, albeit through exhibits.'

'I hadn't thought about it like that. I can see what you mean, but the job will be a little more than that, I think. At least I hope it will. I intend to find more creative ways of presenting some of the exhibits, ways that are less static, and that'll be a challenge in itself. But if I succeed, the displays will attract children into the museum, and when they're here, they'll learn about life years ago. I also plan to visit the local schools and talk to the children about what an item from the past can teach them. So these four walls won't be confining me.'

'How interesting,' Gladys murmured.

Violet nodded vigorously. 'That's what I think, too. In a classroom I'd be limited to teaching the school's curriculum, but here I'll be able to create the curriculum I want to teach, if that makes sense.'

Gladys managed a smile. 'It does. I certainly hope you'll be very happy here, Violet. You're going to bring a fresh perspective to what we do, and that's very welcome. A museum should be a living organism and not allow itself to become as fossilised as many of its exhibits. And even some of the staff,' she added.

They both laughed.

'Well, if you've finished your tea,' Gladys continued, 'we could repair to the office and have a look at some of the files.'

Violet smiled warmly at her. 'I'm so grateful to you for telling me so much about the administrative side of things today, Gladys, and for all your help. You've been brilliant.'

'Not at all,' Gladys said. 'I started working here when the late Dr Russell was in charge, which is a long time ago, and I've come to love the place. I want to see it develop in a way that attracts visitors, which I'm sure it'll do under you, and I'll be happy to help in whatever way I can.'

'That's so kind,' Violet said gratefully.

'Not at all. There isn't anything I haven't done, from showing visitors around, to supervising the cleaning of exhibits, to dealing with the accounts. That's the advantage of being a relatively small museum—you become familiar with every aspect of running it.'

Violet nodded. 'It must be lovely to feel that you're completely in control of everything.'

'Well, almost everything,' Gladys said with a smile. 'The cleaners come in on Friday evenings and I'm happy to leave them to it. We share a caretaker with the secondary school and we can call on him if anything's broken. The security and maintenance is covered by people who know what they're doing, and we've a body of highly educated experts to call upon when it comes to evaluating any possible new exhibits and if we want to build up our specialist collections. But I'll be able to help you with anything else, and I hope you'll let me do so.'

'I certainly will,' Violet said fervently.

'Well, then,' Gladys said, rising to her feet. 'Shall we go to the office and I'll show you the files?'

Violet stood up.

'Oh, dear. It looks as if I've left it too late for a cup of tea!' they heard Edward exclaim from behind them.

Both Violet and Gladys turned at the same time and saw Edward coming towards them.

'Not at all, Edward,' Gladys said quickly. She smiled at him. 'Just give me a minute and I'll get you one. Would you like another cup of tea, Violet?'

'Only if you're having one, too,' Violet said.

Gladys nodded. 'I think I will.' She picked up her cup and Violet's and carried them across to the kitchenette in the corner of the staffroom.

'How's the morning been?' Edward asked as he and Violet sat down.

'Busy,' Violet said with a smile. 'Gladys has been telling me so many important things, all of which she's explained in such minute detail that my head's quite spinning. But it was all really interesting. I'm so impressed by everything I've seen. And she's been so helpful. She's given me one of the lockable cupboards in the staffroom where I can keep my things.'

'That's good,' he said. 'And have you had time to talk to Lucy?'

'Not yet, but I hope to do so tomorrow. She very kindly tossed the rota out of the window today, so to speak, and has been covering the reception desk and the galleries so that Gladys was able to spend the whole morning with me.'

'Here you are,' Gladys said, returning to the table with a tray. She removed the three cups of tea from the tray, gave one to each of them, then propped the tray against the leg of the table and sat down.

Edward glanced at her as he picked up his cup. 'It sounds as if you've been a tremendous help to Violet this morning, Gladys. I'm extremely grateful.'

Gladys gave a dismissive wave. 'It's the least I can do. We want Violet to settle quickly, don't we?'

Edward smiled warmly at Violet. 'Yes, we do.'

'We were about to go into the office, Edward, and have a close look at some of the most important files,' Gladys continued. 'But if there's anything you'd like to talk to Violet about, we can leave the office for another day.'

'If you can, that'd be a great help,' he said. 'I wanted to check that there isn't anything Violet needs for the house.'

'I don't need anything, thank you, Dr Russell. My mother and father brought me in the van yesterday so that I could bring one or two bits and pieces with me, as well as my clothes. They'd been very keen on seeing the house and they thought it perfect. The flowers you'd put on the windowsill in the kitchen looked lovely and were very welcoming. Thank you for them. I'm so lucky that the museum has a house I can rent.'

'It was left to us about six months ago when the woman who lived there died childless,' Edward told her. 'As we hadn't yet got around to finding a tenant, we've been using the house for storage. But we don't really need it as such as there's plenty of space in the museum itself.'

'How fortunate for me,' Violet said.

He smiled. 'The trustees consider themselves very fortunate to have a tenant. It wouldn't be large enough for a family, so it wouldn't have been that easy to let.'

'D'you live in the village, Gladys?' Violet asked.

Gladys nodded. 'I've a house to the north of the village. You go across the marketplace and up past the school. I was born in that house, and raised there, and I carried on living there after my parents died.' She smiled at Violet. 'I'm obviously someone who doesn't feel any need for change. You're different, so you being appointed to run the museum was a very good idea.'

'That's very generous of you, Gladys,' Edward said with an appreciative nod. He looked back at Violet. 'I'd hoped to stop by while you were moving in, and perhaps meet your parents, but one of my patients was taken ill with appendicitis and transferred to the hospital. I had to go with him.' He paused. 'In fact,' he said hesitantly, 'I'm on my way to the hospital to look in on him now, and also to see one of my patients who's in there with a hernia. I know it's your first day, but I wondered if you'd like to come with me?'

'To the hospital?' she asked in surprise.

'That's right. I won't be going there that much in the future—it'll be Jean who makes the visits—so there might not be another such occasion for a while. And while I hope you'll never need the hospital yourself, you ought to know where it is. I thought we could go to the hospital first, and then to Abbeygate Street. I could show you where to find some of the shops you might need. What d'you think? If Gladys doesn't mind me taking you away so soon after you've started, that is,' he added quickly.

'Not at all,' Gladys said brightly.

Violet glanced anxiously at Gladys. 'Are you sure, Gladys? You were going to show me the files. Would it be difficult for you if I went with Dr Russell now, and we left the files for another day?'

'Not at all,' Gladys repeated. 'There's nothing that can't wait.'

Violet beamed at Edward. 'Then I'd love to go with you, thank you. It makes sense to get to know all the important places in the area as soon as I can. Is the hospital near the village?'

'It's in Bury St Edmunds itself, and Bury is near the village. What's more, it's on our side of the town. Unsurprisingly, since we're in West Suffolk, it's called the West Suffolk General Hospital and equally unsurprisingly, it's on a road called Hospital Road. Well, shall we go?' he asked, and he stood up.

'Thank you again for this morning, Gladys,' Violet said, getting up.

'It was a pleasure,' Gladys said, and smiling cheerfully at both Edward and Violet, she put her cup to her lips.

Abbey Gardens, Bury St Edmunds

. . .

In the fading light of the day, Gladys and Stanley Patterson sat side by side on a wooden bench on the eastern side of the Abbey Gardens, each of them holding a small package wrapped in brown paper. The package that Gladys held had been given to her by Stan, and his package had been given to him by Gladys.

Staring ahead of her, deep wrinkles etched into her face, Gladys glared at the darkening water of the River Lark, which was flowing on the other side of the narrow path in front of them.

'I can't tell you how frustrated and angry I was when Edward turned up out of the blue,' she told him bitterly. 'I'd spent all morning with Miss "exhaustingly enthusiastic" Hammond, endlessly stretching my mouth into a smile so wide my face felt as if it was about to split in two, and we'd finally reached the moment where I was to get my reward, the moment I'd been leading towards all morning, when in he came and whisked her off into town!'

'Which is, I imagine, why we're meeting here and not in the shop.'

'You imagine correctly,' she said angrily. 'As he's taking her to Abbeygate Street and the Buttermarket, I thought it wiser to meet here. I'd rather they didn't see me coming out of your shop.'

He shrugged. 'It wouldn't really matter if they did, would it? I've been to the museum in the past, so it'd be reasonable to assume that we know each other and there'd be nothing suspicious about you popping into the shop. Perhaps you were delivering a parcel from the museum.'

'And perhaps not,' she countered. 'Not when Lucy lives in Bury. She's told me that she gets off the bus a stop or two early if she wants to go to the shops. I'd obviously give her anything intended for you, and she'd bring it here herself.'

He shrugged. 'It was only a suggestion.' He paused. 'I take it from the mood you're in that you didn't get her to sign anything?'

'How could I?' she snapped. 'I'd got everything ready in the office. All I had to do was take out the file, give her the papers and ask her to sign them. Her head was so full of all the minutiae I'd stuffed into it in the morning that she wouldn't have been able to read anything—she'd have just signed where I told her.'

Stanley grinned. 'Hats off to you, Gladys. When you want something, you don't waste any time.'

'Much good it did me,' she grumbled. 'With Edward there, I didn't dare produce any forms. I was obliged to sit with the two of them in the staffroom and simper.'

He threw back his head and laughed. 'I don't think I've ever seen you simper. As it's somewhat hard to imagine, I'd be grateful if you'd demonstrate a simper now.'

She gave him a dry smile. 'You were just finishing a sandwich when I got here. I wouldn't want to cause you indigestion.'

He grinned at her, then both turned back to look at the water.

'The timing was such bad luck,' she went on after a few minutes' silence. 'When Edward suggested taking her with him to the hospital, I was tempted to suggest that Violet sign the forms before they left as she wouldn't have had time to read anything properly. But common sense prevailed. I know Edward, and I don't think he'd have let her sign anything she hadn't read. He's a stickler for doing what's both right and sensible. Worse still, he might have looked at what I was asking her to sign. That would've been disastrous.'

'But if you'd pleaded the importance of what you wanted her to do, he might've gone to the hospital without her. If he had, you could've got her to sign.'

'Don't think that thought didn't go through my mind,' she said wryly. 'But it was too much of a gamble. I was just relieved that I hadn't told her that she'd be signing some papers. If I had, when Edward asked her to go to the hospital with him, she might have turned to me, opened those big brown eyes and asked me if she shouldn't sign those very important documents before going out,' she went on, her voice taking on a hesitant little girl voice.

Stanley laughed. 'I may have failed to get a simper, but that wasn't too bad as a second best, Gladys.'

With a slight smile, she inclined her head. 'If she'd said that,' she continued in her normal voice, 'I'm certain that Edward, who shouldn't have even been there today as he's not in charge any more, would promptly have stuck his nose in and asked what papers she was talking about.'

'I probably would if I'd been him.'

She sat back with a sigh. 'You know, Stan, I can see it getting harder to do what we've been doing, and I'm wondering if we shouldn't stop now before we're caught. Perhaps have a word with Eric and see what he thinks. I don't want my final years to be inside a gaol, and I'm sure he doesn't want to end up in one, either.'

'All right, I'll do that,' he said with obvious reluctance, 'but I can just imagine his explosive response. As for Edward turning up when he did, it doesn't really matter, does it? You can get her to sign tomorrow, can't you? And from what you've told me of your plans, it's only one form that actually matters, isn't it?'

Gladys nodded. 'That's right. But I won't be giving her the forms first thing in the day, when she's fresh and full of energy. If she was, she'd be sure to want to read everything first. She'd see it as a way of learning more,' she added, her voice taking on a touch of mimicry. 'I'll present the forms to her in the afternoon.'

'So what are your plans for the morning?' he asked in amusement.

She laughed. 'I intend to introduce her to the extensive storage in the basement of the museum, which is off limits to visitors,' she said with a satisfied air. 'Whatever energy she has when we start our exploration will have evaporated long before we've completed our tour. By the end of the morning, she'll be utterly fed up with anything to do with the museum, and that's when we'll go into the office.'

Stan laughed. 'That's more like it, Gladys.'

6

The Angel Hotel, Bury St Edmunds,
The same afternoon

VIOLET GLANCED at the dainty sandwiches, their crusts removed, and at the selection of small cakes that had been carefully arranged on paper doilies on the silver cake stand in the centre of the table.

She looked up from the cakes and smiled shyly at Edward, who was sitting opposite her. 'This is very kind of you,' she said, smoothing down the white tablecloth on either side of her place setting. 'I didn't expect you to feed me bread and cake as well as feeding me masses of information about the hospital.'

'Well, I hope you've left some space for the food,' he said, grinning. 'I can't eat all this by myself.'

'I'm sure I'll be able to help you out.' She looked around at the wood-panelled walls. 'This is a lovely hotel,' she remarked, 'inside and out. All that ivy on the stone walls when you approach the building gives it a load of character. And that lovely large square between Abbey Gate and the hotel really sets it off. It's beautiful.'

'It is, indeed. And Charles Dickens thought so, too. It's a former coaching inn. In *The Pickwick Papers*, when Mr Pickwick and his manservant Sam arrived at Bury St Edmunds on the trail of the charlatan, Alfred Jingle, Dickens had them pull up in front of the Angel, which he described as a large inn situated in a wide open street that was almost facing the old abbey.'

'Oh, my goodness! So I'm sitting in a building that Dickens visited?' she exclaimed.

'He did more than visit—he actually stayed here. Ah, here's the waitress with our tea. Do make a start on the sandwiches, won't you.' He indicated the cake stand.

'I confess I started *The Pickwick Papers* a few years ago,' she said, helping herself to a couple of cucumber sandwiches. 'I didn't finish it, though. I didn't really like it. I much preferred *Great Expectations* and *Oliver Twist*. Also, I really liked *Dombey and Son*. That made me laugh out loud. It's actually a savage attack on much of the education of the day, but dressed up as comedy.'

He smiled at her. 'We have the same taste. I, too, love the book, and how Dickens says that the boys in Dr Blimber's school are subject to an education force-fed so relentlessly that they've come to see the Romans as their implacable enemy.'

They both laughed.

'The large building on our left as we approached the Angel is called the Athenaeum,' he went on. 'It's a club. There used to be a beautiful, large eighteenth-century ballroom on the ground floor, which was used for dances and lectures and things like that. But during the war it was converted by the townspeople into a canteen for the troops. Volunteers manned the counters, and you could get tea, sandwiches and cakes there. There was even a lending library in one corner of the room, and a mending service in another. But when the war ended, the canteen was closed down.'

She smiled at him. 'There's so much history here. There obviously is in London, too, but when you live there, you don't notice it in the same way. But it's not just the history and architecture here that are interesting,' she said lightly. 'Seeing you at the hospital this morning was also very interesting. So far, I've only seen you as the manager of the museum, or former manager. Seeing you in a white coat and stethoscope gave me a glimpse of you in a different role.'

'So what did you think of the hospital?' he asked when the waitress in a black dress and white apron had finished pouring them each a cup of tea, and had left after placing the porcelain teapot and milk jug on the table, along with a silver jug containing boiling water.

'Really pleasant,' she said, 'if that doesn't sound a mad way to describe a building that's full of sick people. But the wards were light and airy, and the atmosphere warm and friendly. The nurses seemed very knowledgeable and efficient, and although they were busy, nothing felt regimented, if that's the right word. It could've easily done so with that forbidding line of iron beds down each side of the wards.'

He nodded. 'You've described it perfectly. We're lucky to have a hospital like that so near the village. The matron's a stickler for things being done correctly, and that shows. It's quite a relief that the hospital's now part of the new health service and no longer has to rely on subscriptions, donations from companies and payment for treatment by private patients.'

'It must be. I felt sorry for the nurses, though. While the pretty cotton curtains on the screens helped to create a summery feeling in the ward,' she went on, 'moving them looked really difficult. I was sitting on the chair opposite your patient's bed when the nurses were pulling screens around the bed for you to do your examination in private, and I could see them struggling.'

'It certainly isn't easy. The screen itself is cotton, but the frame's made of heavy metal. And as one screen isn't big enough to cover even half the bed, it usually takes three screens to hide it completely and allow sufficient room for me, a nurse and the dressings trolley.'

'You said you wouldn't be going to the hospital as often in the future, didn't you?' she asked him.

'That's right. Under this new system, it's the district nurse who'll check on any of our patients admitted to hospital. The "our", by the way, refers to my partner, Martin Lloyd, and me. I think I mentioned before that Martin lives above the surgery. Sadly, his wife died of an aggressive brain tumour a few years ago.'

'Oh, how sad!' she exclaimed.

'Yes, it is. Florence was a lovely woman.'

'Has your district nurse been with you for long?' she asked.

'It feels like forever, as we knew each other as children. But what about you, Violet?' he said quickly. 'Tell me if it's none of my business, but I understand you lived at home until you moved here. I was wondering if there was a young man back there, desperate at you moving all the way to Suffolk?'

She smiled. 'If I had a suitor I liked, I'd be pretty stupid if I chose to move away from where he lived. There are far more women around than men at the moment, with so many men not returning from the war. It would be foolhardy to jeopardise my chance of marrying a man I really liked.'

He nodded. 'I can see that. It must be hard for women.'

'Also,' she went on, 'my work's been the most important thing in my life for years. I stayed on at school for four years longer than I needed to have done as I wanted to be a teacher, then I helped as an assistant teacher in a local school during the war years. After that, as you know, I went to Avery Hill, a teacher's training college, which was for women only. There weren't a lot of opportunities for me to meet men.'

'I suppose there can't have been,' he said. 'I hope you won't let your work here stop you from having a social life. You're an attractive young woman, if you don't mind me saying so, and intelligent, too. I'm sure that any unattached man who met you would be keen to be a part of your life. You need to make sure that such a man does meet you.'

He took another sandwich, and so did she.

She paused. 'What did you do during the war, if it's not rude to ask?'

'Of course it's not. When war broke out, the Emergency Medical Service started up, giving the government control over voluntary and municipal hospitals. Doctors were a reserved occupation and I was sent to a London hospital. I did think of joining up, though. Although I had a general practice by then, I knew that medical organisations kept a register of doctors who'd volunteered to serve in the forces, and they'd devised a scheme whereby a doctor's practice could be continued by another practitioner. A lot of doctors were able to join up because of that.'

'Did you do so?'

He shook his head. 'No, not at that time. I held back.'

'Did you stay in London, then?'

'Not for long. It soon became clear that the Emergency Medical Service was extremely short of doctors, and the year after the war began, we were told that all doctors might be called up. I promptly put my name forward.'

'Where were you sent?' she asked.

'Nowhere more exciting than Ipswich, Braintree and a few similar places,' he said with a laugh. 'I didn't end up overseas, if that's what you're thinking. But enough about that. The war is well in the past. For the moment, the only other thing you should know about me is that I've got a sweet tooth. I think we should start on the cakes.'

'You don't look as if you have!' she exclaimed. Her hand flew to her mouth. 'I shouldn't have said that,' she said, horrified. 'It was too personal. People shouldn't make personal comments.'

He grinned at her. 'Except when the comment is a flattering one.'

'I think I'll have a cake,' she said, going red with embarrassment. 'As I'm sufficiently well bred to know not to talk with my mouth full, you'll excuse my lack of response.'

She hastily took a cake and bit deeply into it.

7

H*arton,*
The following morning

She was going to be working with Lucy that morning, Gladys told Violet, her voice full of apology, so it would be more sensible to leave the form signing till later in the day. After lunch they could deal with that, plus she would show Violet the storage in the basement. She also wondered if Violet would mind if she and Lucy worked in Violet's office that morning as it was time they removed any out-of-date files.

Delighted to have an unexpected few hours to herself, Violet decided to do something she'd been really keen to do but hadn't yet got round to doing, which was to wander around the museum on her own.

Although she'd been to the museum before she'd applied to work there, she hadn't studied it in depth as she hadn't expected to get the job. She'd mainly wanted to see the sort of exhibits they had, and how they were displayed.

After her appointment, she'd had a quick look round the museum with Edward, and had later, when she'd started working there, been given a very detailed tour by Gladys, who had given her so much information about the running of the museum that she'd stopped being able to take anything in.

But with Gladys and Lucy tied up in her office that morning, it would be the perfect time to take a look at the museum as a whole, and to try to see it as a visitor from outside would see it, while also being available for any visitors who might have a question to ask.

She realised that she'd have to finish her tour when it was time for her to join Gladys, but if she worked systematically through the galleries, she should by then have a pretty good idea about how the museum would be seen by an outsider.

Furthermore, by looking at the structure of the building and the exhibits, she wouldn't be thinking about Edward, and dwelling on how much she'd enjoyed the time she'd spent with him the day before.

But he was such good company, and so attractive, that it was hard to put him out of her mind, especially as he seemed to enjoy being with her just as she enjoyed being with him. And especially as he didn't seem to be married or engaged, which would have put him out of bounds.

Mentally, she pulled herself up.

Thinking about him in a romantic way would only end in misery, and she must stop. Someone like him, with the background he'd had, and all his experience, would never be interested in someone like her, a haberdasher's daughter who'd seen next to nothing of the world. She must force him out of her thoughts and think only of the museum, not of its former boss.

She'd approach the museum from the outside as if she were visiting it for the first time, she decided, and she picked up her notebook and pencil, went across the hall to the front door and opened it. Then she made her way along the short gravel path to the wrought-iron gate at the top of the path and turned to face the museum.

She was struck anew by the gracefulness of the two-storey building, a modestly sized late Georgian house that Edward had told her had once been the home of a successful cloth merchant, and by the warmth exuded by the red-brick walls. Although the house had been subject to a few adaptations to modernise it and make it more suitable to display the exhibits and for the staff who worked in it, she knew from what Edward had said that nothing that had been done had altered the outward appearance.

How unusual to find a building that was both elegant and welcoming, she thought as she started walking slowly back down the path, which was bordered on both sides by bright red petunias and a small lush green lawn.

Above the white-painted front door there was a tiled portico that protected visitors from rain, and on either side of the door there were two white-framed windows. Above that, across the upper storey of the house, there was a line of five windows.

She smiled at the house as she walked towards it, and the house seemed to smile back at her.

When she reached the front door, she opened it and went into the hall. The bright morning light streamed through the open door and fell on to the polished planks of the oak wood floor that gleamed a rich brown beneath the touch of the sun.

There were two galleries to the left of her and a large one to the right. Just before the door to the gallery on the right, there was a reception desk on which there were postcards for sale, and leaflets about the museum.

Further into the hall on the right-hand side, a graceful staircase flanked by a decorated oak handrail and balusters led up to the landing on the first floor.

Beyond the staircase at the far end of the hall, she could see two of the three doors that she knew were there. The third door, which was the door to her office, was hidden behind the staircase. The doors she could see were the doors to the staffroom on the left, and a door ahead of her that opened into the narrow room where Lucy did any typing that had been given to her. The stationery and supplies for the museum were stored there.

She looked back to the foot of the staircase. A framed black-and-white sign on the wall told visitors that they would find more exhibits in a further three galleries on the upper floor, one of which she knew housed most of their paintings.

It was hard to see how the entrance could be improved, she thought as she closed the front door behind her. But she'd walk through the two galleries on her left and see if anything struck her, and then she'd go through the upstairs' galleries, before coming back down and finishing with the large gallery on her right.

She crossed the hall to Gallery One on the left, walked into the airy high-ceilinged room, and glanced up. A central light hung from an ornate white ceiling rose. All round the room, the point at which the apple-green walls and white ceiling met was filled by an elaborately moulded white cornice.

It was a lovely room, and she would have to think very

carefully before making any changes to the way in which items were exhibited in such an elegant space. It certainly wouldn't be suitable for the main display she had in mind.

Her notebook and pencil poised, she went across to the first of the cabinets and looked at the display of wounding knives that had been found in the area. They dated from the ninth and tenth centuries. The blades of two of the knives had been inlaid with a gold pattern that was still visible in places.

Young lads could be interested in those, she thought, but would they bother to look at them in a room that suggested Georgian elegance, and where they were displayed in the same manner as the selection of ancient coins in the cabinet next to it?

She thought not, and she moved to the next cabinet.

As SHE CAME to the last of the exhibits in Gallery Six, the large gallery behind the reception desk, she paused in front of a glass-covered cabinet containing a stone slab dating from the tenth or eleventh century, which had been found in the vicinity of a church not far from the town. She leaned closer to get a better look at the decoration engraved in the stone.

'That claw-like motif is quite distinctive,' said a voice behind her.

She turned and saw Lucy Carr approaching her.

'Why did they engrave it in such a way, do you think?' Violet asked, indicating the stone slab. 'It makes the lump of stone look a bit like a hand.'

'In a way that's what it is. It's so you could fix something into it,' Lucy said, coming to stand next to her. 'A wooden cross, for example. As it was found close to a church, it's quite likely that this was a grave slab, and because it's made of stone, it's survived in the way that the wooden ones haven't.'

Violet stared at the slab. 'That's fascinating. But although it's got a label, the label doesn't say anything more than that it's a stone slab, and it gives it a possible date. Your comment about fixing a cross in it would be interesting for visitors to know. It would help them to understand what they were seeing, and then they'd know how to interpret other similar items.'

Lucy looked pleased. 'I suppose it would,' she said.

'I'd like all the labels to have the sort of details you've just mentioned. On my visit before I applied for the job, I noticed that some of the information given was very sparse, and it was one of the comments I made during my interview. I didn't make it as a criticism, I just remarked on the fact that I'd liked to have known more.'

Lucy nodded. 'I think labels are important, too.'

Violet turned towards Lucy. 'We were introduced so briefly, when I came to look at the museum. I was about to be taken to the house I'm renting, so you and I didn't really talk,' she said. 'I wonder if now would be a good time for a chat over a cup of coffee.'

'I just left Gladys at the front desk. She's sorting out the new museum postcards.'

'In that case, why don't we leave her to keep an eye on the place and take ourselves to the staffroom? It'll be impossible to do so this afternoon as Gladys is going to show me the storage area under the museum.'

'I'd like that. Thank you.'

'Right. Let's tell Gladys where we'll be, and then go for that coffee.'

When they reached the staffroom, Lucy insisted on

making the coffee for them both, and also one for Gladys. 'You're in charge of the museum, so I should be the one to make the coffee,' she told Violet. 'And it's easy enough with the Nescafé that Edward's given us,' she added, pouring boiling water on top of the coffee powder she'd put into each of the cups.

She added milk, and then picked up one of the cups and carried it carefully out to the front hall. Violet heard Gladys thank her.

'I've let you make the coffee today, but in future, we'll take it in turns,' Violet told Lucy when she came back into the staffroom. 'We've a small staff and we share the same goal. I don't think there's any need for hierarchy.'

'We'll see,' Lucy said with a smile. She gave each of them a cup and sat down. 'Did you find anything obvious you wanted to change?' she asked, taking a sip of her drink.

'Some little things, like the labelling. The main change will be with Gallery Five upstairs. There aren't that many exhibits and it looks a little sparse. But being a good-sized space, and right at the top of the stairs, it would be the ideal place to introduce a different way of presenting some of the exhibits. Not only would there be room for an interesting display, but there'd also be room for tables where we could sit groups of children.'

'It's certainly the least interesting of the galleries at the moment,' Lucy said.

'Fortunately, the headmistress of the local secondary school hasn't broken up yet although the pupils have, and I've an appointment to visit her tomorrow morning. I needed to move fast as I'm sure she'll be going on holiday before too long. I wanted to ask her about the areas of history they'll be teaching in the coming school year, and to discuss ways in which the museum might be able to support them.'

'That sounds terrific!' Lucy exclaimed. 'No wonder you got the job. Or perhaps I shouldn't have said that,' she added with sudden alarm.

Violet laughed. 'I'm not surprised people wonder why I was given the post. I've wondered about that, too. I know so little about museums and Gladys so much. Dr Russell must have had a lot of faith in me. I just hope I don't let him down. But let's talk about you, not me. I think Dr Russell said you live in Bury itself. Is that right?'

Lucy nodded. 'Yes, in Westgate Street. It's very easy—the bus takes me there. It goes down Angel Hill, past the Abbey Gardens and the abbey, and it's not far from there to where I live. When you get to the end of the road, you turn left to get to the Theatre Royal and the Brewery, and turn right to get to me. You might have driven past my house yesterday as you can get to Hospital Road from Westgate Street.'

'Then we probably did,' Violet said. 'And maybe we passed it on the way back. After the hospital, we parked in the large square in front of the Angel and walked up Abbeygate Street to Buttermarket and Cornhill, and then along Skinner Street, and round the marketplace. I was pleased to see that some of my favourite shops are there. I'm not a great person for shopping, but I do like Marks & Spencer. And I'll certainly be going to the market. My family started out in markets.'

'That's on a Wednesday,' Lucy told her. 'Perhaps one weekend if you're in town, you can come and have tea with my parents and me,' she added shyly. 'I know they'd like to meet you. My father isn't able to get about very easily so they don't really come to the museum.'

'That's very kind of you. I'd like that.' She paused. 'I

hope you don't mind me asking,' she went on with a hint of awkwardness, 'but since you live in a town, I wondered why at your age you'd choose to work in a village, not in the town, and moreover to work in a museum?'

Lucy laughed. 'My schoolfriends thought I was mad, too.'

'Oh, I don't think you're mad,' Violet said hastily. 'After all, it's what I've done myself. I was just curious as to why you made that decision.'

'There isn't really any one reason. Bury St Edmunds isn't very big and I thought it'd be nice to escape it and go somewhere different from what I'd always known. But I had to be able to get there easily. Harton was somewhere different, and it was only a bus ride away. Also, there weren't really any jobs in Bury that I wanted to do. The men who'd come back from the war had been given their old jobs back and they were the first to be chosen for anything new, so there were lots of women looking for work. They'd enjoyed working during the war and didn't want to go back to just looking after the house, or go into domestic employment.'

Violet nodded. 'I think that's true just about everywhere in the country.'

'So the only vacancies in Bury seemed to be for shop assistants, which I wouldn't like at all, or secretarial work,' Lucy continued. 'I'd done a Pitman's typing course to please my parents, but I knew I'd hate being a secretary. Then someone mentioned to my mother a year ago that they were looking for an assistant in Harton Museum. I thought it sounded really interesting, and I instantly applied.'

'And d'you think you made the right choice?'

Lucy nodded vigorously. 'Absolutely! I really like it here. I know I have to do a little typing, but I don't mind as it's not like being in an office all day. And I like having a short journey to get home. If it's been a busy day, by the time the bus reaches the bottom of Angel Hill, I've completely put work behind me.'

'I'm not surprised. The bus ride must be really pleasant. Talking of Angel Hill, before we came back yesterday, we had tea in the Angel Hotel.'

'You and Dr Russell!' Lucy exclaimed. 'I bet Jean won't like that!'

Violet's brow creased. 'Who's Jean?'

'Their district nurse. She's Dr Russell's fiancée.'

8

L*ater, early afternoon*

THE REST of the morning had felt as if it would never end, Violet thought dejectedly as she returned from walking around the village after lunch in a desperate attempt to rid herself of her overwhelming disappointment at learning that Edward was attached.

She thought she'd succeeded, but as soon as she'd seen the museum ahead of her, she'd thought of Edward and realised that despite her determined efforts, she hadn't completely managed to put him out of her mind, so the afternoon was going to feel endless, too, she realised in despair.

Pausing for a moment under the portico above the entrance to the museum, she tucked the loose strands of her chestnut hair into her French pleat and smoothed down her pale grey cotton dress. Then hoping she looked suitably composed, she took a deep breath, opened the door and went into the hall.

Lucy was sitting behind the reception desk. Giving Lucy a warm smile as she passed her, she went straight down to her office, where she knew Gladys would be waiting.

It was all her own fault that she was feeling as miserable as she was, she berated herself as she approached her office. All the resolutions she'd made in the train on her way back to London after being shown round the house by Edward, and having had lunch with him, had come to nothing. They'd been lost in the air just like the steam that had spewed forth from the train's funnel.

But he was so pleasant to be with.

It had been impossible not to feel a real warmth towards him as she'd followed him into the hospital ward and seen the gentleness and consideration with which he treated his patients. And it had been impossible not to relax and enjoy their conversation in the Angel.

Unlike so many good-looking men, he was really interesting, too, and she'd enjoyed every moment of their time together.

If only she'd accepted it for what it was—an employer being kind to an employee—and had left it at that.

But she hadn't.

When they'd returned to Harton and he'd left her back at her house, she'd walked into the kitchen and immediately seen the flowers he'd put on her windowsill on the weekend of her arrival. It had reminded her of his thoughtfulness, and for the whole of that evening, she'd given in to an outpouring of feelings for him, and had relived their few hours together.

And if she was brutally honest with herself, in doing so

she'd read something behind his words and glances that clearly hadn't been there.

Well, she now knew for certain that there could never be any romantic feelings between her and Edward, and she must urgently take herself under control.

It shouldn't be difficult to get into the frame of mind where she saw him as a friend and nothing more. After all, it was hardly any time since she'd moved into Harton so her knowledge of Edward as a person could only be superficial. Her feelings for him, therefore, must be equally shallow and would easily be dispelled.

From that moment on, she would put him out of her mind and distance herself from him as much as she could without being rude. All that mattered was her work, and firm in her resolution, she opened the door to her office.

Gladys was sitting behind Violet's desk, a pile of papers in front of her. She looked up as Violet entered the room, and promptly rose to her feet, patting the sausage-like roll of greyish hair at the back of her head.

'It's fine, Gladys,' Violet said. 'Just stay where you are. I'll pull up a chair next to you.'

'Old habits die hard,' Gladys said with a self-deprecating laugh. 'I used to sit here when Edward was out and I was in charge. But rather than sit, perhaps we should make a start now, unless you'd prefer not to?'

'Make a start?' Violet stared at her, mystified, and went further into the room.

'You've probably forgotten,' Gladys said in a tone of deep understanding. 'I'm sure you've had a busy morning. But I was going to show you around the basement, which is where we keep artefacts that aren't on display for one reason or another.'

'I'm so sorry,' Violet said apologetically. 'It completely slipped my mind. Of course, let's do that now.'

'And then we can sign a few forms,' Gladys went on smoothly. 'And that will be that for the day.' She went round the desk and across to the door. She held the door open for Violet to go back into the hall, then closed it behind them both.

'I'll lead the way, shall I?' Gladys said, and she crossed the hall to a door set into the back of the staircase. 'You probably hadn't yet noticed this door,' she added.

'You're right,' Violet said in surprise. 'I must have looked at it but assumed it was a cupboard.'

'And why wouldn't you?' Gladys said with a smile. 'You're too young to know that before the wars it was customary for households to have servants. Even modest households would have at least one servant. These days, though, it's different. No one wants to enter domestic employment, so you won't find servants' quarters in any of the houses they're building at the top of the village. But when this house was built, any family which owned such a house would employ a number of servants. This door takes you beneath the house to an area the Georgians would have called "below stairs".'

She opened the door, and Violet followed her down a short flight of stone steps.

'Years ago,' Gladys told her, 'servants spent most of the time in the basement. It can't have been pleasant—you can see how dark it is. This would have been the kitchen.' She led Violet into a large room to the left of the stairs. 'It's the largest and lightest of the rooms. Size and light were needed for the kitchen, which was the busiest room below stairs.'

'I can just imagine a huge kitchen range along the wall here,' Violet said, going across to the side of the room and indicating a wide stone alcove. She pointed to the area above the alcove. 'Hanging above it, I imagine, would be all the pots, pans and moulds that the cook would have had for her use.'

Gladys nodded. 'That's right. As you can see, though, there are now artefacts rather than pots and pans. And there are more shelves today than there used to be. We've had to build a number of shelves to house everything we want to store in here. We've done the same in all the basement rooms. This large wooden table in the centre of the kitchen is the original, though. It's very useful, even today.'

Violet glanced round at the shelves filled with artefacts. Some of them had a small white card in front of them, she noticed. She picked up the card closest to her and saw that it gave the details of when the museum had received the artefact and from whom, and where it had been found.

'Are they down here because there's no room for them upstairs?' she asked, putting the card back.

'That's one of the reasons,' Gladys said. 'We're lucky enough to have been donated a great many finds, and also Edward has made some interesting purchases for the museum. But everything down here needs to be assessed and evaluated before it can be moved out of storage.'

'I see,' Violet said. She glanced around her. 'Who keeps the place clean?'

'The cleaners put in extra time once a month and give it a quick wipe over. Some of the items down here are worth a lot, and mustn't be neglected.'

'It certainly doesn't feel overly dusty. They're obviously doing a very good job,' Violet said.

Gladys nodded. 'They do. To come back to the cataloguing and evaluating, with a small staff, it isn't easy to find time to organise visits by the specialists, who are the ones to evaluate the artefacts. Edward had his patients to look after as well as the museum to run. But you're in a different position, Violet. You won't be doing another job as well as working here, so hopefully we'll soon see more of the items catalogued and exhibited.'

'I'll certainly do everything I can to speed that up,' she said.

'That's what I hoped you'd say,' Gladys said with a smile. 'To continue our tour, over there,' she pointed to the corner of the kitchen, 'you'll find the door to the scullery.'

Violet looked towards the scullery and then turned and looked up at the wall at the foot of the steps. A line of brass bells was hanging from a wooden bar. 'I suppose those are the bells that would ring when the servants were wanted?' she said.

'That's right. Most of the signs of life as it was a few years ago have been removed as we needed the space for storage, but the bells were left. Each has a different sound, so the servants would know to which room they were to go. We also kept the bread oven, too. So if ever the baker runs out, you know what you can do.'

Both of them laughed.

'Along the passageway, you'll find several other rooms, including a wine cellar,' Gladys continued as she started to lead the way through the rest of the basement.

As with the kitchen, all the walls, Violet noticed, were lined with wooden shelves filled with items of different shapes and sizes. Although quite a few had small labels in front of them, there were a significant number that lacked a tag.

'Why aren't they all tagged?' Violet asked.

'They were, but during the war we had to store a lot of extra things in here to stop them from being damaged. It became very cramped and crowded, with everything jumbled together, and a number of tags were lost.'

'I'd forgotten the effect that the war would have had,' Violet said.

'Some of these rooms would have been used for storage in the past,' Gladys went on, 'but others would've been used by the servants. Some servants will have slept in the attic, and others down here. The cook, housekeeper and butler would have their own rooms down here, but any house-maids or kitchen maids who slept in the basement would've had to share a room.'

She paused at the entrance to a small room with a window at the far end of it.

'This would have been the butler's room,' Gladys said. 'He needed to be able to keep an eye on any deliveries and on the servants. All traders and servants will have come and gone through the back door. His room is next to the back door for that reason,' she added, and she continued walking.

'Is the door used at all these days?' Violet asked as they stood and looked at the back door.

'No, never. We keep it locked at all times. I don't know when it was last opened. It's a matter of safety. Outside the door, there're a few steps up to a path, which leads to the marketplace. You can't see the marketplace from here because of the tall hedges. Although there's only a market on Saturdays, the place is generally a focal point for the villagers and visitors on any day of the week. The key to the door is in a box on the wall, but we keep it locked to ensure that no one enters the museum without us seeing them.'

'That's only right.' Violet glanced at the box on the wall next to the door and frowned. 'Where's the key?'

Gladys stared at the box in visible surprise. 'You're right, there isn't one, and there should be. If there was a fire we might need another exit. I didn't realise it wasn't there as I seldom come this far along the basement. I've no idea what can have happened to it.'

'If we can't find it, we'll need a replacement,' Violet said. 'I'll have a word with Edward. He may have the original key, but if he hasn't, he might have a master key.'

'Thank you, Violet,' Gladys said with obvious relief. She looked around them, and then back at Violet. 'Well, I think that's our basement tour over.'

'It's been fascinating, Gladys. Thank you. Seeing all these signs of life in the past while listening to your account of how they lived, and being able to touch the table used by people so long ago, on the very spot where they would've touched it, is really exciting.'

Gladys inclined her head in acknowledgement.

'Are the artefacts stored in any particular grouping when they're put down here—before they've been assessed by the experts, I mean?' Violet asked as they turned and started to walk back towards the kitchen. 'Such as according to when you think they date from, or what you think their likely use was?'

Gladys's face took on an expression of regret. 'As I say, we would've liked to have done that, but it's proved impossible to find the time to do more than put them on the nearest shelf. Lucy and I have done our best, but I'm afraid that most of our time was spent in the part of the museum open to the public, not down here.'

'In that case, I should love to organise some sort of grouping down here,' Violet said enthusiastically. 'Apart from anything else, it'll help me with my plans for display if I know what's in the basement. I'll make a start as soon as I can, and when I've got a large enough group of items about which I'm uncertain, we can ask the specialists you mentioned to come and take a look at them. That would be all right, wouldn't it?' she asked anxiously. 'It seems such a shame to hide so many interesting things away.'

Gladys's mouth stretched into a smile. 'That's an excellent idea. And while you're busy down here, you can rely on me to see that everything upstairs is running smoothly. And talking of upstairs,' she said as they reached the first of the steps, 'perhaps we should return to your office. There are one or two forms for you to sign.'

SITTING at her kitchen table that evening, a cup of coffee next to her, her pen, inkwell and a sheet of paper in front of her, Gladys cast her mind back to the events of the day.

Her plan had been most successful, she thought with satisfaction as she glanced down at the single-page form headed 'Harton Museum Association Account'. Under the heading there were several lines of instruction, an account number and two designated spaces at the bottom for a signature and a date.

Violet Hammond's signature was unmistakable.

And so was Edward's. It was a good copy and would appear to be authentic to anyone who glanced at it. Handwriting experts would obviously determine it was a fake, but they wouldn't be able to say whose hand had held the pen.

This had been the penultimate form she'd presented to Violet. After Violet had signed it, she'd slipped it into her bag while Violet was signing the last one in the pile, all of the forms, bar that one, having been signed by Edward a few days earlier. When she was sure that Violet was watching, she'd placed the rest of the signed forms in the filing cabinet.

The effort involved in getting Violet into a suitable state to be presented the forms for signing had certainly paid off.

Only a fool or someone young and inexperienced would sign a pile of documents they hadn't been in the mood to read before signing. But she'd counted on Violet, who'd been plied with knowledge for several hours, not wanting to do anything that would delay her return home.

And she'd been proved right.

Anyone more experienced would simply have said they weren't in any state to go through the forms that evening, and would do so the following morning, after which they would sign. They'd realise that a day's delay wouldn't matter.

But that hadn't occurred to Violet, cowed as she was by her lack of experience and urged on to sign by someone more knowledgeable than she, and a form she would never have signed had she first read it now bore her signature.

Stanley *would* be pleased, she thought, and she allowed herself a moment to gloat at her success and at Violet's stupidity, then she stood up and began to return her writing implements to the old mahogany bureau in the corner of the room.

9

T*he following day*

After a fitful night, throughout which Violet had berated herself for her stupidity in signing documents she'd hadn't first read, she'd had to pull herself together before the two meetings planned for that day.

When she reached the museum, Gladys was opening the post that had just arrived.

'I always used to sort out the correspondence when Edward was here,' Gladys told her apologetically. 'I'd give him anything addressed to him, and distribute everything else. I assumed you'd like me to continue doing so, which would free up a little more time for things you want to be doing, but I should have asked you first. If you'd rather I didn't—' Her voice trailed off.

'Oh no,' Violet said hastily. 'Carry on doing what you used to do.' And she headed for her office, relieved to have time to go through the signed forms before she had to leave for her first appointment.

Her first meeting was with the headmistress of the local school and the second with Brian Armstrong, the manager of Lloyds Bank in Bury St Edmunds. Her signature had to be recorded with the bank. Gladys was going to go into Bury with her for that. They'd go after they'd had lunch, Gladys had told her. It wouldn't take long, and Lucy was proficient enough to hold the fort on her own.

She opened the door to her office, went straight across to the filing cabinet and opened it.

Her first appointment had gone well.

The headmistress had been so enthusiastic about Violet's plans that she'd gone even further than Violet had dared to hope by volunteering that the school's art teacher could paint the necessary scenery. To have such support had partially revived her good spirits.

But now that she'd left the school, her guilt had flooded back, and her anger at herself, and as the morning was warm and pleasant, and she wasn't going to the bank till the afternoon, she decided to take the long way back to the museum. With luck, by the end of the walk, she'd have lost the irritation with herself that had been building since the moment she'd watched Gladys close the drawer of the filing cabinet the night before.

She should never have signed those forms without reading them first.

It had been the one piece of advice her father had given her before she'd left London, and she'd ignored it, she thought miserably as she left the school and strolled down Church Road in the direction of the village hall.

Reaching the drive that led up to the hall, she paused in front of the noticeboard and looked up at it to see what was happening in the village.

It was a busy community, she thought, seeing notices about a sewing and knitting circle, a gardening club, an amateur dramatic club and a group for keen cake-makers. In one of the bottom corners, a somewhat tattered card with a picture of a maypole, from which the sun had leached the colour, announced May Day celebrations that had obviously already taken place.

She looked beyond the noticeboard to the garden at the top of the drive on the left. Seeing a wooden bench that faced the small central plot filled with flowers, she went up the drive and sat on it.

Why, oh why, had she been so unprofessional as to sign forms without first checking what she was signing?

Gladys had asked her to sign about eight forms, which was only to be expected as she was taking over from Edward and it was now her signature that would be required for the various roles she'd be filling in the future, not his.

But as she'd started to read the first form, she'd found it hard to concentrate, having spent a morning making notes about the exhibits in each of the galleries, and an afternoon exploring the extensive storage in the basement, and it had been an effort to try to take in the meaning of the legalistic terms.

And everything had been made even harder by the fact that she was still reeling with disappointment at learning that Edward was engaged to his district nurse. Not even the fascinating afternoon in the basement had been able to dispel her lingering sense of depression that Edward was already spoken for.

By the time she'd reached the end of the first of the

forms, she'd realised that she was no longer aware of what she was reading, and had given up and just signed on the dotted line.

Gladys had promptly handed her another long form to sign. She'd remarked as she'd taken it that all would be satisfactory, she was sure. She'd glanced at it, and then seeing where she was meant to sign, had signed the form. Thereafter, she'd abandoned any pretence at reading the forms and had signed them all.

Gladys had taken the signed forms from her, put them into her filing cabinet, and suggested that, as it was closing time, they go through the files on another occasion. Relieved to be rid of them and longing to be outside and alone with her thoughts, she'd agreed.

Thank goodness the museum staff was so few and friendly, she'd thought as she'd gone into her house. Nothing would be amiss. Nevertheless, anxiety had frustrated her attempts to sleep, tired though she was, and she'd used the time she had before leaving for the school to take out everything she'd signed and read through each of the forms.

Nothing *had* been amiss.

She sat in the village hall garden for a few more minutes, staring at the flowers, and then, feeling a little better in herself, she stood up and went back down the drive to Church Road.

At the end of the drive, she paused and looked left. Her gaze went past her house and down to the museum. She hadn't been out that long, and could stay out a little longer if she wanted. Gladys and Lucy didn't know how long she'd be at the school so they wouldn't be expecting her back at any particular time.

She turned her head and looked to her right towards the

surgery and thence to the road beyond the surgery. That was the road in which Edward lived, she knew. She wondered if he was at home. She could stroll past the surgery and then past his house, and if he happened to be coming out of either building at the time, he would see her and would be bound to stop and talk.

The idea of possibly seeing him lifted her spirits. Perhaps she could even unburden herself of the stupid thing she'd done the day before. It was a very tempting thought, and she took a few steps in the direction of the surgery.

Then she stopped abruptly, turned and walked back down the road.

Edward was an engaged man.

Instead of trying to bump into him, she should be doing the reverse. The fewer times she saw him, the better. She'd done one stupid thing in the past twenty-four hours, and she certainly shouldn't do another!

She'd go back to the museum, tell Lucy and Gladys what the headmistress had said, and then have lunch. While she waited for Gladys to take her to the bank, she'd make a start on her report for the board of trustees, which had to be done before their September meeting, which she'd been asked to attend. If she immediately wrote up the result of her visit to the school that morning, she wouldn't forget any details, and it would almost certainly wipe any lingering thoughts of Edward from her mind.

As she went past the noticeboard again, she paused. A leisure activity might help with the Edward problem by reducing the role he played in her life. If she joined one of the many clubs, it would be a diversion and it would help her to meet more of the people who were now her neighbours. It was something she'd certainly think about, she decided as she resumed walking down the hill.

She'd also write to her parents and invite them to come for Sunday lunch in the not-too-distant future. She'd enjoy cooking a meal in her little kitchen, possibly something simple like toad in the hole. After the meal, they could all go for a walk around the village. If they went past Harry's Inn, she could explain how it got its name. That would amuse them, she was sure.

She'd also confess to her parents how stupid she'd been over the forms, and that should get it out of her system. Then she'd tell them her plans for a new style of display. She'd omit, however, any mention of her feelings for Edward.

She also wanted to hear more about their visits to Rose in Jersey and then to Iris in France. They'd told her how much they'd enjoyed spending time with both of her sisters, but there was bound to be more to say than they'd put in a letter, and she'd like to hear every single detail of the visits they'd recently made.

Greatly comforted at the thought of seeing her parents again before too long and hearing more about the lives of her sisters, her steps to the museum speeded up.

Bury St Edmunds

'We're very lucky to have a bus service from Harton into Bury,' Gladys remarked as she and Violet walked up Abbeygate Street with Gladys carrying the forms in a narrow leather briefcase that Violet had once seen at Edward's side.

'It was my mistake that I got the time wrong and we had to wait a while for the bus,' Gladys went on, a note of apology in her voice. 'Fortunately, it's an excellent service.

It's why the museum's used Lloyds Bank for years,' she added as they turned into the Buttermarket and crossed to the other side of the road.

Violet saw that they were heading for a large multi-windowed brick building.

'I hope they're still open,' she said anxiously. 'It's almost three o'clock.'

'Don't worry, we'll be just in time,' Gladys said, and gave her a quick smile. 'And they're expecting us. I'll go in first, shall I?' she suggested as they reached the entrance door, which had a night safe built into the wall at the side of it. Without waiting for a reply, she promptly pushed open the door, and went inside.

Violet followed Gladys up to the nearest counter, where Gladys asked to speak to Mr Armstrong, adding an apology for it being so near to their closing time. 'It was the bus,' she said. And she smiled at the teller.

A moment later, the door to a glass-fronted office at the far end of the bank opened, and a tall, grey-haired man came out. Gladys hurried up to him, followed by Violet.

'I'd almost given up on you,' Mr Armstrong said.

'We missed the bus, I'm afraid,' Gladys said ruefully. She pulled Violet slightly forward. 'May I introduce you to Violet Hammond, Mr Armstrong. Violet, I'd like you to meet Mr Armstrong, who's the manager of a bank to which we've owed many kindnesses throughout the years. Violet's taken over from Edward, Brian. Both she and Edward have signed all the necessary forms to that effect.'

Violet and Brian Armstrong shook hands. 'It's a pleasure to meet you, Miss Hammond,' he said.

'Likewise,' Violet replied.

Gladys took a folder from the briefcase and handed it to Mr Armstrong.

'Come in,' he said, taking the folder and indicating that they should go into his office. He followed them in, closed the door and sat down behind his desk. 'Do sit,' he said, pointing to the chairs.

'I'm delighted you've had the chance to meet Miss Hammond today,' Gladys said, and she began a long description of Violet, extolling the changes she'd planned for the museum.

Violet saw him glance at the clock on the wall.

Violet was going to introduce a new form of display, Gladys told him in a tone of voice replete with pride. It was designed to appeal to children and capture their imagination, she added, and it was to be hoped that the manager and his charming grandsons would visit once the display was open, or even before if he wanted to see how things were progressing.

She took a deep breath to continue, but the manager got in first, Violet noticed with amusement.

'So these are the forms you want me to substitute for those originally signed by Edward, are they Miss Hammond?' he asked, his smile embracing Violet as well as Gladys.

'That's right,' Gladys said. 'Edward's work prevented him from coming with Violet today, which is why I'm here. So much is expected of GPs these days. Too much, in fact. I can't tell you how much everyone who has anything to do with the museum respects the time that Edward is still managing to give to the museum, despite how busy he is with all the changes caused by the new health service. The way he interested himself in Violet's appointment, for example.' She smiled at Violet, and then turned back to the bank manager.

Violet saw the manager's eyes go to the clock again.

'You must let Violet tell you herself about her plans for the museum,' Gladys went on with audible enthusiasm. 'You'll be most impressed. Violet,' she said turning to her, 'perhaps you'd like to tell Mr Armstrong what you've been doing since you took up your position?'

An anguished look crossed the manager's face. He glanced at the clock again.

Suppressing the desire to laugh, Violet opened her mouth to speak.

'I regret to say,' he said, quickly standing up, 'but it's one minute to three. I suggest, given that we're about to close, you leave these with me and I'll go through everything later on. We've known each other for long enough for this to be an acceptable way of attending to such matters, given the lateness of the hour, and the fact that it's the monthly governors' meeting at my grandsons' school this evening. I'm one of the governors, Miss Hammond. If I've any queries, I'll contact you. And I'll post the paying-in books to you.'

'I'm so sorry to have been late for our appointment,' Gladys began, standing up.

Telling her not to worry, he hurried across to the door and held it open for them. 'I'm delighted to have met you, Miss Hammond,' he said. 'I look forward to doing so again before too long.'

They'd hardly got through the doorway when he closed the door behind them.

They left the bank, crossed to the other side of the road, and glanced at each other. Both burst out laughing.

'I've never heard you talk as much,' Violet said in awe. 'You seemed determined to go on for ever.'

'Fortunately, that's what he also thought. But I've been through the forms with him before, and he goes into every minute detail, and looks at every little loop of the pen and dot on an “I”. We would have expired with boredom,’ she said as they turned back into Abbeygate Street.

‘It’s lucky we got the time of the bus wrong, then,’ Violet said with a sly glance at Gladys.

Gladys met her eyes, and both laughed again.

‘Why didn’t you tell me what you were going to do?’ Violet asked.

‘You might’ve given the game away by mistake. I don’t know about you, but it’s been a busy few days and I want to get home and put my feet up. I didn’t want to be stuck in the bank for hours.’

‘I agree,’ Violet said. ‘How lucky that he had a governors’ meeting this evening,’ she remarked as they reached Angel Hill.

‘Wasn’t it just?’

10

H*arton,*
The following day

THE FOLLOWING morning when they were looking at the museum rota for the day, Violet suggested that Gladys and Lucy went to lunch at the same time, and that she stay on the reception desk and go for her lunch when they returned. But before the day really began, she wondered if they'd like to sit with her in the reception area and she could tell them what the headmistress had said.

They had promptly agreed, and she ran through the main points of her morning discussion, telling them how she'd be using artefacts from the basement to form a very visual, lifelike sort of display in Gallery Five, and that the headmistress had told her the historical periods they'd be covering that year.

She added that she didn't expect them to keep going up

and down the basement steps, and said she was prepared to take it upon herself to find the items she needed.

Lucy jumped in at once saying that she really wanted to help her, and that with three of them sorting out the artefacts, they'd get through everything much more quickly.

Gladys had corrected her, a trace of amusement in her voice. There'd be two of them running up and down to the basement, she told them, not three. She'd leave it to their young legs, hers being rather too old for stone steps, and she volunteered to sit instead at the reception desk for as long as they wanted to be downstairs.

'That's very kind of you, Gladys, thank you,' Violet said, her voice warm with appreciation. 'We could make a start this morning, Lucy, don't you think?'

'I WASN'T SURPRISED to learn that the school would be focusing on the Angles and Saxons this term,' Violet told Lucy as they stood in the basement of the museum, 'given the area in which we live, and that they'll be doing the Romans next year.'

'There're masses of exhibits from the Anglo-Saxon period on display upstairs,' Lucy volunteered, 'and Gladys always said there were lots more down here.'

Violet nodded. 'When she showed me the basement I noticed several. The trouble is, they're all over the place. There's no real order here. I'm surprised there isn't a separate area for each period, and shelves within that area for groups of items with the same function. It would make it so much easier to find things if, for example, you wanted to replace one exhibit with another that was similar.'

'That would be really good,' Lucy said. 'It would certainly help us to keep track of them. I imagine the cleaners move them around, but if everything had a designated space, they'd be less likely to do so. Especially when they've all been catalogued.'

'To be honest, I'm surprised it hasn't already been done,' Violet said.

'Edward asked Gladys several times if he could have a list of everything in the basement,' Lucy told her. 'But although she always said she would draw up a list, when it came to it, she was invariably busy doing something else. I volunteered to help her, but she never took me up on it. Edward obviously assumed she was working on it, and it was usually a while before he realised she wasn't and brought the subject up again.'

'I'll bet the enormity of the task deterred her,' Violet said. 'Even with two of us coming to the basement whenever we've got a moment it'll take at least three or four weeks to sort out everything, if not longer. And then the experts will have to check what we've done when we've finished, and we'll have to wait to find out if we were right. Then we'll have to work out what to say on the labels. I'm not surprised that Gladys couldn't face doing all that.'

Lucy pulled a face. 'Nor me, when you put it like that.'

'On the bright side, when all that's done, we'll know what we've got, and we'll have established a good routine,' Violet added.

'With so much to do, it's just as well that we're making a start today,' Lucy said.

Violet nodded. 'It certainly is. Looking around, in this room alone, pottery, jugs, carved stone, metalwork and jewellery are jumbled up together. Why don't we begin by taking everything off the shelves and putting it all on the table? Then we can decide if we think they're Anglo-Saxon or Roman, and put them on the appropriate shelves.'

'This will be fun,' Lucy said. 'I feel like a detective.'

Violet laughed. 'Me, too. But some pieces could be quite difficult. The Romans had a Latin influence, and the Angles and Saxons a German influence, since they came from Germany, so anything in the middle of their periods should be easy to spot. Where we might get it wrong, though, will be with artefacts from around the fifth century. The Romans had left by then, and it's early in terms of the arrival of the Anglo-Saxons, so there'll be some overlap. It may be difficult to say what's Roman and what isn't.'

'This is going to be interesting,' Lucy said, and she reached up to a small horse carved out of stone.

'Anything made of iron is probably later—the Romans preferred bronze whenever possible. And items like spears, swords and helmets are most likely Anglo-Saxon as they're known to have been proud warriors. I don't think I noticed any helmets, though.'

'How d'you know all this?' Lucy asked.

'I've always liked history. It was my special subject in college. Right, to work.'

Bury St Edmunds

Sitting in the fading light of day at the wooden table in the small yard at the back of Patterson's Antiques, which was made even smaller by the amount of furniture piled up around the perimeter, all of it covered by dark grey tarpaulins, Stanley ran his fingers through his wiry grey hair.

'I don't mind telling you, Gladys,' he said, 'that for a moment or two, caught in the onslaught of Eric's anger, I was quite alarmed. It's why I dropped you a line and suggested you come over after work.'

'I'd been going to stop by anyway as I wanted to tell you about the success of my little foray into the bank.'

'I'm very glad to hear that,' he said tetchily. 'I wish I could say that my visit to Eric was equally successful. But I can't. I'd explained to him why we were wondering whether to call it a day, and he stood very still and stared at me. His eyes were two black slits. He looked evil. Were we seriously contemplating ending our profitable business merely because some young girl got the job that Gladys had wanted, he said in a sneering way, and because neither of us felt able to deal with it?'

'How did you answer?'

'He didn't give me time to reply. Before I could say anything, he assumed a tone of great concern and suggested he instantly smash the copy of the fourteenth century jug he'd just finished firing and consign its ashes to the dustbin. And perhaps he should give back the thirteenth century tile I'd just given him, he said, and he offered me the tile. What did it matter that there were buyers for both the originals, he said, feigning solicitousness, compared with your mental distress?'

'I assume you didn't take the tile from him,' she said drily.

He gave a wry laugh. 'You assume correctly. On the contrary, I assured him that he'd misunderstood me. We'd felt he should know that there was a new manager at the museum, but that's all it was. I told him you were going to be even more cautious than usual, but nothing else would change.'

'And what did he say?' she asked.

'He raised an eyebrow and said good. He managed to

make that one word sound like a threat. Then he added that he was delighted to be told that he'd misunderstood me. It would've been a shame to have turned our backs on the money we've been making without good reason, he added nastily. Then he gave me the two packages I'd been expecting, and effectively closed the workshop door in my face.'

'So you've now got the original fourteenth century jug and also the copy?'

'That's right. I'll get in touch with my buyer tomorrow morning. We'll get good money for an item like this. There aren't that many jugs where the suggestive pouring spout illustrates the bawdy sense of humour prevalent in medieval times. All you've got to do is return the copy to the museum.'

'You make it sound very easy,' she said, annoyed. 'I've not yet told you but it's got even more difficult since today. Violet Hammond's virtually taken up residence in the basement, and Lucy's almost as bad. They've been going through the artefacts as Madame Hammond is planning to use some in the displays she's been so boringly trumpeting about. And by taking the equally enthusiastic Lucy into the basement with her, there are now two more people who'll have an idea of what's down there. Before that eager beaver got the job, there was only me.'

'It's annoying, I admit.'

'And with the time they're giving it, it won't be long before they've finished. I've been going back to the museum in the evenings, using the back door to the basement so I'm screened by the hedge, checking that none of Eric's creations have ended up among the items on their shelves.'

'So there's nothing to worry about,' Stanley said, shrugging. 'Or not enough to make us pack it in. Not with a partner like Eric, who has some very dubious friends. A little more cunning will be required, but that's all. And I've every faith in you, Gladys.'

'I obviously won't remove anything she might want for her first active display, now that I know what she's doing. Active's her word, not mine.'

'There you are,' Stanley said, and he leaned back in satisfaction.

'Also, I could make a note of any items in Gallery Five that won't be used for her display as they'd eventually have to be put in the basement. I'll make sure I'm the person who takes them downstairs, and I'll stow them as far from the kitchen as possible. They could be worth copying, and I'd rather she and Lucy didn't keep seeing them. In fact, it might be an idea to give some of those items to Eric while both are tied up with plans for the display.'

He nodded approvingly. 'I agree. I'll draw up a list of the things that seem to be particularly in demand at the moment, and you can look out for them.'

'You'll have to be quick. She's moving fast. She wants to prove that she's up to the job.'

'Then that's something else you could do,' Stanley said. 'If she's moving as fast as you say she is, slow her down.'

'And how exactly am I meant to do that?' Gladys asked cuttingly.

'By giving her something to work on that keeps her in her office. You say she's new to this, well use your experience to think up something administrative for her to do.'

'It's an idea.' Gladys stared thoughtfully at the table. 'The board of trustees must be kept informed of what she's doing,' she said at last. 'They'll know she's introducing a new sort of display, but I'm guessing they won't be able to visualise it.'

'Then it would be a kindness for Miss Hammond to help them out,' he said with mock gravity.

'You could be right,' she said, amused. 'She's been invited to the board meeting at the end of the month, and she should have something to show them. Obviously, she'll have to produce a report, and she'll know that, but also having something pictorial to explain her display would be an idea. Pictorial depictions take time to prepare, and only Madame Violet can do them as only she knows the details of what she's doing.'

He nodded. 'It sounds as if we've a plan. And I think it's time I got to know your Miss Hammond. I feel the urge to call at the museum tomorrow morning. If nothing else, it should guarantee me an invitation to the reception.'

'What reception?' she asked in surprise.

He raised his eyebrows. 'Why, the time-consuming one we're going to persuade her to organise.'

She smiled at Stanley. 'I think I *will* have that gin you were about to offer me.'

11

Harton,

The following day

At the sound of a light knock on her office door, Violet looked up from the article about how to handle artefacts, especially those that were porous.

'Hello, Gladys!' she said, smothering her annoyance at being forced to pause at an interesting point in her reading. 'Come in and sit down. Can I help you with anything?'

'I was going to ask you that very question,' Gladys said as she sat on the chair on the opposite side of the desk from Violet. She smoothed her brown tweed skirt over her knees and gave a slight cough. 'I've been leaving you alone as much as possible as I was sure you'd want to find your feet in your own way and wouldn't want me leaning over your shoulder.'

Violet murmured what she hoped sounded like gratitude.

'But it occurred to me that, by now, you might have compiled a list of questions you'd like to ask,' Gladys went on.

'That's very thoughtful of you, Gladys. But I think for the moment I'm all right. As you know, Lucy and I have made a start on sorting out the artefacts downstairs. But I'm afraid there are a huge number to get through so it'll be some time before we've finished.'

'It's something I always intended to do but never actually got down to it. I'm delighted you've taken it on.'

Violet laughed. 'You make it sound more noble than it is. We need to know what's down there and integrate what we can into the museum. Plus it's the only way I'll find what I need for my display. I'm so glad Lucy's willing to help.'

'I hope you know that you can always call on me for assistance,' Gladys said, sounding anxious, 'even if it'd be a bit too much for me to go down there as often as you.'

'Of course I do,' Violet said hastily. 'It's better that you're at the reception desk, though. If you and I were both in the basement, Lucy would be completely on her own upstairs. She's very competent, of course, but she doesn't have your breadth of knowledge over all aspects of the museum. If she had to come down to ask you something, which would likely happen, it'd leave the museum unattended.'

To her relief, she saw Gladys look mollified.

'That's very true,' Gladys said with a slight inclination of her head.

Violet glanced at the clock on her wall. 'It's about the time that I go to the staffroom and make a cup of coffee. Lucy's on the desk all morning, so when I've given her a coffee, we could have ours together in the staffroom, if you'd like?'

'That would be very pleasant,' Gladys said.

Both stood up.

'There's something I'd like to suggest regarding your

report for the trustees,' Gladys said as she followed Violet out of her office. 'It can wait till we have that coffee, though.'

'WHAT AN EXCELLENT IDEA!' Violet exclaimed and clapped her hands. 'Apart from the fact that I'd enjoy doing it, having a pictorial depiction of both displays will make it so much easier for the board to visualise what I'm talking about.'

Gladys smiled. 'I thought so, too. And as you clearly have some artistic skill, it—'

At the firm rap on the staffroom door, Gladys stopped talking.

'Come in,' Violet called.

Both glanced towards the door as Lucy came into the staffroom, followed by a man.

'Why, Stanley!' Gladys exclaimed, her voice shrill with surprise as she saw him. She stood up and took a step towards him. Then she turned back to Violet. 'I don't believe you've met Stanley Patterson yet,' she said.

Violet rose to her feet.

Lucy stood for a moment or two, hovering near the entrance.

Gladys turned to Stanley and indicated Violet. 'Meet Miss Hammond, Stanley, who's taken over the running of the museum from Dr Russell. Stanley Patterson is the owner of Patterson's Antiques, Violet, one of the best antique shops for miles around. And once or twice over the years, he's kindly advised us about auction purchases.'

Stanley went forward and held out his hand to Violet. 'I'm delighted to meet you, Miss Hammond.'

'Please call me Violet, won't you?' she said, shaking his hand. Sitting back down, she indicated one of the empty chairs at their table. 'Do join us, unless you'd rather come to my office?'

'Not at all. This is only a casual visit. I was in the area and felt it time we met. And it's always good to see Gladys. I can't remember when I last saw you, Gladys, it's so long ago.'

'Nor me,' Gladys said with a smile. 'It's certainly an age. Let me get you a coffee, Stanley.' As she went across to the kitchen area, she glanced towards Lucy. 'You'd better get back to the reception desk now, Lucy,' she said.

Lucy nodded and left the room.

'Is your shop near here, Mr Patterson?' Violet asked.

'It's Stanley, please,' he said. 'The answer's yes. It's in the heart of Bury St Edmunds.'

'How lovely! It's such a beautiful little town.'

'And my shop is in one of the best positions. Go along Abbeygate, turn right into the Buttermarket and walk up to the marketplace. Stand with your back to Marks & Spencer, and look to your left. Parallel to the Buttermarket, there are three narrow roads running into the marketplace. My shop is on the corner of Skinner Street, the closest of the three to Marks & Spencer. The chemist shop, Croasdale's, is on the corner of the next street along.'

Violet laughed. 'Something tells me that it isn't the first time you've told someone how to get to your shop.'

Stanley smiled. 'You're right, it isn't. I'm always happy to help people find my shop, and I'm more than willing if they want to leave me some of their money.'

She laughed again.

Gladys came back with a coffee for him, put it in front of him and sat down again.

'So how are you settling in, Violet?' he asked her.

'If you mean how am I settling into the house I'm renting,' she said, 'I'm very comfortable, thank you. It isn't large, but it's perfect for my needs. And I'm sorry to tell you, it has all the furniture I want,' she added with a smile.

'Darn!' he exclaimed, slapping his knee in mock dismay.

Gladys looked from one to the other in amusement.

'And how are you settling into the museum?' he continued. 'All seemed to be running very smoothly when I came in. The atmosphere was one of calm and academic tranquillity, if that makes any sense.'

She nodded. 'It does. But a little liveliness, too, at the right time would be desirable. We want to attract children into the museum, and they tend to come with a degree of noise.' And she told him about her plans for two displays, each of which was to capture graphically a moment that typified the lives of the Angles and Saxons.

His lined face took on an air of respect. 'That's an excellent idea,' he said. 'I'll be keen to see what you do. When d'you expect it to be ready?'

'Hopefully, late October.'

'Violet will be telling the board of trustees about her plans when she meets them later this month. I'm sure they'll be as excited about them as I am,' Gladys cut in.

Stanley smiled. 'And knowing the fondness of the trustees for social occasions, I imagine they'll be looking forward to the grand opening.'

'Grand opening?' Violet echoed in sudden alarm. 'What d'you mean?'

He looked a little uncomfortable. 'I assumed that on the evening before you open the display to the public there'd be some kind of reception for the trustees, and maybe for important people in the village and in Bury, too. It'd be a private viewing, accompanied, of course, by something to drink and a bite to eat. But perhaps you weren't planning to do this?'

Violet looked hesitantly at Gladys. 'You know everything there is to know about the museum's finances, Gladys. D'you think there'd be the money to pay for that?'

'To pay for what?' a man's voice asked.

Violet turned instantly towards the door, and saw Edward coming into the room.

Her spirits soared, and despite her conscious effort to avoid feeling anything at seeing him again, a warm glow of pleasure crept through her. Trying not to show how pleased she was to see him, she cleared her throat. 'To do something Stanley's just suggested,' she told him.

He pulled up a chair.

'Hello, Stanley,' he said, sitting down. 'And what's that?'

'Would you like coffee?' Violet asked.

He shook his head. 'No, thanks. I had one at the end of my morning surgery. So what did you suggest, Stanley?'

'That Violet, or the board perhaps, holds a reception here on the night before Violet's new display is opened. It would be a good way of getting word out about what sounds as if it's going to be very imaginative. There's no point in opening something if people don't know you've opened it.'

'That's an excellent idea,' Edward said. 'And in answer to the question I overheard as I came into the room, yes, there would be money for it. At least, I believe there's still a fund for such extra expenses, Gladys, isn't there?'

She nodded. 'That's right. And I can't think of a better use for the money. If you design some leaflets advertising the new display in the next week or so, Violet, we'll work out where they should go, such as to the schools in Bury, and to the Bury town councillors, and then we'll have an idea of how many we'll need to get printed. We could also use the designs as a basis for invitations to the reception. After that, we can work out how to distribute everything.'

'That's great, Gladys,' Violet said with a broad smile. 'Thank you so much for your support. And thank you, too, for such an excellent idea, Stanley, and you, Edward, for making it possible. You arrived at exactly the right moment.'

Stanley stood up. 'I ought to get back to the shop. It's been closed for long enough. It was a pleasure to meet you, Violet, and I hope we meet again before too long. You've an open invitation for a coffee at Patterson's Antiques, or a gin if you leave it late enough in the day.'

She smiled.

Gladys rose to her feet. 'I'll see you out, Stanley, and then I'll take over from Lucy.' And she led the way out of the staffroom.

Alone with Edward, Violet suddenly felt awkward. She got up. 'Would you excuse me if I go back to my office now, Edward? I've rather a lot to do.'

'I'll come with you. I stopped by as I've a couple of things to pass on to you that were sent to me by mistake,' he said, and he stood up and followed her out.

STANDING at the front door with Stanley, Gladys saw Violet go across the end of the hall to her office, accompanied by Edward.

'Well, that's well and truly put paid to any more rummaging down in the basement for a while,' she said with satisfaction. 'I hope that for some time to come, I'll be the only person down there moving objects,' she added drily. 'You'd better give me that list you promised as soon as you can.'

12

A *short time later*

VIOLET SAT in her chair behind the desk, her emotions divided.

On the one hand she was desperately trying to suppress the pleasure she felt at being alone with Edward again, something she'd no right to feel as he was an engaged man, but at the same time, she couldn't help the delight that welled up at the sight of him sitting at the other side of her desk.

If only he hadn't been so attractive!

Keeping her eyes resolutely on the papers in front of her, she determined that her best course of action was to avoid looking at him.

For a weighty few moments, neither said a word.

Violet broke the silence. 'You had some things to give me, I think you said?'

Shifting uncomfortably, Edward gave a slight cough. 'It seemed the easiest thing to say. Really, I wanted to ask you if you needed any help. I've left a couple of messages telling you to call me if you need help, but you haven't.'

Violet managed a smile. 'That's because I haven't needed any help. I've been very busy here, and on the occasions when I've wanted advice, Gladys has been able to tell me what I needed to know.' She paused. 'In a way, that's a tribute to you. Before I started here, you'd told me so much. And on the day we had lunch at Harry's, you covered a lot more of the stuff I might need to know. That helped me enormously.'

Edward nodded. 'That's good to hear.' He paused. 'How are you getting on in the house? Is there anything you need?'

'No, nothing, thank you. I feel really settled there. My parents are coming in just over a couple of weeks, and they're bringing me some touches from home. Not things I need, but things I'd like. Such as the only doll I had as a child. I thought we'd take a walk around the village after lunch. I'm sure they'll love it as much as I do.'

He smiled. 'That's good to hear. And what about the work? I'd like to know more about what you've been arranging with the school, and about your display.' He paused. 'Look, I've an idea. I've finished my morning surgery, and as I don't have any house calls to make, I'm free till my afternoon surgery. I've got to eat lunch. Would you care to join me at Harry's? This time you'd be the one giving out information, rather than the reverse.'

She stared at the top of her desk. 'I'm not sure that your fiancée would be happy at me having lunch with you,' she said bluntly, not looking up from the desk.

Silence hung in the air between them.

'She'd realise that it was about museum business,' he said at last. 'You're an employee of the board of trustees, and I'm a trustee. What's more, I probably still know things you don't know, that might be helpful to you. I can't see how anyone could take exception to that. Jean certainly wouldn't.'

'I can see people thinking it a bit strange,' she said quietly.

'That's because you're looking at it in the wrong way. This is business.' He leaned slightly towards her. 'It's a lovely day, Violet. Why don't you tell Gladys that you're bringing me up to date and will be back in a couple of hours? You could take a file with you for appearances' sake, if that made you feel better.' He picked up the file closest to him and offered it to her. 'How about this one?' he suggested.

She hesitated, took it and then put it back on the desk. 'I'll take this one,' she said, picking up a different file. 'It shows the table I've drawn up as a way of classifying each item in the basement. There's a logbook for the exhibits on show in the museum, but nothing, as far as I could see, for those that are hidden below. Lucy and I are making such a classification.'

'That's an excellent idea,' he said getting up. 'I've long regretted that we've rather ignored the items downstairs. Well done.'

'When it's finished,' she said, and she, too, stood up, 'we'll have a full list of everything in the museum, upstairs and downstairs. It could be used for education and display, and possibly even for research.' She clutched her file to her chest. 'So I accept your kind invitation to lunch.'

Their eyes met.

He turned away and they left her office.

Guilty at how much she was looking forward to having

lunch with him, her file and clutch bag in one hand, she grabbed her straw hat with the other, and hastily followed him.

'I ENJOYED THAT, EDWARD,' Violet said, sitting back in her chair. 'Thank you for the invitation.'

'It was my pleasure,' he said with a smile. 'And it really *was* a pleasure,' he added warmly.

She gave a slight nod of acknowledgement. 'Perhaps we should talk about work now?' she suggested. She opened her file and showed him the table she'd drawn up. 'These are the categories I've put. I did the same as you'd done for the items in the galleries.'

He turned the file to face him and quickly scanned her headings. 'That all looks good. I think you'll have a problem, though, with giving an acquisition date and source for everything in the basement. The items down there have come to us in a number of different ways, and some of the tags were lost in the turmoil of the war years.'

Violet nodded. 'That's what Gladys told me.'

'The physical description and distinguishing features will be easy enough for you to do, though, and they're very important,' he went on. 'So fill in what you can, and the experts will do the rest.'

'In what way are they important, apart from being a part of our records?'

'They're the starting place for everything. There are several groups of specialists we can call upon, each with an in-depth knowledge of a different area. Your descriptions will help us know upon whom to call.'

'But calling in experts will cost a lot of money,' she said with dismay.

'Don't worry. The trustees will see that you have the money for it. Get it done if you can before you open your new display. You'll want to be able to say with confidence that everything on display is genuinely Anglo-Saxon.'

'And the trustees won't think I'm extravagant?'

He smiled. 'Not at all. I'll make sure that they know it's essential work, and they'll be happy to give you their support.'

'Even though I'll also need money for the reception?'

'You're doing what they want, Violet. They want more people to come into the museum, and that's what you'll bring about. When I got here today, I saw one person in Gallery One and two in Gallery Six. It's summer. Bury St Edmunds is full of tourists, and we're only a short bus ride away. This is a well-stocked museum, with a display of keys, coins, weapons, ornaments and so on, and some excellent paintings. It's easily equal to Moyse's Hall in Bury St Edmunds. People go to Moyse's Hall, but few bother to come here.'

'I do hope I can increase the number of visitors we get,' she said anxiously.

'You will do. We'll advertise what we've done, or will have done. From what you said at the interview about your vision, your display is going to be unique. Stanley Patterson had the right idea. A private reception to which the so-called important people of both Bury and Harton are invited, held in the gallery with the new display, will be a superb way of advertising the museum. And so will the leaflets we'll distribute around the town.'

'The work with the school should help, too,' she said. 'Their art teacher is going to be doing the background scenery, which I hadn't expected, so that's one aspect of the display that I don't have to worry about. When it's open, the children will come to the museum, a class at a time, and see what their school has helped us to do. Hopefully, they'll tell their parents, who might also want to come.'

'You certainly sound as if you have everything in hand,' he told her.

'There are still one or two things I need to sort out, but not many.'

'Can I help you with them?'

'I don't really think you can, Edward,' she said. 'But I'm so grateful for the help you've already given me. I'm loving what I'm doing.'

'So no regrets about not being a schoolteacher?'

She shook her head. 'None at all.'

'And I've none at all about appointing you, Violet. Everything feels so much more vibrant since you moved here.'

She blushed. 'You mustn't talk like that,' she said. 'It's too familiar.'

He studied her face.

Beneath the intensity of his gaze, she went a deeper shade of red.

'I don't think it's too familiar,' he said at last, 'it's a matter of fact. But if it were a little familiar, in the way that one friend is to another, would that matter?'

'Of course it would,' she said. Hearing a tremor in her voice, she cleared her throat. 'There's nothing wrong with familiarity if a person's in a position to be familiar. But you're not, Edward. You've a fiancée who'd be annoyed if she heard your tone of voice when you speak to me, and who, despite the official-looking file on the table, would be sure to be upset that you were lunching with another woman.'

She paused. 'When we first met, you had several occasions to tell me you were engaged, so why didn't you?'

He gave her a wry smile. 'Now who's being familiar?'

She coloured again.

'But you're right. I should've told you from the start that Jean was not only my district nurse, but also my fiancée. I don't know why I didn't.'

'I shouldn't have just asked you that,' she said quickly. 'There was no reason for you to tell me. Ours is a working friendship.'

'You're absolutely right—there was no reason for me to tell you. And no reason for you to feel upset that I didn't. Yet I feel that I should have told you, and you're clearly upset with me that I didn't, and rightly so, I think. But why should that be?'

Each stared at the other across the table.

'I think it's time I went back to the museum,' she said at last, and she stood up. 'Thank you very much for lunch. I'll walk back on my own.'

She picked up her file and headed at speed past the school towards the marketplace, and thence to the museum, glad that Edward was some distance behind her and couldn't see that her eyes had filled with tears.

When he reached the local school, where he had to turn left to get back to Church Road and his surgery, Edward stood and watched Violet retreating across the marketplace. He saw her pass the tall hedges at the back of the museum and turn down Museum Road to the high street.

Long after she'd disappeared from view, he was still standing there staring at the spot where he'd lost sight of her.

. . .

Gladys had been at the reception desk when Violet walked back into the museum.

'I thought to do some work in my office,' she told Gladys.

Gladys nodded. 'That's a good idea. It's better that you get on with your report for the board, and the pictures to accompany it, than that you sit here. Lucy's going to take over from me in about half an hour, and I'll go down to the basement to help with the sorting.'

'That's very kind of you. Thank you.'

'Not at all. I really should have made an effort before now. Lucy's put me to shame. She went down as soon as she'd had her lunch, rather than take a proper break, and she's been below stairs ever since then. She lacks experience, though, so it might be better if she did a stint up here while I went downstairs, had a quick look at what she's done, and then did some more sorting myself.'

Violet smiled gratefully at her. 'It's very kind of you both. I'll be in my office, then. Will you tell her that if either of you needs anything, not to hesitate to knock?'

She started to move away, then paused. 'It was very pleasant meeting Stanley Patterson this morning,' she said. 'I'll pop into his shop when I'm next in Bury. I'll wait till my parents have been to lunch, but I'll make a point of going there soon after that.'

Gladys nodded. 'On the few occasions over the years that I've been to his shop, I've been most impressed by his stock. It's genuine antiques, you know. These days, you find a number of places calling themselves antique shops, but what they're really selling is junk.'

'I imagine one has to be really careful. I'm so glad he mentioned the idea of a reception. Obviously, he'll be invited. But now I must get on. And here's Lucy!'

With a smile at Gladys, she went across the hall to her office.

'DID you get much done down there?' Gladys asked as Lucy came over to the reception table and took the empty seat next to hers.

Lucy pulled a downcast face. 'Not as much as I'd hoped. I was able to identify one or two things, but I don't know enough to be confident about many of them. I picked out a few obvious things, and put them on what I think is the right shelf. I kept hoping other items would scream at me that they were twelfth or thirteenth century, but they didn't. I'm quite relieved that you're going to look through what I've done. You're much better than I am at knowing what's what.'

'The museum's lucky to have you, Lucy. You're intelligent, eager to learn and hardworking. That's an ideal combination.'

'I think I'm so lucky to have the job,' she said earnestly. 'My schoolfriends thought I was nuts to want to work here and not in Bury, but I've always liked history and I thought the job sounded interesting.'

'And *do* you find it interesting?' Gladys asked.

Lucy nodded vigorously. 'Oh yes,' she said. 'Even more than I thought I would. And identifying the artefacts is fascinating.'

'That's good to hear.' Gladys gave a slight cough. 'It's just occurred to me, as you're finding it difficult to place the artefacts, would you prefer it if I went down to the basement and you stayed on the reception desk? I think my aged legs would just about cope with the steps.'

'That's very kind of you, Gladys, but I'm happy to carry on going downstairs. It's the only way I'll learn. My goal is to be able to identify the date and purpose of everything we have in the museum, whether upstairs or downstairs. When the experts come, I'll find out if I was right, and that'll teach me a lot.'

Forcing a smile to her face, Gladys stood up and left the reception desk to Lucy.

13

H*arton,*
Sunday, two weeks later

AT THE SOUND of her father's van pulling up outside her house, Violet rushed to the front door and flung it open. 'Welcome!' she cried as she rushed forward to help her mother from the van.

Mabel Hammond held Violet at arm's length and studied her face. 'The country air suits you, love,' she said. And she hugged her daughter.

'Your mother and I were saying how pleasant it was to be able to get to you fairly easily. It's a long journey, but not a difficult one,' John Hammond said coming round the side of the van. He, too, gave Violet a big hug.

'Your mother's right. You do look well, love,' he said. He glanced beyond her to her small front garden. The grass had been cut and the hedge trimmed. 'I see you've got the garden in shape,' he remarked. 'Well done.'

'Thanks, Father. But why are we standing here? Come on in and see the house. I know you've been here before, but that's when I was moving in, so it was in a mess. But there's a place for everything now. I've learnt that when you live in a small house, it's essential that everything has a home, and that you keep it tidy.'

They followed her into a small lobby, and into the sitting room through a door on the right.

'Sit down and make yourself comfortable,' she said.

'I always think an empty fireplace looks very sad,' John said, nodding towards the grate as he sat down in a floral-covered armchair. Mabel sat down opposite him.

Violet nodded. 'Me, too. I sometimes put a vase of flowers in front of it to make it look better, but they don't last long. But perhaps this is something for you to think about, Father. Unlit fireplaces look woeful in summer. You could get one of your shop assistants to make an interesting screen that would hide most of the grate. She could do it when it was her turn to sit in the emporium window. If the passers-by saw what she was doing, they might want one, too. You could do a roaring trade in framed tapestry screens.'

John smiled. 'It's certainly a thought. We get a lot of customers coming back again, and we need new ways of tempting them into spending their money. It tells me, too, that you can take a girl from the heart of a haberdashery store but you can't take the love of haberdashery out of the girl.'

Violet laughed. 'As my new display is inspired by the displays that Iris did for your shops during the war, that could be true.'

'How are they coming, love?' her mother asked.

'Very well, thank you. At least, I think they are. I've solved all but one problem.'

'And what's that?' John asked.

'The display figures I need,' Violet said. 'They're pretty important. I need six fairly life-size figures, I think it is. I thought to go to the Theatre Royal in Bury to see if they had any mannequins. If not, I'll go to shops like Marks & Spencer and try my luck there. If the worst comes to the worst, I'll have to go to London. As for clothes for the mannequins, I'm sure I'll be able to get them from Bury market. They should be quite straightforward. They're Angles and Saxons, and it's not like they'd be wearing elaborate costumes.'

John sat back. 'I can probably help you with the mannequins, love. Between my contacts in the market and the local shops, and what we've got in the emporium, I can find you six good-sized models, or more if you need them. And between your mother and me, we can provide some clothes for them. Just give me a detailed list of everything you want, and leave it to us.'

'Thank you so much, Father,' Violet cried. She hugged her father hard, and then drew back. 'I must've been more worried about it than I'd thought as I feel so hugely relieved. Thank you so much. You, too, Mother.' And she went across and gave her mother a kiss.

'Right,' Violet said. 'Let me make you some tea—you must be thirsty after your journey. And I've made some little scones. I hope you like them.'

'I hope you didn't go to too much trouble, dear,' her mother said anxiously. 'We know how busy you've been.'

Violet waved her hand dismissively. 'It's only a simple meal, and I enjoyed making it. I'll get that tea now.'

. . .

'THAT WAS A DELICIOUS PLUM TART, LOVE,' Mabel said as she put her spoon and fork together on the empty plate.

'I'm glad you enjoyed it. I thought I ought to do something very Suffolkish, and as Victoria plums grow in profusion in Suffolk, and I love plum tart, that seemed the obvious pudding to make.'

'I didn't realise you were such a good cook,' her mother said. 'If I'd known, I'd have let you take over from me years ago.'

'Then I'm glad you didn't know,' Violet said cheerfully. 'I enjoy making the occasional meal and odd cakes and things, but I don't think I'll ever be the best of cooks. Not like you. In the war years you did amazing things with very little.'

'That feels a long time ago now. Doesn't it, John?' Mabel said.

'Yes, it does, love. He paused. 'You know, Violet, if I'm being truly honest with you, when you sprang it on your mother and me that you were going to run a museum, and not be a teacher like you'd always wanted, I thought you were making a big mistake,' John said folding his napkin and putting it next to his plate.

Violet smiled. 'I seem to recall you saying as much at the time, and more than once.'

'Well, I was wrong. I think it was the right decision. The work clearly suits you, and has given you a new interest. Your mother and I felt the same desire to do something different when we sold two of our shops and expanded the third. We'd reached a point where we needed a fresh challenge, and building an emporium was just that. In the same way, your museum job is obviously a challenge for you, and that's invigorated you, if I may say so.'

'I'm glad you think so, Father. Rose and Iris probably felt

the same at some point about taking a path they could never have predicted, and from what you've told me about your visits to both of them, it's worked out very well for them, even if they had some shaky moments,' Violet went on.

'They both live in lovely places,' Mabel said, 'and they seem so happy. You mustn't leave it too much longer before you visit them.'

'I'll go next year, doing like you did, starting in Jersey and going from there to Dinan. But there's too much to do in what's left of this year for me to be able to leave the museum for the couple of weeks I'd need. We've only a small number of staff.'

'What are the people working with you like?' John asked, taking his worn leather tobacco pouch from one of the pockets in his jacket and his pipe from the other.

'Dr Russell is extremely nice,' Violet said enthusiastically. 'He's been ever so helpful, and very thoughtful in making sure I'm comfortable here and in the museum. He's still on the board of trustees and pops in from time to time to see how I'm managing. If I need any advice I can call him. But I haven't needed to do so as Gladys is so helpful.'

John nodded. 'You've mentioned Gladys several times since you started there. She's proving to be a good colleague, isn't she?'

'That's right. She knows all there is to know about the museum and she's helped me a lot. And there's Lucy. She's a general assistant, and also does any typing that's needed. She's lovely, too. She's working closely with me. She helped me measure up for the display cabinets last week.'

'Your ideas sound excellent,' John said, starting to fill the bowl of the pipe with tobacco. 'I just hope the museum realises that they've hired a gem.'

'Not that you're biased, Father,' Violet said lightly. She

hesitated, watching her father gently tamp the tobacco in the half-full bowl with his tamper. 'I *have* made one mistake, though, and a true gem wouldn't have made that. Fortunately, Edward—that's Dr Russell—doesn't know about it, and there's no harm done. I was very silly, though.'

Mabel frowned. 'What did you do, Violet?'

'It's more what I didn't do,' Violet said morosely. And she told them about signing the forms without reading them.

'But as you say, you've now read through the forms,' John said, lighting the pipe and drawing in a couple of breaths, 'and you've seen there isn't anything you wouldn't have signed, so there's nothing to worry about. Everyone makes mistakes, but they learn from them. You'll never make such a mistake again,' he added, filling the rest of the pipe and tamping down the tobacco more firmly.

Violet nodded vigorously. 'You can be sure I won't.'

'But your Gladys is partly to blame, too, from what you said,' John went on, taking the pipe from his mouth. 'She knows you're inexperienced so she should've been more protective of you. She'd been with you all afternoon, so she must have realised you'd had enough for the day. And the end of the day is the wrong time to sign anything, anyway. She was at fault in the first place.' He put his pipe back in his mouth and drew in deeply.

Mabel squeezed Violet's hand. 'Your father's right, love. Don't be too hard on yourself.'

Violet frowned. 'I never thought about it like that, but yes, you're right. I wonder why she gave them to me at such a time.' She shrugged. 'It was probably because there was nothing of major importance among the forms, and she was keen to get them out of the way. She's a very efficient person. Now, shall I make us a coffee?'

'That would be lovely,' John said. 'And then what about

that walk you mentioned over lunch? It'd be good to have a little exercise before we start for home, and I'm keen to see the village. So far, we've seen your house and the outside of the museum, but nothing more.'

'Your father's right, Violet. If we see the rest of the village, we'll be able to picture what you're talking about when you tell us what you've done and where you've been.'

'Shall we get off now, then?' Violet said getting up. 'We can have our coffee or tea when we get back. We'll go as far as the pub that Edward and I call Harry's Inn. When we get there, I'll tell you why.'

'A walk first and coffee later sounds a good idea,' John said, putting his tobacco pouch into his pocket.

'We'll go up Museum Road to the marketplace, where you'll find the butcher's, bakery and grocer's,' Violet said as her parents stood up. 'I'll show you the school, which is on the other side of the marketplace, and then we'll go up to Harry's, and from there walk along the outer edge of the village. There's a small wood in the top right-hand corner, which is very pleasant to walk in, especially if it's hot. It's a little way back from some new houses they're building.'

'More visitors for the museum,' her mother said with a smile.

Violet laughed. 'I do hope so. Then we'll come back down Church Road. If you want to look at the church, we can turn off Church Road and walk along Church Lane. The local church is very old. Then we'll come back, passing Edward's house and his surgery, which is almost next to his house, and then the village hall. It sounds a long walk, but it isn't. The village is really quite small.'

'It sounds lovely, dear,' her mother said.

. . .

'ARE you sure you don't want tea before you leave?' Violet asked her parents as the three of them stood by the van.

John shook his head. 'Quite sure, thank you, love. As we told your Dr Russell when we turned down his kind invitation, we've a long drive ahead and we shouldn't leave it too late to start for home. Your mother and I have very much enjoyed the day,' he told her. 'And you're right, it's a very pretty village.'

'Wasn't it lucky that Edward saw us passing by?' Violet said happily. 'I was so surprised when I heard him calling out to us. And then offering us tea. He's helped me so much that I'm delighted you had a chance to meet him. And also that I could ask him to stop by at the museum on Tuesday. There are costings and items he needs to approve before I can order them.'

Her parents exchanged glances.

'We're pleased to have met him, love,' Mabel said. 'He seems a very pleasant man. You've mentioned him several times today. I was quite surprised he invited us to tea, though. He's only your boss, after all.' She smiled questioningly at Violet.

Violet blushed. 'He's helped me with a lot of things, so I've obviously mentioned him more than once.' She heard the defensive note in her voice, and coughed. 'What you're hinting at couldn't be further from the truth—he's engaged to the woman who's his district nurse.'

Her mother glanced again at her father, and then turned back to Violet. 'In that case, love,' Mabel said firmly, 'I'd join one of those clubs you were talking about. It'd be good to meet other people in the village.'

14

T*hat evening*

EDWARD SAT AT HIS DESK, staring with unseeing eyes at the pieces of paper spread out in front of him. He should never have rushed out to speak to her parents, he scolded himself.

If only he'd been able to ignore the fact that he knew she intended for them to take a walk around the village after they'd had lunch and would probably take a route that would bring them past his house.

But he hadn't been able to do so, and as a result, he'd taken his agenda for the next meeting of the board of trustees to the chair next to the window and had sat down. Apart from an occasional glance at the agenda, he'd watched for them to appear.

Then, as soon as he'd seen them, he'd run out and offered them tea!

He must have been crazy!

Had they accepted, Mavis would have been most annoyed as she'd had no warning of possible visitors. But worse than that, she might have started to wonder about his feelings for Violet.

She had worked for him for long enough to know him very well, and not for one minute would she believe that his interest in meeting Violet's parents was for themselves alone. They weren't doctors. They weren't in any way connected with museum administration. Their sole interest to him must be that they were Violet's family.

Mavis would have been bound to come to the conclusion that his motive was simply to meet Violet, and to talk to her, even if it was for a few minutes only.

And he dreaded to think what Violet's parents must have made of it.

If they thought about it for more than a minute, they, too, could easily suspect that Violet was the reason behind the invitation. After all, it was quite a coincidence he was asking them to swallow, that he'd happened to look out of the window at the exact moment they were passing.

With luck, as they'd turned down the invitation, they wouldn't see it as anything more than an act of friendliness, and they'd soon forget about it.

But what about Violet?

She could easily wonder why he'd gone out of his way to meet her parents. There'd been no need for him to meet them, and she'd know that. Her hasty attempt to make their conversation about work was proof of this.

She knew he was engaged to Jean, so what must she have thought of him?

Angry with himself, he pulled one of the pieces of paper towards him and glared at it.

Whatever Mavis and Violet might think they knew

about his feelings, they were wrong. How could they know what he felt when he didn't even know it himself?

But every bone in his body told him that he'd be wise to avoid seeing Violet for anything other than work. Stopping by the museum merely to say hello must end. To do otherwise would be unfair to Jean.

And to Violet, too.

THE LUNCH DISHES washed and everything put away in their drawer or cupboard, and the drop-leaf table back against the wall, Violet sat in her sitting room and enjoyed the fresh air drifting into the room through the open window.

The sunlight, so bright in the middle of the day, was losing its lustre and fading into a pale yellow glow as the afternoon moved inexorably towards dusk. Shadows were creeping from the corners of the room but she felt no impetus to switch on the lamp.

It had been a really successful day, she thought.

It had been the first time she'd entertained in her home, and she felt the meal had gone well. Her parents had been comfortable in the house and the room hadn't felt too cramped. Also, by being in such a lovely village, she'd had something to do with them in the afternoon and she knew they'd all enjoyed their walk.

Even without Edward's intervention, it would have been a really satisfying day.

But he had intervened. He'd come out to meet her parents.

He hadn't needed to do so.

Nevertheless, it was pretty obvious that he'd kept an eye out for them, knowing they'd be taking a walk after lunch.

After her pleased surprise at seeing Edward, she'd been

disappointed at hearing her father decline his invitation to tea. But upon reflection, it was probably just as well he'd done so. Her parents and Edward didn't have a lot in common, and conversation could have been difficult.

Fortunately, because she'd had a genuine work matter to bring up with Edward in the few minutes they'd spoken, she had been able to alter the tone of the meeting and prevent it from seeming purely social.

But what must her parents make of him appearing like that, and then issuing an invitation to tea?

She straightened up. It was really important that she didn't mention him as often as she must have been doing. Her mother hadn't directly asked her about her feelings for Edward, but she'd certainly implied that Violet felt an attraction towards him. And now they knew he was engaged, it would be awful if they thought she'd fallen in love with him.

And they'd be wrong, because she hadn't.

If he hadn't been engaged, she would have been able to accept that she had feelings for him that kept her awake at night, and if she found that he felt the same about her, it could have been so different.

But he *was* engaged.

He wasn't the sort of man to show an interest in a woman when he was engaged to someone else. She wasn't the sort of woman to chase after a man who was spoken for. Their friendship was built on a shared interest in the museum, and it could never be anything more than that.

But he had been watching for them to pass his house that afternoon, and had come out to them when he needn't have done.

And when she'd seen him coming towards her, her heart had been so full that she thought it might explode.

So what did that say about his feelings for her, and what did it say about hers for him?

She was going to have to be very strong with herself, she resolved. To admit to herself how much she liked him, really liked him, and even more so to reveal the depth of her feelings to him, would be walking with her eyes wide open into a situation that could only end in unhappiness.

She burst into tears.

15

T*he following Tuesday*

VIOLET SAT in her office and surveyed the lists in front of her with relief.

Having told Edward on the Sunday that she needed to see him on Tuesday about some costings, she'd had to have something to give him for his approval, so she'd worked solidly for the whole of the previous day and well into the evening.

Thanks to Gladys's advice, she'd already drawn pictures of the structures she'd need for her displays, and had sketched out the items she hoped to exhibit within them, all of which would be attached to the report she'd give to the trustees, but which she could show to Edward that morning.

But now she'd also drawn up a list of items to purchase and tasks for the caretaker, the first of which would be to check the measurements for the display cabinets that would take up almost the whole of two walls.

She and Lucy had done a rough measurement the week before, and although they'd later checked their figures and thought them accurate, someone practical like the caretaker would know if they'd made any mistakes.

A separate list contained everything relating to the catering.

She was now at the stage where she had to ask Edward, on behalf of the trustees, to approve the expenditure she'd suggested, which made their meeting that morning a genuinely needed one, not something spurious to justify a change of tone at the awkward meeting between him and her parents.

Hopefully, he would also approve the suggestion made by Lucy's mother of using her close friend, Wendy Ives, to do the food for the reception. She was a baker in Bury St Edmunds, who did occasional catering, and she had sent in a quote through Lucy. But the board of trustees must have a caterer they used, so Edward might prefer to contact them.

He would also have to tell her where to get the special glass they used in the cabinets, and from whom to order the wooden frames. She would need a number of very slender stands of adjustable heights for positioning the items within the cabinet so they conveyed the effect of a scene trapped in a moment of time. Edward would know where to get those, she was sure.

On her desk she also had a proposal for a leaflet advertising the museum that could be delivered to shops and hotels in Bury St Edmunds, and distributed around Harton. To illustrate it, she'd taken a small drawing from the leaflets given to visitors to the museum on their arrival, and had put it in the corner of her proposed leaflet.

When she showed her idea to Edward, she'd also show him the list of people, from both Bury and from Harton, whom she and Gladys had thought should be invited to the opening reception. She was sure he would want to add to the list as he'd be familiar with those responsible for running the town in the way that she wasn't.

She glanced at the clock on her desk. Hopefully, he wouldn't be late in arriving. He'd telephoned the museum the previous day and told her that unexpectedly he had to look in at the hospital that morning, but would stop by beforehand. He'd take all her proposals and costings with him and get back to her when he'd had time to look at them properly.

After he'd left, she was going to walk up to the school and give the headmistress her sketches for the background for inside the display cabinets, which would be passed on to the art teacher. The end of October looked like being a good date for the opening of the display, and she'd pencilled that in as it would give the teacher something to work towards.

At the same time, the headmistress was going to give her copies of what the pupils were going to be taught about life in Anglo-Saxon times when the term started the following week, which would help her with the contents of her display and with the workbooks she intended to prepare for pupils' visits.

She and Lucy had been going down to the basement whenever they'd had a moment, and had already put aside a number of items relating to Anglo-Saxons at home and at war. She'd been amazed by the number of really interesting artefacts they'd found, to which there was nothing similar already on show in the museum. It would add to the feeling of something new in terms of content, she thought gleefully, as well as something new in the way the exhibits were displayed.

She'd sent her father the details he needed in order to source suitable mannequins and the clothes they'd be wearing, and he'd sent back word that there'd be no problem in getting what she'd asked for.

As she looked at the pile of papers in front of her, she felt a strong sense of satisfaction. It was all starting to take shape.

The only other thing left to arrange was when to go into the school to speak to the children at their morning assembly. She'd suggest the middle of October. If she built up a sense of excitement in the children at there soon being something different to look at in the village, that momentum should still be fairly strong by the time the display was opened at the end of October and the first group of pupils came to the museum.

As she glanced again at her clock, there was a knock on the door.

Her stomach lurched. 'Come in,' she called.

Edward came into the room.

She promptly stood up.

For a brief moment they stood facing each other, discomfort etched in their faces.

'Sit down, won't you?' she said at last, and sat down herself. He took the seat opposite her. 'Thank you very much for coming out to say hello to my parents on Sunday,' she began. 'And for the invitation to tea.'

He nodded. 'I was pleased to meet them.' He paused. 'I'd just come out of my house as I'd thought to call in on Martin to see if he wanted a walk, and then I saw you. The timing was a pleasing coincidence.'

She blushed. 'I thought it must be something like that.'

He coughed. 'Anyway, where are those documents you wanted me to look at?'

She handed him the pile she'd gathered. 'I think it's all self-explanatory. The food quotation is per head. It's from someone Lucy's mother knows. Lucy thought it a low quote as a favour to us. You would know if that's right or not.'

'What about tea and orange juice? Would she provide those, too?'

Violet went red, and bit her lip. 'I'd forgotten about drinks. I'll have to ask her. She'd have to bring urns.' She looked at him anxiously.

'Don't worry,' he said. 'When we have a final number, I'll have a word with her. And I'll arrange for the leaflets and invitations to be printed. We've always used the same printer, and at some point when there's less going on, I'll take you there and introduce you.'

'Thank you for all your help!' she exclaimed, sitting back heavily in her chair. 'Thank you very much.'

He smiled at her. 'I'm glad to do something to help. I think it's really impressive what you've managed to do in the relatively short amount of time you've been here.'

'I've only managed to get this far because Gladys and Lucy have helped so much. We're all responsible for this.'

He laughed. 'Don't worry, if it goes well, we'll give you all the credit. But if it doesn't, we'll blame Gladys and Lucy as well.'

She laughed, too.

As their laughter died away, they stared at each other without speaking.

'I'm going to have to go now,' he said at last, getting up. 'I've got to check on a villager who was taken to hospital last night. Jean would have gone but one of her patients is close to delivery. It looks as if there might be problems, so it's best she stays in Harton today.'

'Of course,' she murmured, standing up.

He took the papers she handed to him.

'Will you let me know as soon as you've checked my figures?' she asked, feeling the need to say something to fill the awkward silence that had fallen again.

He nodded. 'Of course.' He glanced down at the pile. 'I expect you've remembered to do so, but if you haven't, don't forget to include an RSVP on the invitation. We'll need to have some idea of how many are planning to come.'

'I won't forget.'

He glanced at her face. 'I'm sorry, Violet,' he said quietly, 'I'm not sure why I'm saying it, but it feels the right thing to say.'

She gave him a rueful smile. 'So am I, Edward,' she said.

An aura of wistfulness hovered between them.

'I'm sorry,' he repeated.

Their eyes locked, then he turned and left the office.

16

L*ater that day*

'DID you give Edward your drawings and the various lists?' Lucy asked as she and Violet went down the steps to the basement.

'He took the whole lot with him. When we were talking, he asked about the drinks, and I realised I'd forgotten about them. Happily, he's going to speak to Wendy himself, and he said he'll get everything printed when it's ready.'

'Not long now,' Lucy said cheerfully.

'You can say that again! It's frighteningly close. We're thinking of having the reception and opening on the twenty-ninth of October.'

'That *is* soon!' Lucy exclaimed.

'Indeed, it is,' Violet said as they walked into the basement kitchen. She looked around them with satisfaction. 'There isn't an item on a shelf in here or in most of the other rooms that doesn't now have a pencilled label. When we know if our designations are correct, we can write everything in ink. We'll know how close we are to being right on Friday as that's when the specialists are coming in.'

Lucy smiled. 'I'm looking forward to that.'

'Me, too. There's only the butler's room left to do, and we should get that finished today or tomorrow,' Violet said, and they started walking towards the end of the corridor. 'It's lucky that Gladys is happy to be on the desk all afternoon, as well as having been out there this morning. She said she prefers that to being among the cobwebs down here.'

Lucy stopped and looked around her. 'Except there aren't any cobwebs, are there? It's amazing how clean it is down here. We're never dirty when we go back up.'

'I said the same thing to Gladys,' Violet said. 'It must be down to the cleaners. Apparently, they come down here once a month. They obviously do a very thorough job, which is important as Gladys said some of the items here are very valuable.'

'I'm impressed,' Lucy said. 'I may even ask them their secret. Our house gets dirty almost as soon as my mother's finished cleaning it. But I suppose it's different down here. No one comes to the basement except for us.'

When they reached the butler's room, Lucy continued walking past the opening and went up to the back door.

'There's no key in the box,' she remarked. 'But to look at the door, you'd never think it wasn't being used.'

'I was going to ask Edward if he had a master key, but I've been so busy that I forgot. I'll make a note of it and get down to it as soon as I can. But for now, let's see what there is in the butler's room. I doubt there's anything much of interest this far into the basement, but you never know.'

. . .

'THERE ARE some lovely items in here,' Lucy said when they finished working their way through the butler's room. 'And we didn't think we'd find anything of interest! It's quite a surprise that we have. At a glance, they'd be all wrong for your display, but it would be lovely to find a home upstairs for some of them.'

'I agree,' Violet said. 'The way the cabinets are placed in the galleries is a bit wasteful of space. Once the display is open, I'll see about having another line of cabinets in some of the other galleries. And the art gallery doesn't have any exhibits. We might be able to find a few that relate to the period or subject of the paintings and put them in there.'

Lucy indicated a figurine in the far corner of the top shelf. 'I mean, look at that—it's beautiful.' She went up to the figurine and glanced at the label. 'Apparently, it was found in a church near here. It's made of copper alloy and gilt, and it dates from the fourteenth century.'

She turned and smiled at Violet. 'The work's been done for us,' she said cheerfully. 'And for most of the other artefacts, too, in here,' she added, looking around the small room.

She took a tall, rounded goblet with a dome-shaped cover from the shelf next to her, and scanned the label. 'We know this is a ciborium that was used to take the consecrated host to sick people and to anyone else who was unable to go to Holy Communion. It dates from the fifteenth century.'

Violet ran her eyes along the shelves. 'You're right. A lot of them appear to have more than the most basic of details on their label. Not all, though. I wonder what this is.' Very carefully she lifted a small rectangular metal board from a shelf near her, and read the label. 'All it says is "Pax Board, fifteenth century". I wonder what it's for?'

'I can tell you,' Lucy said, taking it from her. 'There was a pax board in one of the galleries when I started. I don't know why it was removed, so it would be good to exhibit this one. It's an excellent example of a pax board as it's got a clearly defined picture of Christ on the cross on it. They're an English invention and this would interest people.'

'What were they used for?' Violet asked.

'You know in the church service, how people sort of kiss each other when it gets to the kiss of peace. It's particularly done in Roman Catholic churches. Well, the idea was that instead of kissing a person, you kissed the board. If people hadn't washed, it would certainly be preferable to kiss a board than kiss an unsavoury person,' she added with a giggle.

Violet pulled a face. 'I totally agree. So why did they stop using them?'

'Because they caused so much unrest over hierarchy. There were so many disputes about the order in which the board should be kissed that in the end they fell out of popularity.' She glanced again at the board. 'This one certainly looks as if it's seen some trouble—there's a noticeable indentation in the right-hand corner, as if it was thrown at someone and hit the target.'

'That's really interesting,' Violet said as Lucy put the pax board back on the shelf.

Violet glanced around her again. 'Given the better labelling of most of the items in here, it's not going to take us long to see if there's anything we'd want for the display.'

'So, that's where you are!'

They turned and saw Gladys standing in the open doorway.

'We were just going to do this room,' Violet told her. 'This is the last room. We've done all the others. I don't think we'll need to spend much time in here as the labels seem to be more detailed than elsewhere.'

'They would be,' Gladys said with a smile. 'As you know, Edward asked me more than once to see that everything down here was catalogued. When I'd done a few, we called in the experts to see if I was doing it correctly. These are the items they evaluated, and when they'd done them, they wrote the details on the labels. Unfortunately, owing to a lack of time, we haven't yet moved the artefacts upstairs.'

'It makes me even more keen to hear what the specialists say at the end of the week,' Violet said. 'Obviously, it's going to take them a while to get everything done, but I'll ask that they start on the things I've set aside for the display. I'm hoping they won't take too long.'

'I'm sure they won't. You may well be correct in the details you've pencilled in. You've obviously been quite thorough. I've seen you reading the auction catalogues we've been sent, and they'll have built up your bank of knowledge.'

Violet nodded. 'I hope so. I found the catalogues very interesting.' She paused. 'You said you were looking for us, Gladys. Is anything wrong?'

'It's that I've got toothache. I feel guilty asking it, seeing how hard you're working down here, but I feel I ought to go to the dentist before the pain gets worse. I'd also like to get to the chemist before it shuts as I might need aspirin tonight. I go to a dentist in Bury, in Hatter Street. I know it's early, but would you mind if I left now?'

Violet stepped forward, her face concerned. 'Of course, you must leave at once,' she said. 'Toothache's really awful. I do hope they can sort it out before it gets worse. And if it's not right tomorrow, you must stay at home.'

'Well, if you're sure,' Gladys said hesitantly. She looked around again. 'I do feel guilty, though.'

'Well, you mustn't,' Violet said firmly. 'You're such a help and such a hard worker that you're more than entitled to leave early. Lucy and I will go back upstairs now. There's no need for us to go through this room.'

'I do hope your tooth feels better soon, Gladys,' Lucy said as she and Violet followed Gladys back through the basement.

'I'm sure it will,' Gladys said. Reaching the foot of the stone steps, she turned to them, her hand pressed against her cheek. 'Thank you, both of you, for your kindness.'

17

B*ury St Edmunds,*
Later that day,

'WELL, THIS IS UNEXPECTED,' Stanley said as Gladys hurried into Patterson's Antiques. 'Aren't you usually still at work at this time?' he asked as he shut the door behind her and turned the sign on the door to "Closed".

'I told them I needed to see the dentist as I had to speak to you urgently,' she said, panting.

'How intriguing, Gladys, but somewhat alarming, too. Come through to the back and we'll talk there.'

He led the way into the small room behind the shop and indicated for Gladys to sit down. Then he poured a glass of water and put it on the table next to her. 'You look as if you could do with that,' he said as he sat down at the other side of the table. 'We'll have something more interesting later when you've told me what this is about.'

She clutched her bag on her lap. 'I'm really worried,

Stan. It's about Violet and Lucy again. They've almost finished going through the items stored in the basement and have got experts coming in on Friday. But I'm not worried about the specialists, though, as I've been checking what they've set aside and removing anything made by Eric.'

He held out his hands questioningly, palms upwards. 'What's the anxiety, then?'

'After lunch, I decided to visit them in the basement. I thought I ought to look as if I was interested in how they were getting on. If I appear uninterested, they might not keep me up to date with their plans regarding that wretched display.'

'That seems very wise,' Stanley said.

'To my great alarm, I found them in the butler's room!' she exclaimed.

'Does it matter that they were there?' he asked in surprise.

She nodded impatiently. 'Yes. No one ever goes there so it's where I've been putting the items destined for Eric. I know the sort of things you can sell. Everything in the butler's room has been through the hands of the experts so I know their worth. And there are quite a lot of them. The experts don't come that often, so after each visit, I've been setting aside anything I think you could sell.'

Stanley frowned. 'I see.'

'You can imagine how excited they were at finding such a hoard!' she said angrily. 'I'm just glad that I went down there when I did or I might not've known they'd been in there. Fortunately, they hadn't yet started on the room, and the detailed labels had made them think it might not be necessary to do so.'

Stanley stared at her intently. 'Are you sure they didn't find anything that could cause us a problem?'

She shook her head. 'I'm sure they didn't—I got there in time. But now that they know there are artefacts in the room, even if they haven't had a close look at them, it's all got much riskier. Also, we'll soon have to move everything from Gallery Five to make a space for the blasted display. I'd been planning to put anything that would be suitable for Eric in the butler's room.'

'Isn't there anywhere else to store them?'

She shrugged. 'I've occasionally put one or two of the less valuable items in the scullery. It's not the nicest of rooms and we don't go into it if we don't have to.'

He thought for a moment.

'When the time comes to move items from Gallery Five to the basement,' he said slowly, 'it might be possible, using sleight of hand, for only the less valuable items to reach the basement.'

She nodded slowly. 'I suppose it could be done, so long as I was the one who was moving the items downstairs. But how will I know what's most valuable at the moment?'

He gave her a wry smile. 'I'd tell you, of course.' He sat back. 'I feel the urge to visit the museum again in the not-too-distant future. In fact, I think I'll do so tomorrow. You can give me a quick tour of Gallery Five, and at the same time, you can discreetly hand me a couple of items from the butler's room in case Violet and Lucy decide to inspect the contents of the room after all and the artefacts become lodged in their memory. How does that sound?'

'It sounds fine. But that's not the only thing worrying me. I think we'll have to do something about Lucy, Stan. She's far too interested in everything Violet's doing. We've managed to distract Madame Violet a little, but there's a limit to what we can do to rein in Lucy.'

'She's harmless, isn't she? She doesn't know the first thing about artefacts, you told me a while ago.'

'Unfortunately, that's not strictly true any longer,' Gladys said bitterly. 'She's made an effort to learn about them by reading books on the subject. She even goes down to the basement on her own when she doesn't have to, and tries to identify the period they date from. She hopes to compare what she thinks with what the experts say. That's the way she'll learn, she tells me.'

'You're worrying for nothing,' Stanley said tetchily. 'Reading a few books won't make her an expert.'

'The point is, she'll know what's there, and more importantly, she'll know what isn't,' she said with exaggerated patience. 'With two people now poking their noses into every dark corner and recess, it's all become more dangerous for us. They're studying the originals, Stan. In the future, if they come across a copy, one of them is sure to notice if there's anything different from the original.'

He raised his eyebrows. 'And you feel brave enough to tell Eric to be sure not to make any mistakes in his copies?'

She slumped back. 'Obviously not. At least, not in those words.' She paused. 'So you think we should continue as we've been doing and not stop immediately, before we're caught?'

'We've already broached that once with Eric, and you know what he said. I can imagine what he'd say if I suggested pulling the plug on our little enterprise again. He'd tell us we have a choice—either we put an end to what has been a profitable venture, or we get rid of the cause of our problem. According to you, two causes of our problem.'

'What're you thinking of doing?' she asked sharply.

'Relax, not what you're fearing,' he said drily. 'Finding another job for Lucy, and disgracing Miss Hammond. The first I should be able to deal with, but you'd have to give me two or three weeks. The second would be down to you. But as you've been preparing for such an eventuality since she started at the museum, that shouldn't be too difficult.'

'What *are* you talking about?' she asked irritably.

He raised his eyebrows. 'You're making Miss Hammond look guilty of theft, aren't you?'

'That's true,' she said slowly.

'So we've been protecting ourselves against a situation like this for some time now. In addition to the bank statements, it might be an idea to plant some physical evidence against her. Just in case. So I suggest that while I deal with the problem of Lucy, you think about a second way to incriminate Miss Hammond.' He paused. 'So what do you think? Should we again ask Eric to agree to us stopping, or should we continue?'

'If it can be done as you suggest, then I'd prefer to continue. The two or three weeks you mentioned won't be a problem. With the evaluation over, they'll be so busy till the end of October, dealing with the reception and the active display, and liaising with the school as the art teacher there is doing the background scenery, that they won't have time to dig around in the basement.'

Stanley smiled. 'So we're carrying on as we've always done?'

She finished her glass of water. 'Of course. When we've got both of them out of the way, we can take a short break to let the dust settle, then start again. After the mistake Edward will think he made by appointing the soon-to-be disgraced Miss Hammond, he's bound to give me the job of running the museum. It will all be much easier then.'

'That sounds good to me.' Stanley got up, went across to a wooden dresser and opened one of the top drawers.

'Before you leave, I've got some money for you.' He took out an envelope and handed it to her.

Gladys took it from him. 'I thought you might have,' she said with a thin smile. 'And I know exactly where to put it. It just so happens that I have everything I need with me, so I'll drop it into the night safe at the bank on my way to the bus.'

She counted the money, slipped some of it into an envelope that she'd brought with her, added a signed paying-in slip, and sealed the envelope.

WHAT A STROKE OF LUCK, Lucy thought, as she walked up Abbeygate Street to the Buttermarket, her shoes clattering loudly on the cobblestones.

If Gladys hadn't mentioned aspirin, she'd have completely forgotten that she'd promised to get some for her parents. Faced with a choice of going to Harton Pharmacy in the marketplace and thereby missing the bus to Bury that she normally caught in the evenings, or catching her regular bus and getting off a stop or two early to go to Croasdale's, she'd decided on taking her usual bus.

As she passed Ridley's grocery store, a heady aroma of coffee beans and cheese reached her. It reminded her that her mother had also mentioned that they were low on cheese, so she went inside, and in the absence of any selection, bought a piece of what she and her friends called 'government cheddar'.

Her packet of cheese in her hand, she continued up Abbeygate Street. When she passed Hatter Street, she glanced down the hill.

Poor Gladys, she thought.

She was somewhere down there having goodness knows what being done to her tooth. Going to the dentist was something she always dreaded, and Gladys had looked so ashen that she was obviously similarly fearful.

Reaching Buttermarket, she turned right, and passing Lloyds Bank on the other side of the road, and the Suffolk Hotel on her right, headed for Marks & Spencer, which opened on to the large space where the twice-weekly market was held. At Marks & Spencer, she turned towards Skinner Street to go to Croasdale's, which was just beyond it.

At that moment, the door to Patterson's Antiques swung open and she saw Gladys come out, followed by Stanley.

With a gasp, she stopped abruptly.

Instinctively, she put her head down and backed into the shadowy recess of the Marks & Spencer doorway. Pressing close to the wall, certain she couldn't be seen, she watched Gladys and Stanley.

They were speaking to each other in a very friendly manner, and then Stanley put his hand across his heart. Gladys laughed, tapped his hand away, and started walking towards the Buttermarket.

Lucy pressed even closer to the wall, but Gladys didn't so much as glance in her direction.

Instead, Gladys turned to her right and went down Buttermarket as far as Lloyd's Bank. Stopping outside the main door, she glanced quickly around her. Then she took an envelope from her bag, slipped it into the night safe and resumed walking down Buttermarket towards Abbeygate Street.

Lucy looked back at Stanley, but he'd gone into his shop.

She lingered there for a few minutes, feeling a vague sense of disquiet.

While Gladys might have been to the dentist and had treatment before calling on Stanley, it was very unlikely. There hadn't really been enough time for her to have done that, even assuming she'd been seen straight away. Furthermore, she didn't look like a person who'd undergone dental work that was bound to have been painful.

It could only mean that Gladys had lied about having toothache.

But why would she do so?

Why not just ask for time off? Gladys worked hard and took little time off, so she was entitled to leave early occasionally if she wanted. It would have been more honest to have been open about it.

Of course, she might have felt uncomfortable at asking to go early without a good reason as others would have to do her work, Lucy decided as she hurried past Patterson's Antiques, desperately hoping to avoid being seen by Stanley, should he still be in the shop, crossed over Skinner Street and pushed open the door to Croasdale's.

It was her other lie that was more surprising. And the fact that Stanley, too, had lied.

He had said quite clearly that he hadn't seen much of Gladys for quite a time, and she hadn't disagreed. Yet they obviously knew each other very well, and clearly had seen each other more frequently that Stanley's comment suggested. The easy way that each had been with the other showed a familiarity that gave the lie to what both had said.

Could they be romantically involved, she wondered as she joined the queue, and she giggled inwardly at the thought. Could Gladys, who had a rather wrinkled face and salt-and-pepper-coloured hair, who was probably a few years older than Stanley Patterson, be the object of his affection.

It would make sense of what she'd seen if they *were* romantically close. They might fear ridicule at publicly acknowledging they felt something for each other at their ages, so were pretending not to know each other.

But in the few minutes she'd seen them together there'd been nothing to suggest a romantic involvement. It had appeared to be no more than a friendship of some standing.

Having said that, people who loved each other and had been together for years often appeared to outsiders to be no more than very good friends. Her parents were an example of that. They were undemonstrative, yet they loved each other deeply.

It must be that Gladys and Stanley were in love, she decided. There was no other explanation. As for the lie about her toothache, it would merely be Gladys's reluctance to ask to leave work ahead of time. She shouldn't attempt to make more if it than it was.

18

T*hursday, two weeks later*

HALFWAY ALONG THE road that led from Bury St Edmunds to Mildenhall, Stanley Patterson reached the shop owned by Tom Bradley, a fellow antiques dealer.

He drove into the large open space in front of the shop, parked his van, went up to the entrance and paused to look at the display on either side of the door. It was a somewhat disorderly sprawl, he thought, and smiling to himself, he went into the shop.

Seeing that Tom was busy serving a customer, he wandered around the area closest to the entrance, picking up the occasional plate or decanter and examining it.

When the sale had been completed, he stood aside to let the customer leave the shop with the tall glass vase he'd bought, and then went up to the counter where Tom was noting down the item he'd sold and the amount he'd put in the cash till.

'Hello, Tom,' he said.

Tom looked up. Seeing Stanley, his face broke out into a smile 'Well, this is a pleasant surprise!' he exclaimed.

'It's good to see you again. I don't often come this way, but I had to go into Mildenhall today, so I thought I'd stop by and say hello.'

'I'm glad you did. It's so long since we've met that I'd almost forgotten what you look like.'

'Just as well I came in today, then, isn't it?' Stanley said cheerfully.

'Funnily enough, I have to go into Bury this afternoon,' Tom said. 'I've got to deliver something to a customer. It's a good job you stopped by this morning or you'd have missed me. Anyway, how are you? Business good?'

'I can't complain,' Stanley said with a smile. He looked very obviously around the shop, and then back at Tom. 'Nor can you, by the look of it. You've expanded, I see. Last time I was here, you were only displaying items for sale on one side of the entrance. Now you're displaying on both sides. And it's pretty full inside the shop, too.'

'But not with furniture, unfortunately. I've not really had the time to add to the furniture stock, and without new stock in the shop, you don't get the business. The eighteenth-century bureau I'm delivering this afternoon is the first piece of furniture I've sold in over a month,' Tom said, with a strong note of regret. 'People are now looking for china and glassware, and I've plenty of that, but it's much less interesting than your genuine antique furniture. Dad would turn in his grave at what I'm selling now. I mean, just look at that!'

He indicated the wall at the back of the shop where

three wooden structures with glass shelves from top to bottom were crowded with blue-and-white plates and similarly patterned cups, saucers and jugs. The tops of the shelves were lined with large oval serving dishes that stood upright against the wall.

On one side of the three structures was a fourth that was narrower than the other three. It was filled with small painted figurines of animals and children.

'I see what you mean,' Stanley said, turning back to Tom. 'It's a shame as there're some excellent bargains to be had at auctions these days. With a number of people turning to modern designs made of woods such as teak, antique pieces are increasingly up for auction, and the auction houses have become a rich source of stock for traditional dealers like us. There's such a plentiful supply that we're able to buy at a lot less than a few years ago. Believe me, there's still a solid market for genuine antiques, particularly among people with money to spend.'

'I know, and I'd like to get to auctions more frequently, but I can't. It's probably why we've not bumped into each other for a while. And I'd also like to do more house clearances. But the problem is, Mother wants to do less in the shop, rather than more, and I don't want to put upon her—she's not getting any younger.'

'I'd heard that your mother was less visible these days,' Stanley murmured. 'I'm afraid it'll come to us all. But perhaps your wife or young lady would be willing to relieve you in here so you could get out more?'

Tom laughed. 'We really *are* out of touch! There isn't a wife or young lady, as you put it. If I haven't been able to find the time since Dad died to search for antiques, I certainly haven't been able to find the time to search for a wife.'

'Then you need to pay someone to help you in the shop,

Tom,' Stanley said bluntly. 'I know it's none of my business, but if you're selling stock, which you obviously are, you should be able to afford to pay for help. I'd a lot of respect for your dad, and I have for you, too. I hate to see you missing good business opportunities. Or dying a decrepit old bachelor like me.'

Both laughed.

'No, you're right,' Tom said. 'You're only saying what I ought to have been thinking. Thanks, Stan. You're a good friend. The trouble is, being stuck out here isn't exactly a dream job for anyone. Not when you've got towns in easy reach. Both Mildenhall and Bury St Edmunds are only a bus ride away. But I do need to get some paid help in the shop. It makes good sense.' He paused. 'Have you got time for a drink?'

Stanley looked at his watch. 'Yes, provided I don't stay too long.'

'Let's go to the inner sanctum, then,' Tom said, and he led the way to a cramped office at the back of the shop.

'You know,' Stanley said, moving a mantel clock with a brown marble Bakelite case from the nearest chair and sitting down, 'you'd be wise to look for a young woman to help you, rather than a man. What you need is the energy of youth combined with a woman's instinct for tidiness. And that's actually given me an idea.'

HARTON, early that afternoon

'EXCUSE ME,' the voice said, breaking into the afternoon's silence in the museum.

Lucy looked up from the book on the history of the

Anglo-Saxon period that she was reading while at the reception desk. Her stomach gave a sudden lurch at the sight of the tall dark-haired young man standing in front of her, his grey eyes staring intently at her.

She blushed. 'I'm so sorry,' she said, closing the book. 'I shouldn't have been reading while I was working.'

He leaned over the desk and saw the title. 'I would have thought that counted as work,' he said with a smile as he straightened up. 'After all, you work in a place that's full of relics of the past, which is about as historical as you can get, so the more you learn about the background to your exhibits, the better. You'd certainly be a more interesting guide for any visitors who asked for further information about items in the museum.'

'That's what I think!' she exclaimed. 'And Violet—that's Miss Hammond, she runs the museum—agrees.'

'Is it only the Anglo-Saxon period that interests you, or are more recent periods of interest, too?' he asked, sitting down on the chair placed in front of the desk for visitors.

She shook her head. 'No, I like all periods. It's just that we've got a lot of Anglo-Saxon artefacts. We're doing—or rather Violet's doing, and I'm helping—a different sort of display. It'll bring to life the Anglo-Saxon period. At least we hope it will,' she added, and laughed.

'That sounds a really good idea,' he said. 'Suffolk is where the Angles first settled in the fifth century, and there's lots of evidence of their time here. I expect your book or your school will have told you that the first place they settled in was Ipswich. When they died, the kings were buried at Sutton Hoo, and look at what archaeologists found there ten years ago. And even more recently, the unearthing of the Mildenhall Treasure, which is not that far from where I live. Finding thirty-four masterpieces of

Roman silver tableware from the fourth century was quite astonishing.'

'As you're local to that area, I imagine that whenever you do any gardening, you have a storage bag and a magnifying glass in your pocket, just in case,' she said lightly.

'You must have been spying on me,' he said with a grin. 'And if you have, you'll know my name is Tom.'

Lucy coloured more deeply. 'I'm Lucy.' She paused. 'Bury St Edmunds, where I live, is also very historical, but it's more Georgian than Anglo-Saxon.' She hesitated. 'Like me, you're obviously interested in history. Are you a history teacher?'

'I'm an antiques dealer. An interest in history helps with that.'

'It must do. And modern history is interesting, too,' she continued. 'I've been helping Violet sort out the exhibits stored in the basement. The rooms down there give us a glimpse into the life of a servant in Georgian times. I intend to learn more about that, too, but not till I've finished reading this book. And also a book I've got about the Romans.'

'You did the Anglo-Saxon period and the Romans at school, didn't you?'

'Yes and no,' Lucy said with a giggle. 'They were on the timetable for more than a year, but every time I heard the words Angles, Saxons, Romans, I inwardly stopped listening. Boring, I thought. I now wish I'd paid more attention in history.'

'I've one or two letters for you to type, Lucy,' Violet said, coming up to the reception desk. 'If you'd like to do them now, I'll take over from you here.'

'Of course,' Lucy said, standing up. She glanced at the pile of leaflets on her desk. 'I'm neglecting my job,' she told

Tom with a smile, and she picked up a leaflet and offered it to him. 'This will tell you what you'll find in the different galleries.'

Tom rose to his feet. 'Thank you,' he said, and he headed in the direction of the first gallery.

Trying not to show her great disappointment at having to end a conversation she'd really been enjoying, Lucy headed for the narrow secretarial office at the back of the entrance hall. Halfway towards the door, hearing footsteps running up behind her, she stopped and turned round.

'Tom!' she exclaimed in pleased surprise.

'This is going to sound completely mad as I've only just met you,' he said. 'But as I told you, I've got an antique shop and I need someone to help me with it. It's between here and Mildenhall. You can get buses there from Bury. My mother works there part-time, but she wants to do less. It hadn't really occurred to me to get in an assistant so I haven't advertised the post or anything, but talking to you, feeling your interest in the sort of things that I like, it suddenly occurred to me to wonder if you'd like to come and work for me.' He paused. 'Would you?'

Lucy stared at him in shock.

'You don't have to decide now,' he said quickly. 'I could come back tomorrow or the next day—whatever you wanted. My offer's rather come out of the blue for both of us.'

'I can answer you now,' she said shakily. 'If I wasn't so happy here, I would've loved to work for you. But I *am* very happy here. Violet has some exciting plans for the future, and I want to help her make the museum a vibrant source of history in a way that it's never been before. So, I'm really sorry, Tom, but I'll have to say no.'

'I'm really sorry, too,' he said with obvious regret, 'but I understand. Violet is very lucky to have someone like you working here. I wish you well with all your plans.'

Giving her a rueful smile, he turned away.

She went up to the door to the secretarial office and stood facing it for a moment, knowing how much she wanted to see Tom again, but knowing also that she couldn't leave the museum.

But she and Violet could invite him to the reception, she suddenly realised. Antique dealers were important people. Stanley Patterson was on the list of those to be invited, so Tom could be, too.

Instantly feeling more cheerful, she started to open the door.

'One moment!' She heard Tom's voice behind her again.

'This is nothing about work,' he said running up to her. 'That subject's as dead as the artefacts in your museum. When I got outside, I realised that there was something else I could have asked, that I very much wanted to ask, so I came back in to ask it. It's about eating.'

'Eating?' she echoed.

'That's right. I really enjoyed our conversation and I'd like to continue it over dinner one evening. What about Saturday night? Would you allow me to take you to dinner on Saturday?'

'Oh, yes!' she exclaimed in delight.

And they stood there, smiling broadly at each other.

19

A *little later*

Lucy put her cup of coffee on the table, sat down opposite Gladys and opened her lunch box.

'Violet's on the reception desk. She said there's no need for us to hurry,' Lucy remarked, taking out her cheese sandwich.

'That's very kind of her,' Gladys said with a smile. She cleared her throat. 'That was a good-looking young man you were talking to this morning,' she said with studied casualness. 'You seemed to be getting on very well. May I be extremely nosy and ask if you're walking out with him?' She paused, waiting.

Lucy opened her mouth to say that they'd be having dinner together on Saturday, but on an instinct, closed it again. 'His name's Tom. He's got an antiques shop on the way to Mildenhall,' she said, and left it at that.

Gladys nodded. 'Ah, that must be Tom Bradley. I've heard of him, but never actually met him. It was his father's business, I believe, and Tom took it over when his father died a few years ago. But they're not a family I know anything about.' She paused again. 'I don't recall ever seeing Tom here before, and I noticed that he didn't actually go into any of the galleries, but left after he'd spoken to you. I wondered why?' Cocking her head slightly to one side, Gladys left the question hanging in the air.

'I think he intended to have a look around but got side-tracked.'

'Side-tracked?' Gladys raised a questioning eyebrow.

Lucy slumped back. 'He offered me a job, if you want to know.'

Gladys smiled at her. 'How exciting! You must have impressed him by what he saw and by what you said.' She paused. 'Well, what answer did you give him?'

'I told him the truth. I'm very happy here, and I want to carry on helping Violet with what she's doing.'

'So you're not going to work for him, then!' Gladys said. A look of displeasure swept fleetingly across her face, to be replaced almost at once by a look of surprise.

Gladys was disappointed she hadn't taken the job, Lucy realised with a shock.

But why would she be, she wondered.

If she'd gone to work for Tom, the trustees would have had to go to the trouble of finding someone to replace her, and that wouldn't have been easy. She remembered the bewilderment shown by her friends when they'd learnt she was going to work in a museum. And it would mean more work for Gladys if it took some time to find a suitable replacement.

What's more, the person they found might not be so

keen on helping Violet, and that could slow the progress that Violet was hoping to make. Surely Gladys wouldn't want that. She'd worked in the museum for years and must want to see it improve. What's more, she'd said more than once that Violet was opening the windows and sweeping away the cobwebs, and was the future of the place.

So why would Gladys be sorry she hadn't taken up Tom's offer? For she obviously was, despite her rapid change of expression.

Lucy shook her head. 'No, I'm not. I don't want to leave the museum.'

'I'm so glad,' Gladys said heartily. 'You're an asset to the place, Lucy, and we wouldn't want to lose you.' She hesitated. 'Perhaps I shouldn't say this, but Tom Bradley's a handsome man and a most eligible one, which is why I was initially surprised at you turning down the chance to work for him. I'm delighted you did, though,' she added warmly.

'It would make me very shallow if I left a job I enjoyed just because someone with a very pleasant face asked me to work for them,' Lucy said cheerily.

Gladys laughed. 'Yes, it would. I shouldn't have said that. It suggests, though, that in my youth, I was more taken by looks than perhaps I should've been.' She took a bite of her sandwich. 'I couldn't help noticing that Tom left the museum but returned almost at once?' she remarked when she'd swallowed it.

Her words were an unmistakable question.

'He'd taken one of our leaflets by mistake and wondered if I wanted it back,' Lucy promptly replied. 'I said he could hang on to it.'

. . .

Why had she held back from mentioning that she was going to have dinner with Tom on Saturday evening, Lucy wondered as she left the staffroom. Going to dinner with him was a harmless enough thing to do, given he was unattached and so was she. And the need for a chaperone had virtually died out, certainly for people like her.

It was such a pity that Edward was engaged to Jean, she mused as she made her way to the reception desk, where Violet was sitting. Jean was really pleasant, but so was Violet. And Violet and Edward seemed to have so much in common, both of them liking history the way they did. Of course, Jean and Edward had a lot in common, too—they shared a knowledge of medicine, after all. But Edward and Violet seemed to go particularly well together. And she sensed that each felt something for the other.

But if she was right, where did that leave Jean?

Jean was officially engaged to Edward so she could sue him if he broke off their engagement, not that Jean was the sort of person to do such a thing. Nevertheless, they'd been engaged for a couple of years, and had been close friends for a lot longer than that. Jean was no longer as young as she'd been, and if she and Edward parted, she wouldn't find it easy to attract another man, not when there were so many more women around than men.

She mentally shook herself.

Just because she'd met someone who was both interesting and very attractive, who seemed to want to get to know her, it didn't mean that she should start trying to pair off all the unattached people she knew. She'd become like Emma in Jane Austen's book, which she'd read at school. And look at what happened when Emma attempted to matchmake!

Mind you, Emma did get lovely Mr Knightley in the end,

she thought as she reached the desk. She smiled at Violet, who got up, picked up some sketches and headed towards her office.

Her book on the history of the Anglo-Saxon period caught her eye as she sat down behind the desk, and she pulled it towards her. How fortunate she'd been reading that book when Tom arrived, as it had led to them having a conversation. It had indeed been her lucky day meeting a man like him and how very fortunate that he was unattached.

She frowned.

How did Gladys know he was eligible? She said she'd never met him, and knew nothing about the family?

She mentally shrugged. It must be that the friendly way in which he spoke to her suggested a lack of commitment to anyone else, she decided. Also, in a small community, such as that shared by museums and antique shops, Gladys would probably have heard if Tom had married, even if she hadn't known him.

Furthermore, his shop was on the road to Mildenhall, which wasn't far away. Being on a bus route made it easily accessible for villagers from Harton, and if they'd been talking among themselves and the subject of Tom's family had come up, Gladys might have heard them.

Nevertheless, it was a little strange.

And it was also strange that Gladys had been sorry she'd turned down Tom's offer. She was sure she hadn't been mistaken about that.

VIOLET LOOKED up at the sound of a gentle knock on her office door. 'Come in,' she called.

The door opened and Gladys's head appeared in the crack.

'Come in, Gladys, and sit down,' Violet said, putting down her pen. 'What can I help you with?'

As Gladys came into the room, Violet saw she was carrying a cup of tea.

'I thought you might be thirsty,' Gladys said in a solicitous tone. She put the cup on the desk next to Violet, and took a step back.

'That's very thoughtful,' Violet said. 'I *am* quite thirsty, but I've been working hard and I hadn't realised it till now. The tea's very welcome, thank you.'

'Not at all,' Gladys said. 'I was in a good mood, and I thought that making you a cup of tea would be the perfect way to celebrate.'

'Celebrate?' Violet sat back and smiled at Gladys. 'You can't leave me in suspense. What are you celebrating?'

'Why, that Lucy isn't leaving, of course.'

Violet straightened up. 'What d'you mean, leaving?'

Gladys looked apologetic. 'I'm so sorry, but I thought you knew. She had an offer from Tom Bradley this morning. He's a local antiques dealer. He wanted her to go and work for him. She's turned him down, though, which is such good news. Little Lucy has become quite indispensable.'

Violet bit her lip. 'She certainly has.'

'Mind you, there's always a risk that she might give more thought to the offer, despite originally turning it down,' Gladys said with exaggerated hesitation. 'It'd be wise to avoid saying anything to her that shouldn't go outside the museum. Just in case.'

'I can't think of anything secret, but I'll remember your advice. Thank you, Gladys. It's a relief to know that you've got the museum's interests so much at heart. Learning that

Lucy might leave us before long has actually given me quite a shock.'

Gladys looked distressed. 'Perhaps I should've kept it to myself?'

Violet shook her head. 'No, you did right to tell me. But we won't tell Lucy that I know about the offer. She'll tell me when she wants me to know.'

'I'll let you drink your tea in peace, then,' Gladys said. 'If you want to continue working in here through the afternoon, I'd be happy to take your turn on the desk.'

'If you really don't mind, I'll take you up on your kind offer. I've a lot to do.'

Gladys turned and went out of the office.

For a few minutes after the door had closed behind Gladys, Violet stared hard at the door.

Why would Gladys go out of the way to tell her that Lucy had turned down an offer of work and perhaps shouldn't be trusted? What could Gladys possibly have hoped to gain by passing that on? It was mystifying.

Unable to come up with an answer, she shrugged and turned back to her work.

20

Thursday evening, a week later

WITH AN AIR OF DEJECTION, Jean leaned her bicycle against the wall of the surgery building, lifted her brown leather Gladstone bag from the wire basket, unlocked the surgery door and went inside.

She paused for a moment and stood still, listening to the welcome emptiness, then she started to cross the hall to the room that had been designated for her use.

Hearing footsteps coming down the wooden staircase, she stopped walking and glanced up the stairs.

'Martin!' she exclaimed, surprise tinged with displeasure as she saw him coming down towards her.

Suppressing her irritation at having to be sociable for even a moment or two when she wasn't in the mood for company, even though she very much liked Martin, she forced herself to wait for him to reach the bottom step. 'It's unlike you to use this staircase. You usually avoid it in case you're trapped by a patient when you're off duty,' she told him.

'An emergency situation calls for emergency action,' he said.

She tightened her hold on her bag and looked at him in alarm. 'What emergency?'

'You,' he said.

She stared at him for a moment, then gave a dismissive laugh, turned away and continued to her surgery. 'You're talking in riddles, Martin,' she called back without looking at him, 'which is also most unlike you.'

She opened the door to her surgery and a faint smell of disinfectant drifted out.

He followed her into the room and stood waiting while she removed her uniform hat and serviceable navy cloak, both of which she hung on wooden pegs just inside the door. Then she pulled out the tortoiseshell clip that kept her red hair hidden under her hat and let her hair fall to her shoulders.

'I wish I knew what this was about,' she said, keeping her back to him as she put her bag on the table that stood between the medicine cabinet and her store cupboard.

'Everything about you at the moment, Jeannie, suggests that you *do* know what this is about. But in case I'm mistaken, why don't you come upstairs, and we'll talk over a cup of tea?'

'I can't. I've had a busy afternoon and I need to re-equip my bag,' she said sharply. She unlocked the bag and pushed down on the brass button that opened it.

'Then I'll wait while you do your bag.'

He sat on the chair intended for patients and folded his arms.

She glanced at him over her shoulder. 'Haven't you anything better to do?'

He shook his head. 'No.'

Shrugging her shoulders, she turned away, unlocked both the medicine cabinet and the store cupboard, opened her bag more widely, and very slowly started to go through the contents.

Having checked the soap she kept in a special box in the outside section of the bag, she started on the rest of the items in the bag. First she made sure she had sufficient Dettol and methylated spirits, then she changed the two aprons, cap and mask in her bag for clean ones.

Taking what she needed from the store cupboard, she made sure that she had a complete set of dressings, a sterilised thermometer, a full set of hypodermic needles and instruments, including scissors and forceps. Finally, she replaced her sterilising tray, white enamel cups and hand towels with fresh ones.

Then she closed her bag, locked it again and stood facing the wall, motionless.

'That's about it, I would say,' Martin said. 'Now that you're out of delaying tactics, why don't we have that tea?'

'If you think it's really necessary,' she said stiffly, turning round to face him. 'But I wasn't trying to delay anything—we have to check our bag at the end of the day, as you well know.'

'Which you always do so diligently, and usually in half the time.'

Their eyes met.

Her body relaxed.

'You're right,' she said with an awkward laugh. 'Maybe I *have* been quicker in the past. I've no idea what you want to talk about, but I've a feeling I'm not going to like whatever it is.'

'Let's go back up those stairs I so seldom come down, and find out,' he said, and he stood up.

'WELL, that's the small talk done, wouldn't you say?' Jean said. 'I think we've covered everything anyone could say about the weather. Suppose you now tell me what's bothering you?'

He smiled at her. 'You took the words out of my mouth. I think something's worrying you, and I want to know what I can do to help.'

She gave an embarrassed laugh. 'You're mistaken. There's nothing troubling me. I can't imagine where you got that idea.'

'Could it be that you've seemed increasingly unhappy every time I've seen you these past couple of weeks? That's not like you, Jeannie. You're always so cheerful.'

'There's nothing bothering me,' she insisted.

'I think there is,' he told her gently, and he moved from his armchair to the sofa where she was sitting and sat down next to her. 'We're friends, aren't we? Why don't you let me be a friend to you by helping you in any way I can?'

To her horror, she felt her eyes fill with tears.

She blinked them back. 'There's nothing you can do, unless it's in your power to sack that paragon of enthusiasm and ideas from the museum,' she said, failing in her attempt to laugh the words into a joke.

He nodded. 'I thought it might be about Violet.'

'Is that because he goes on and on about her to you every time he sees you?' she asked, looking at him with watery eyes. 'Is it because every time he opens his mouth these days it's to praise her? Because that's what he's like with me.'

'I admit he's a bit full of her at the moment,' he said.

She burst into tears.

He put his arm around her shoulders.

'Oh, Martin,' she cried, tears rolling down her cheeks. 'I hate myself for feeling like this. I'm sure she's very nice, and I should be pleased that Edward can relax about the museum, confident that he's handed it to the right person. But I'm not. I wish she'd never applied for the job. I wish that grim-faced Gladys was running the place.'

He hugged her. 'All his praise for Violet doesn't mean anything, Jean. Just now, you used the word "relax". I believe you're right about Edward now feeling more relaxed about everything, and very relieved. I think a part of him had been aware of the limitations he would've placed on the museum's development if he'd appointed Gladys to the role, and he'd been worried about it. It was an instinctive feeling, rather than anything sufficiently formed to put into words.'

'So you think all that praise for Violet is just an outpouring of relief rather than anything else?' Jean asked, wiping her eyes.

'I do. Although it was Edward's workload that forced him to stand down from a position he enjoyed, I know he felt upset about letting the museum down, as he saw it. Having a successor who looks competent, and more important than that, who sounds excited about what she can do for the museum, he's bound to be relieved and enthuse about it.'

'But it's not as if she's only just arrived, is it? Surely his relief, if that's what it is, should've worn off by now, but it hasn't.'

'I imagine that's because there's so much going on at the

moment that he feels obliged to help where he can. It means he can't yet put the museum behind him. The reception and the opening of the display aren't much more than a month away. The museum's full of life and movement, and the school's involved, too. This is what Edward wanted.'

'I realise that,' she said.

'He told me after the interview that it was as if Violet had plucked thoughts from his mind that he hadn't known he had. Naturally, he's thrilled to see them come to fruition.'

'Gladys is competent and could've done it. And she's experienced, much more so than Violet.' Her voice caught.

'But what Violet's doing wouldn't have occurred to Gladys. And if it had, I'm not sure she'd have had the energy to do it. Or the personality. She's not the easiest of women, you must admit. Believe me, Jeannie, Edward's effusiveness isn't about Violet as a person, it's about what she's bringing to the museum.'

Wiping her eyes with the back of her hand, she shook her head. 'I'd like to believe you're right, but I don't think you are.'

'Think about this, then,' he went on. 'Edward's father was the main reason why a small village like Harton has such a good museum. His father's memory is bound up in the museum, and in its success. And Edward was very close to his father.'

She thought for a moment.

'Everything you say makes sense,' she said at last, 'but my instinct is saying something else. You've talked about Edward's instinct. Well, I've got an instinct, too. It's an age since Edward's come out to me when I'm passing his house on my way home. After he'd finished his surgery and house calls, he used to watch for me to go by, and ask me in for a chat.'

Martin nodded. 'I know he did.'

'Well, did you also know that the last time he did so was before she arrived? When we go out together these days, which isn't often, it's because we made an arrangement when we happened to bump into each other in the surgery. There's no more going out of the way to meet me, or planning to do things together. It's now as if he feels it's his duty to take me out.'

'I'm sorry, Jean,' Martin said quietly.

'Whatever you say, I'm sure he has feelings for her, even if he doesn't realise it. No matter what the museum means to him, the way he talks about her is excessive. And it's not surprising. She's very pretty, after all.'

He looked at her with surprise. 'I know she's been here a while, but I didn't think your paths had crossed.'

A pink haze spread over her face, and a couple of tears trickled down her cheeks.

'They haven't, and I've not exactly met her. But I've seen her. I don't know what got into me, but a couple of days ago I stood outside her house where I couldn't be seen, waiting for her to return from the museum. I wanted to know what she looked like.' A sob escaped her. 'You probably think I'm awful.'

'Of course I don't,' he said, and he leaned across and hugged her again. 'It's only natural for you to be curious about someone you've heard so much about. And I agree, she's very pretty. But so are you, Jean, and you're the woman he loves. You're the woman he asked to marry him.'

'But he hadn't yet met that paragon of perfection when he did so!' She brushed angry tears from her cheeks. 'If he feels so strongly about me, why's there still no date for the wedding? Ages ago he said we'd set a date as soon as things had calmed down, but although they've now done so in a lot of respects, on the rare occasions I've seen him and tried to bring up the subject, he's been too busy to discuss it.'

Martin tightened his arm around her. 'I don't know what I can say to reassure you, Jeannie, except that I know Edward loves you and wants to marry you.'

She pulled back slightly and stared into his face, tears clinging to her lashes. 'You think he does, but you don't know that for sure. You say you're my friend, Martin, so I'm going to trust you to tell me the truth. If at some point in the future you find you're mistaken about Edward's feelings for me, promise me you'll be a true friend and tell me.'

'I promise.'

'Even though it might mean telling me something that Edward wasn't ready for me to know?'

He hesitated. 'I would never be disloyal to Edward,' he said slowly. 'He's my closest friend, and I don't know how I'd have got through losing Florence if it hadn't been for him. But if I came to believe that he wasn't being honest about his feelings, then for both your sakes I'd do my utmost to get him to be open with you. I'd do everything in my power to prevent you from continuing to believe in something that was no longer true.' He paused. 'Is that an acceptable answer?'

'Yes, it is. Thank you, Martin,' she said, wiping her eyes with a handkerchief. 'You're a good friend.' She leaned forward and kissed him lightly on the cheek.

He touched her cheek and looked deep into her eyes. 'You're worrying unnecessarily, Jeannie,' he said reassuringly. 'Edward loves you. How could he not?'

STANDING UPSTAIRS at his bedroom window, Martin watched Jean cycle down the short drive in front of the surgery, turn right on to Church Road and cycle up past Edward's house, heading in the direction of the new development at the top of the village and beyond that, the large house in which she lived with her parents, which stood just outside the village.

Then he hurried down the back staircase, went out of the side entrance to his flat and headed down the path to the road. Turning right, he made straight for Edward's house.

A part of him was screaming out that he shouldn't say anything, that it was none of his business. But screaming even more loudly was his awareness that as a friend of both Edward and Jean, he ought to do what he thought best for the two of them, and that meant speaking to Edward. But he was acutely aware that if he didn't do so quickly, he might give in to cowardice and change his mind.

When he reached Edward's house, he took a deep breath, grasped the brass door knocker and rapped on the door. A couple of moments later, the door was opened by Edward's housekeeper.

'Hello, Mavis,' Martin said. 'Is Dr Russell at home?'

'He is,' Edward said, appearing behind Mavis. 'That's fine, Mavis, thank you.' He took over the door from Mavis and she disappeared back into the house.

The smile he gave Martin was tinged with surprise.

'Did we arrange to meet and I forgot all about it?' Edward asked, frowning.

Martin shook his head. 'Not at all. It's just that there's something I wanted to bring up with you. I didn't want to leave it till the next time we happened to meet.'

'How intriguing,' Edward said. He stepped back and held the door wider open. 'Come on in, then. We'll have a whisky and you can tell me what it's about.'

Martin followed him into the sitting room and sat down,

while Edward went across to a cabinet and poured them each a whisky.

'This is a lovely room, Edward,' Martin said. 'I know I've said it before, more than once, but it really is splendidly furnished and very comfortable.'

'You'll have to credit my parents with that. Personally, I think the ceiling's over-ornate, and I'd never myself have chosen a chandelier as the central light. One of these days, I'll change it.'

Having put a whisky on the table next to Martin, he slumped into the armchair opposite him. 'Your health,' he said, raising his glass.

'And that of our patients, too, though perhaps not too healthy or we'd soon be out of business,' Martin said with a smile. He took a sip of his drink and put the glass back on the table.

'So what's this about, then?' Edward asked.

'It's about Jean,' Martin said.

Edward looked at him with surprise. 'What about her?'

'I couldn't help noticing how unhappy she's seemed these past few weeks. You must've noticed it, too.'

Edward frowned. 'I can't say I have.'

'That's probably because you've been so busy waxing lyrical about Violet,' Martin said drily. 'At least you have to me, so I assume you'll have regaled Jean in the same way. A few weeks ago you said you were going to tone down what you said about Violet and fix a date for the wedding. But from Jean's expression these days, you've not yet done either.'

Edward straightened up. 'You're right, I haven't,' he said a trifle coldly. 'I meant to do so but I've been too busy. I intend to get down to it soon, though.'

Martin nodded. 'That's good. I don't like seeing Jean looking as miserable as she has done recently.'

Edward leaned forward. 'I appreciate that as a good friend you've both our interests at heart, but really, what happens between Jean and me is a matter for Jean and me alone. You've alerted me to something I've been too busy to notice, and that was remiss of me. But now that you've told me, you can stop worrying.

'It's also possible,' Edward added, a touch defensively, 'that what you saw as Jean's unhappiness was actually tiredness. Her workload's greatly increased, just like ours, and having to visit our patients in hospital now, in addition to all her house calls, is quite demanding.'

'You could well be right,' Martin said. He finished his drink and stood up. 'I must be getting back. I haven't yet finished writing up my notes on the patients I saw this afternoon.'

Edward got up and walked him to the front door.

'I'm grateful for your concern, Martin,' he said as he opened the door, 'but from now on, I'll be the one who does any worrying that has to be done. I'll see if Jean's free on Saturday evening, and if she is, we'll go up to the Brown Hare Inn and I'll have a word with her then.'

'As you say, it's a matter for you and Jean, not me,' Martin said, and with a slight wave, he turned and walked back towards the road.

21

L*ater that evening*

Reclining in his armchair, Edward stared morosely at the glass of whisky he was holding.

Martin had been absolutely right in what he'd said, even though it had been none of his business to say it.

Deep down, he, too, had noticed how unhappy Jean was looking, but he'd forced himself not to see it. And because he was refusing to see it, he'd been able to avoid doing anything about it.

Martin was right—he should have done something. He shouldn't have had to be shamed by Martin into facing up to the fact that it was almost certainly his gross insensitivity that was causing Jean's misery.

Insensitivity was the right word.

If he'd been thinking about anyone other than himself, he'd have reined in his enthusiasm about Violet as soon as he'd told Jean and Martin that Violet had been appointed, and had given them the reason why. There'd been no need to mention her again. Yet he had, again and again and again.

Obviously, he felt grateful to Violet, and he'd felt that others should also realise how much she'd done in so little time. But instead of mentioning that in passing, he'd clearly overdone it. Jean shouldn't have had to listen to him praising Violet every time they met each other. It was no wonder she hadn't been her usual cheerful self for a while.

He was acutely conscious, too, that he hadn't made the same effort to see Jean in recent weeks as he used to. She must have noticed that, and that was also bound to have caused her misery.

And so was his failure to fix a date for their wedding.

A sharp sense of guilt stabbed him.

It was several weeks since he'd told both Jean and Martin that he'd find a date for the wedding, but he'd made no attempt to do so. Yes, he'd been busy, but not so busy that he couldn't find the time to devise reasons for popping into the museum. And not too busy to take Violet to the Angel Hotel, or to bump into her and her parents when they visited.

Was it possible that Jean had picked up on an emotion he'd been trying not to face in himself since he'd questioned why he'd been so keen to see Violet and her parents that afternoon? Was Violet in some way the reason why he'd drawn back from Jean and wasn't yet ready to fix a date for the wedding?

He ran his finger slowly round the rim of the whisky glass.

He'd have liked to have been able to tell himself that he didn't know the answer to the questions, but he couldn't lie to himself, not after Martin had forced him to open his eyes.

From the day he'd met Violet, which had been the day of her interview, he'd felt himself drawn to her. He'd fought hard against feeling that way, his loyalty being to Jean, and when he'd left Violet at the station after her interview, he'd been confident that he'd overcome what had momentarily threatened to be an unwelcome infatuation.

At the end of their first lunch together at the Brown Hare Inn, he knew he'd failed. And every time he'd seen her since then it had only made his feelings even stronger.

But was it merely infatuation, or something more than that, something more lasting?

He didn't yet know.

Violet had blown into his life like a breath of fresh air with her lively mind and her head full of ideas. Having been with Jean for so many years, Violet was a novelty, a very pretty novelty. And that may well be the attraction she held for him, and nothing of any greater depth.

If so, novelties wore off, and when the novelty of Violet had worn off, it would be Jean alone who filled his thoughts, and that would be the time for him and Jean to discuss a date for their wedding.

But where did that leave him with Jean at the moment?

He loved her. He had done for years. He had never once in all the time they'd known each other questioned his love for her. But could it be that what he felt for her was a very deep friendship, but not the love a man should feel for the woman who was to be his wife?

It was the only way he could explain the romantic feelings he harboured for Violet.

He mentally shook himself. He was getting everything out of proportion.

All he knew for sure was that in his current state of mind, setting in motion the arrangements for a wedding was totally out of the question, and would be until he understood himself better.

It was also out of the question that he left things as they were with Martin.

Martin had spoken out of line that evening. But feeling guilty at the truth of what Martin had said, he'd been sharp in his response. Looking back, he regretted the tone he'd taken, and he would certainly make a point of apologising when he next saw him. Martin was a good friend, and he'd only been trying to help both him and Jean.

But what Martin had said was right, and although he wasn't going to let Martin's words push him into making a decision for which he wasn't yet ready, they'd made him realise that he must be open with Jean about his inner turmoil.

He'd see her at the surgery the following day, and he'd suggest they have dinner at Harry's on Saturday evening. Over a pleasant meal, he would tell her something about the quandary he was in with regard to his feelings.

It was the very least he could do.

He finished his whisky and stood up.

MARTIN STOOD at his bedroom window, staring out at Church Road.

If Florence hadn't died, he would have been looking at a very different view for the past three years. But the familiarity of being above the surgery, in a place that held so many memories of Florence, had been a great comfort to him, and had helped him through his grief. It was for that reason, not for anything financial, that he'd stayed where he was for so long.

But three years was long enough to need the support of

a view, he decided. It was time for him to move on. Not from the surgery, he swiftly told himself. He was very happy working in partnership with Edward, and he very much liked living in Harton and wouldn't want to live in any other village, and certainly not in a large town.

But he'd realised as he'd walked back to the surgery after speaking to Edward, stinging from Edward's ill-concealed annoyance with him, that Edward's irritation was giving him the push he'd needed.

He and Florence had been in the process of buying an old house when she'd died, and she'd been full of plans for how they'd have it decorated. So his starting point was that he wouldn't want to buy the same sort of house that he and Florence had chosen, not if he was trying to put the pain of losing her behind him. He needed a different sort of house.

And he might actually have seen some possible houses.

There were some new houses in the process of being constructed in the north-east corner of Harton, just before the small wood that lay beyond the village, and they could be of interest. Jean passed them every night when she cycled home, and she'd told him more than once how attractive they looked, and how well laid out they were.

He had nothing planned for after his surgery the following afternoon, so he might as well go up to the new development and see what was on offer. And if, when he'd taken a look at the houses, he found one that seemed a possibility, he might ask Jean if she'd be kind enough to visit it with him.

It would be sensible to have a woman's viewpoint before he made a decision. After all, if he married again, he'd want his wife to like the house in which she'd be living.

He felt a sudden shortness of breath.

If he married again, he'd said to himself.

Turning, he looked at his bedside table, at the silver-framed photograph next to his fringed lamp. His knees felt weak. It was the first time he'd considered the possibility that he might remarry.

At the thought of a wife who wasn't Florence, he felt a sharp pang, and his heart racing in anxiety, he went across to the photograph of Florence, picked it up and looked at it. As he stared at her smiling face, he felt himself relax.

Wanting to marry again didn't mean that he no longer loved Florence, because he did. He would always love her. But loving Florence didn't mean that he'd never be able to love anyone else. Hearts were big enough for people to love more than one person. He'd loved both his parents and Florence, too, hadn't he?

And he *did* want to marry again, he realised.

He felt ready to love again, to experience again the happiness he'd enjoyed with Florence. And Florence would want that for him.

He smiled at the photograph as he put it back on the table. He'd definitely go up to the new houses the following afternoon, he resolved. It would be much easier to find a house than a wife, so he'd start with the easier task.

22

F*riday, the following day*

THE NUTTY TANG in the early morning air suggested that autumn was on its way, which was borne out by the touches of gold that were breaking up the dark green of the hedgerows fronting the garden, when Edward hurried up the path to the surgery, hoping like mad to catch Jean before she started on her rounds.

Her bicycle was propped up against the stone wall at the side of the entrance. She hadn't left yet, he thought with relief.

As he approached the front door, it opened and Jean came out wearing the pale blue-and-white-striped cotton dress of her uniform and her district nurse's hat, and carrying her Gladstone bag.

'I timed it well,' he said cheerfully, and he went up and kissed her on the cheek.

'If you mean that I'm still here,' she said, a trace of anxiety in her voice, 'then you did. A few minutes later and you'd have missed me—I've several calls to make and I won't be back till late in the morning.'

'That's what I *did* mean. Where are you off to?' he asked, watching her fit her bag into the wire basket on the front of her bicycle.

She shrugged. 'Just the usual,' she said. 'First of all, the residential care home. I've got to test Mr Smallwood's blood and then inject him with insulin. And I've been told that one of the residents fell out of her bed in the night and has a minor head injury. I expect it'll just be a matter of checking the wound for infection and applying the appropriate dressing. And then I'm going to call on Mrs Groves.'

'Is that for her asthma again?'

'No, it's for her ears this time. I need to syringe them. I can't do much to help her with her movement and breathing, but at least I can help with her hearing. So, like I said, just the usual.'

She smiled up at him brightly.

The smile didn't reach her eyes, and he saw nervousness in their depths.

'I was thinking that it's been quite a while since we've had time to sit down and chat,' he said, 'and I wondered if you were free tomorrow night. We really ought to talk. If you were, I thought we could have dinner together.'

'I'd love that,' she said quickly. 'Thank you.'

'I thought we could go to the Brown Hare Inn. If it's a nice evening we can walk there, which would be very welcome after being indoors for so much of the week. If it isn't, we'll take the car. I could pick you up at about seven. How does that sound?'

'Lovely,' she said. She took hold of the handlebars and

pulled the bicycle away from the wall. 'I'd better be off now. I'll see you tomorrow evening, then.'

'We might even meet again today,' he said with a smile.

'I doubt we will. We don't often do so these days, do we, Edward? After all, I seldom need to go to the museum, and that's where you seem to be when you're not in your surgery. In fact, I imagine you're on the way there now,' she said, glancing ostensibly at the papers he was holding, on some of which Harton Museum was clearly visible.

'That's right, I am,' he said with a trace of awkwardness. 'I've sketched some ideas for invitations to the reception. We've got a tasting in Bury tomorrow morning after a visit to the printer, and there's a lot to be done beforehand.'

'Of course there is,' she said, and she turned away. But not before he'd seen that the nervousness had stayed in her eyes. If anything, it had intensified.

EDWARD PUSHED OPEN the museum door. Violet was standing at the reception desk, talking to Gladys, her back to him. As if she sensed him there, she turned towards him and their eyes met.

She stepped forward.

'How lovely to see you, Edward,' she said. 'I didn't know if you'd stop by today, or if you'd leave anything to be said till we go for the tasting tomorrow.'

'As I've arranged for us to go to the printer first, we need to decide about leaflets and invitations. I hope you don't mind but I've drawn up a few ideas for both. I used some of the sketches you did for the school when you wanted to show them what you were aiming for. If you've a moment, I thought we could run through them now.'

'That's very kind of you,' she said, 'and a relief, to be

honest. I was beginning to get worried that we hadn't done them. But I'm afraid it's my turn on the reception desk,' she said apologetically. 'Gladys has been doing far more than her share recently.'

'Don't worry about me, Violet. I'm fine here,' Gladys called to her. 'Lucy's explaining something to a visitor and will then be on hand to help if anything else turns up. Off you go with Edward.'

'If you're sure, Gladys,' Violet said. 'That's very kind of you. Thank you. Let's go to the office then, Edward.'

A LITTLE LATER, standing side by side behind her desk, with Violet holding the leaflet that they'd chosen for printing and distribution around both Bury and Harton, they both stared down at six specimen invitations on her desk. Each of them had somewhere on the invitation the same small design that had been used in the corner of the leaflet they'd chosen.

'They're excellent, Edward,' she said, 'all of them. But one stands out more than the others.'

He held up his hand to stop her from saying more. 'Don't tell me,' he said, and he swiftly wrote something on the back of a notepad on her desk, making sure she didn't see it. He straightened up. 'I've written the one I think you'll choose,' he told her. 'We'll see if we both have the same idea.'

She laughed. 'I'll do the same for you.' Shielding what she wrote from his eyes, she noted down what she thought would be his favourite.

'Right, at the same moment, we'll show each other what we've written,' he said. 'On the count of three. One, two, three.'

He turned over the notepad so she could see what he'd written, and she put her small piece of paper on the desk in front of him. The same favourite had been written on each.

They burst out laughing.

'So we *do* have the same ideas!' Violet exclaimed.

'It would seem to be so,' he said. 'So this is it.' He picked up the design they'd chosen. 'All we've got to do now is run through the names of the people we're inviting, add any we think should be on the list but aren't, and then drop the invitation and leaflet at the Bury printer's tomorrow. By then we'll know the number we need of both. After that, we'll go to Wendy Ives and decide on the food to be served.'

'I'm so excited,' she said happily. 'I would've been excited anyway, but I'd also have been terrified, never having done such a thing before. But because of your help, I don't feel panicked or anxious, and I'm actually looking forward to the reception. I'm so grateful for your help.'

'I'm the one who has reason to be grateful,' he said, his voice thickening. 'Look what you're doing for the museum. You're bringing it alive. We're going to get more visitors, and among them more children, who're the future of the museum,' he said, his voice full of emotion.

He stared down into her eyes. 'You're wonderful, Violet. I'm so glad you answered my advertisement. I can't thank you enough for everything you've done.'

For a heart-stopping moment, she wondered if he was about to kiss her.

But he didn't move.

They stood very still, gazing at each other, their hearts beating loudly.

Then she stepped back and gave a shaky laugh. 'I'm just doing what you pay me for,' she said. 'Now let's look at the list of guests.'

. . .

It was almost a week since her evening with Tom, Lucy realised as she ran a feather duster over the glass cabinets in Gallery Two. And what an evening that had been.

He'd come to Bury and met her parents, who had thought him utterly charming. Which he was. Then he'd taken her for dinner at the Suffolk Hotel.

They hadn't stopped talking all evening, but if anyone had asked her what they'd talked about, she wouldn't have been able to tell them. As for what she'd eaten, she was sure it had been delicious but she couldn't remember what it was.

One thing stood out clearly, though, and that was that Tom was the most pleasant, easiest of people to be with.

She'd had a slightly more serious moment on the Saturday afternoon when she'd been getting ready to go out, though. Her mother had come into her room and warned her that she must keep in the back of her mind the fact that dinner that evening might be Tom's way of trying to get her to change her mind about working for him.

She mustn't let her feelings run away, her mother had cautioned.

She'd waved her hand dismissively. What feelings, she'd asked.

'The ones that have been shining out of your eyes ever since you met him,' her mother had told her. 'The ones that have led to you punctuating just about every sentence with his name.' Then her mother had attempted a knowing look.

She'd giggled.

However, after her parents had met Tom, her mother had whispered in her ear when she and Tom were on the way out that she thought she might have been mistaken about his motives. He seemed to be someone who was very open and honest, and unlikely to be given to anything as underhand as she'd earlier suggested.

It hadn't been that easy to forget her mother's suspicion, though, and soon after they'd sat down at their table, she had asked Tom directly whether or not the dinner was about her changing her mind.

Not at all, he'd said, sounding quite surprised. It was about having a pleasant evening with someone who seemed to share his interests, and nothing else. Except, he'd added going slightly pink, there might have been an element behind his invitation of wanting to spend the evening looking at someone so attractive.

She knew she'd blushed. That was the problem with fair hair.

Any concerns about his motives were immediately gone, and she'd been able to relax completely and enjoy the evening.

And she'd be meeting him again the following Tuesday!

He was going to pick her up at the museum. He wouldn't be able to get there until just after they'd closed, so she'd tell Gladys and Violet that he was coming, and that she'd lock up when they left.

When he got there, she was going to show him where they'd be putting the display, and she might even take him to the basement. She was sure he'd find it as interesting as she did. And then he was going to take her back to Bury, and they'd have a bite to eat in The Fox.

She hugged herself in delight.

THE LATE AFTERNOON sun was still warm when Martin exited the surgery. Seeing that Jean was cycling down the path towards him, he stood to one side so she could cycle straight up to the building.

Then he strolled across to her as she was getting down from the bicycle.

'It's quite a coincidence, you arriving as I was leaving,' he told her. 'There's something I've been meaning to ask you but I'll keep it for another time as I imagine you'll want to put your things away and write up any notes before you sign off.'

'If you think I'm going to let you leave it at that, Martin Lloyd,' she said with a laugh, 'you're mistaken. That was far too intriguing a thing to say. What were you going to ask me?'

'If you'd like to look at a house with me. I was on my way to the houses in the new development. You've said several times how attractive they are, and I agree. I went up there yesterday, and one house in particular caught my eye. I was about to go up there now and take a closer look at it.'

'Are you planning to move?' she asked in surprise.

He nodded. 'I think it's time I did. If I like the house as much as I think I might, I was going to ask you to come up there with me tomorrow. I wouldn't expect you to do so now, but it could be helpful to get a woman's viewpoint. If you think it's an imposition, though,' he added hastily, 'or don't want to, just say.'

'I'd love to come with you,' she said happily. 'It'll be fun. And I'll also come with you now. But I'll have to re-equip my bag first. If you can't wait, I'll understand.'

'It doesn't matter when we leave, provided we get there during their working hours. I don't have an appointment, so I don't even know if it'll be possible to go into the house. If it's not possible, I thought to wander around and get used to the feeling of being up there.'

'I think that's really sensible. I'll be as quick as I can. You've already seen how slowly I can go,' she added with a laugh. 'Now you're going to see how quickly I can move when I want to.'

And she almost ran into the surgery.

23

B*ury St Edmunds,*
Saturday morning

THE AUTUMN SUN was shining in a sky that was a beautiful clear blue.

Edward took off his jacket as they came out of the office of the small bakery run by Wendy Ives, rolled the sleeves of his white shirt up to his elbow, and slung his jacket over his shoulder. Then he took the carrier bag from Violet that he'd asked her to hold for a moment, and they made their way down towards Angel Hill.

'It's turned out to be a glorious day,' he said as they walked. 'I thought you were being over-optimistic when I picked you up this morning and saw you were wearing only a light cotton dress and a thin cardigan, but not so. You were right. It's much too hot for my jacket.'

Violet glanced at him and smiled. 'You certainly look a

lot cooler now.' For a moment, her eyes lingered on his profile, then she dragged her gaze away and turned back to look towards Abbey Gate, which they were fast approaching. 'I thought the tasting went very well, didn't you? Wendy's very nice. She bent over backwards to help with ideas, and to keep the price reasonable.'

'I noticed that, too,' he said. 'I'll thank Lucy for her recommendation when we get back.'

'And so will I. We were really lucky to be told about her. With sugar still being rationed, I've no idea how she'll be able to make baby scones and fairy cakes as well as gingerbread and seed cake, but she's sure she'll manage. And I really liked the sandwich fillings we tried, and her idea of cutting the sandwiches and bridge rolls into small sizes, and also the gingerbread and seed cake, so everything will be easy for the guests to eat.'

'And delicious, too,' Edward said cheerfully, holding up the carrier bag.

As they reached the bottom of the large square in front of the Angel Hotel, he tucked the carrier bag into the fingers holding his jacket, took her hand with his free hand, and hurried them across Angel Hill, on the opposite side of which stood Abbey Gate, its large stone arch forming the entrance to Abbey Gardens.

Their hands still entwined, they walked beneath the arch and came out into the gardens.

Violet stopped at the sight of the large expanse of green lawn encircled by wooden benches and by trees that were turning from green to red and gold. Circular beds filled with chrysanthemums, dahlias and hydrangea, and occasional outcrops of grey stone, broke up the sweep of the lawn.

She looked around her with pleasure. 'What beautiful gardens!'

Edward nodded. 'Yes, they are. We ought to come here one day when we aren't so rushed and stroll through all the gardens. But they're quite extensive, and given the limited time we've got, we'll have to leave that for another time. Why don't we take one of the benches close to us and eat our sandwiches here?'

'That sounds perfect,' she said. 'I don't know how I can be hungry after all that tasting, but I am.'

Still holding hands, they went across to a bench that faced one of the circular beds of flowers. As they walked, her gaze slid down his powerful forearm to their two hands linked together, and a strange sensation stirred low in her stomach. She drew in her breath and found herself tightening her hold on his hand, not wanting to let him go.

Too quickly they reached the bench and sat down.

He released her hand, and she suddenly felt bereft.

Then he put his jacket on the other side of the bench from her, opened the paper carrier bag and looked inside.

'Wendy's put our sandwiches in separate bags,' he told her, taking out one of the paper bags and handing it to her. 'I'm sure both will have the hard-boiled eggs, sardines, cheese and potted ham fillings that we chose for the reception. I hope we like them as much as we did earlier today.'

'I'm sure we will,' she said, her voice sounding strange to her ears. 'If anything, we should like them better this time as we're eating them in such a lovely place.' She stared around her. 'I suppose those clumps of grey stone were once part of the walls of the original abbey. It gives a real sense of history to the gardens.'

He nodded. 'I agree. But even though the ruins extend over a wide area, they don't do justice to what was once one of the largest and most splendid of monasteries in England. It was a very important destination for pilgrims. Sadly,

Henry VIII closed the abbey in 1539 and had it demolished to show his power and control.'

'St Edmund was martyred near here, wasn't he?'

'He's supposed to have been killed at Hoxne, near the Norfolk border. He was king of the East Angles. The Danes killed him in the ninth century when he refused to renounce Christianity. His remains were brought here in 903, and the abbey was established in his honour. Legend has it that after the Danes shot the young king full of arrows, they cut off his head and threw it away. His followers found his body and eventually found his head, too. It's said that a wolf was guarding his head, which explains why the arms of St Edmund have two arrows running through a crown, and the crest is a wolf guarding a human head between its paws.'

'I love that story!' she exclaimed. 'Is he buried near here?'

He shrugged. 'We don't really know. It's said that a few faithful monks secretly buried St Edmund's body in the nearby St Mary's Church one night, just inside the north door. Over the years, there've been lots of excavations around the church and they've found the bones of a number of abbots, but there haven't yet been any excavations inside the church itself. If ever there were, who knows what they'd find.'

'If they looked north of the altar, they'd find Henry VIII's sister, Mary Tudor, wouldn't they?' she said. 'I read that she was buried there.'

'That's right. Confusingly, though, the church is dedicated to Mary, the mother of Jesus, not to Mary Tudor. But listen to me!' he exclaimed, hitting his head with his hand. 'Once again I'm sounding like a schoolteacher!'

'I don't mind,' she said with a laugh. 'Everything you say is interesting.'

'You're probably just being kind, but thank you for not making me feel as if I'm boring you.'

'You're certainly not,' she said.

They looked at each other and slowly smiled. Then they turned back to their sandwiches.

'I know I keep on saying thank you,' she said after a few moments of silence. 'But you can't know how grateful I am for your help. Getting everything done before the reception had been starting to weigh on me. The twenty-ninth of October isn't that far away. But we've got through a lot this morning, and I've really enjoyed it.'

'So have I,' he said quietly. Gazing at her face, he opened his mouth as if to say something else, but closed it again.

For a long moment, neither spoke, then he glanced at his watch.

'Reluctant as I am to think of moving, I think we ought to be getting back to Harton,' he said.

Both stood up and turned to face the stone arch that would take them back to the town, and the village.

Harton

'The houses are designed extraordinarily well,' Jean said as she and Martin sat on a bench at the edge of the new development. 'They've certainly stood up to a second viewing. And the development's very well landscaped. Between all of the gardens and the numerous trees, it's going to look really lovely here when it's finished. The houses are bound to sell very quickly.'

'That's what I think. It means I need to move fast.'

'In the house you like, the entrance hall alone could be really impressive. I can just see it with a gleaming parquet floor and panelled walls,' Jean went on. 'The salesman called it a lounge hall, and suggested some easy chairs and occasional tables, but I don't see it as an area where one would want to sit. I see it rather as a beautiful space in which to greet guests. In my head I imagined a large mirror above a gleaming mahogany table on which there'd be an arrangement of gorgeous flowers. It would be near the staircase running up to the first storey.'

He smiled broadly. 'I love the picture that conjures up.'

'Then, if you don't mind, I'll go a little further. The salesman said they were planning a stained-glass staircase window, perhaps with an imitation coat of arms. Personally, I'd prefer clear glass, and I think a lot of women would. I can see a simple vase with a few wild flowers on the windowsill in front of it. I'm not keen on the stained-glass idea.'

'Nor am I,' he said. 'Everything you're suggesting is the sort of thing I like, Jeannie. I don't know that it's what I want, so couldn't suggest it, but as soon as you say it, I know it's exactly what I'd choose. Does that make sense?

'Not really,' she said, laughing. 'But I know what you mean.' She paused. 'I hope you genuinely don't mind me running away with ideas for what's your house, not mine. But it could be so lovely that it's difficult not to do so,' she added, suddenly feeling awkward.

He smiled at her. 'I promise you, I don't. I asked you to come with me again because I want your ideas, so keep telling me what you think. The sitting room runs for the depth of the house so I'll certainly need your advice with that. I feel guilty asking as you've already been such a help, but if you could come up here with me again in a day or so, I'd be really grateful. I'd ask you to dinner tonight as a thank you, if I wasn't pretty sure that you'd be seeing Edward.'

'Oh, what a shame, I am,' she said. 'If I wasn't, I'd have been happy to go with you. Very happy.'

Their eyes met... and held a moment. Then both looked away.

Jean wiped an imaginary piece of dust from her skirt.

'I suppose we'd better make a move, then,' he said with a regretful smile. 'As you seem to like the house, I'm tempted to put a deposit on it.'

'Oh, yes, I'd certainly do that,' she said enthusiastically. 'You don't want anyone else to beat you to it because you were hesitating.'

'And you think a woman would be happy living here?' he asked.

Jean nodded. 'I know she would.' She paused. 'But she wouldn't just be happy because she liked the design of the house, she'd be happy because she was living with you.'

'I don't know, Jean,' he said slowly. 'I've been alone for several years now, and I'm probably fairly set in my ways. That wouldn't be attractive to a woman. Also, it would be my second marriage, and I imagine a lot of women wouldn't like the idea of being the second wife.'

'If someone felt like that, then they wouldn't be worthy of you,' Jean said indignantly. 'As for being set in your ways, if you were with someone you loved, who loved you, the two of you would work it out. Anyone would be lucky to be married to you. You're a good man and a good doctor, and you're very attractive. Oh!' She went red. 'I shouldn't have said that. What would Edward think if he heard me? He'd be appalled.'

'But he didn't hear you,' he said quietly. 'I did, and I'm pleased that I did.'

Her hand fell to her lap and they sat on the bench and stared at each other, the silence between them charged with unspoken words.

24

T*hat evening*

EDWARD ARRIVED at Jean's house as planned, and as it was a pleasant mellow evening, they decided to walk to the Brown Hare Inn, taking the long route there by following the winding lanes bordered by flowers and shrubs that traced the outer rim of the village.

As they walked, they commented on the brilliance of the blossom in the hedgerows, and on the striking displays of dahlias and hydrangeas in front of several of the houses they passed.

Several times he'd glanced across at Jean, surprised at how cheerful she seemed. He'd assumed that the concern he'd seen in her the day before would have been festering ever since then and would have manifested itself in an extreme awkwardness when they met.

But there was no trace of her previous depression or anxiety.

On the contrary. Although their conversation had been on fairly mundane things, such as the beauty of the flowers and the loveliness of the evening sky, it had all flowed quite easily and there hadn't as yet been any awkward silences.

But the evening wasn't yet over, he thought ruefully, and what lay ahead wasn't going to be easy. He still hadn't decided exactly what to say to Jean, but he knew that he had to say something that evening to prepare her for what he now felt sure was inevitable.

The fact that he was so torn indicated that he genuinely did love Jean, and he wanted her to know that. She'd had a place in his heart since they'd met in school as children, and always would. But he no longer wanted to marry her.

He knew by now that there was nothing transitory about his feelings for Violet. She had a permanent place in his heart.

Furthermore, he was pretty sure that she had similar feelings for him.

That morning, he'd taken her hand without thinking as they were about to cross Angel Hill. Not only had she let him continue to hold her hand as they walked into Abbey Gardens, but her fingers had tightened around his! It hadn't been his imagination, he was sure.

And when they'd sat there having the sandwiches that Wendy had made them, he had felt so at ease, so happy, so consumed by love that he'd been on the point of telling her how much he adored her.

It was only his awareness that as an engaged man he had no right to speak to her in such a way, and the excellent timing of her question about St Edmund, that had prevented him from embarrassing them both.

But although he had managed to stop words of love from pouring out, he hadn't been able to stop his feelings for Violet from flooding through him. She'd been all he'd been able to think about since he'd left her, and he knew he had to resolve the situation by being open with both Violet and Jean.

Even if Violet turned him down, he knew now that his feelings for Jean would never be more than friendship, and it would be grossly unfair to her not to take steps to prepare her for this.

As Harry's Inn came in sight, he began to rehearse mentally how he would open the conversation by telling Jean that he now felt less sure about the future. He'd then wait to hear what she said in response. He might even have to go as far as to confess that his indecision dated from the arrival of Violet, he realised.

Ideally he'd rather leave any reference to Violet for a later occasion. The forthcoming evening was about sowing a few seeds to stop it from being too great a shock when he broke off their engagement. Any mention of Violet that evening could deny Jean the time to prepare herself.

Feeling tremendously guilty, as well as very nervous, he reached out to take her hand as he always did when they went into the inn. But she was holding her straw bag in one hand and her yellow cardigan in the other, so after a moment's hesitation, he slid his hand into the pocket of his lightweight jacket.

'For a country inn, it's amazing what they can do with the limited amount of meat we're allowed,' he said, sitting back in satisfaction.

'It certainly is. The meal was delicious,' she said. 'It was a good idea to come here. Your invitation yesterday made it the perfect ending to what turned out to be a lovely day.'

'You mean that syringing the ears of Mrs Groves made it a lovely day!' he exclaimed in mock surprise.

'I take it you don't know that my day was further enhanced when I ended up having to bind a badly ulcerated leg with crêpe bandages,' she said lightly.

They both laughed.

'So really, what made it such a good day?' he asked, trying to ward off the moment when he'd have to confess his uncertainty about the future.

'Martin.'

Edward frowned. 'Martin? What did he do?'

'It wasn't so much what he did, but what he said,' Jean said, beaming. 'He was coming out of the surgery when I got back yesterday afternoon, and to my surprise, he said he'd been hoping to see me. He said that he would have even come up to my home if he hadn't caught me at the surgery. He wanted my help, you see.'

'Your help?' Edward echoed.

She nodded. 'That's right. He's going to move from the flat and he wanted my advice about a house he's thinking of buying.'

'He didn't tell me he was moving!' Edward exclaimed, straightening up.

A wave of guilt washed through him.

This must be Martin's response to his visible irritation at being told how he should be behaving towards Jean. He'd go and see him the following day and apologise.

'I think it was a very recent decision,' Jean continued. 'He said he'd been walking around the village the day before and had found himself up by the new houses at the top of the village. He remembered I'd told him several times that I thought they looked very attractive. Well, apparently, he was quite impressed by what he saw, and by one house in particular. So I went to see it with him yesterday and today.'

'You did?' Edward said, surprised.

'It's a really lovely house, Edward,' she said enthusiastically. 'It's a little way back from the others, and it looks over the village in one direction and towards the woods in the other. It's on slightly higher ground, which is why it has such a glorious view.' She settled back. 'Just think, I'll be cycling past it every day,' she added with a giggle.

He couldn't remember the last time he'd heard Jean giggle. She wasn't really a giggling person. He stared at her in amazement.

'I think I know the house you mean,' he said, feeling some comment from him was expected.

'I'm sure you'll have seen it. It's the detached one at the top of the development. They're still building it, so if he buys it now, he's got time to make suggestions about the walls and flooring, for example. And he wants my help with this. Not immediately, of course, but in about three or four weeks' time, when they reach that stage of the construction. It's going to be such fun,' she said, and she laughed gleefully.

'If it's the house I think it is, won't it be a little large for Martin?'

'Maybe at the moment, but possibly not for much longer. He told me that he's started to think about marrying again. Can you believe it?' she said in excitement.

Edward opened his mouth to make an appropriate comment, but as she'd started to speak again, he refrained.

'It's time he remarried,' she continued. 'He's such a nice man. He'd make someone a wonderful husband, and he'd be a superb father. I'm sure he'll want children. With the right wife, he'll be able to leave the past behind him and face a future with a family. His life won't be as lonely as it must surely be now. I'm so pleased for him.'

Edward stared at the glow on Jean's face, at the light shining from her eyes, at the pink haze on her cheeks. Well, well, he thought, and he felt himself start to relax.

He turned, caught sight of the waiter and mouthed a request for two brandies. Then he sat back, adopting a thoughtful expression.

'Good for Martin,' he said. 'And you're just the person to help him, Jean,' he added. 'You've a good eye for the sort of colours that make for a comfortable home. Martin will be a lucky man to have your advice.'

Jean smiled broadly at Edward. 'Thank you for saying so, and for not minding if I spend some time helping him, especially as it'll obviously be at weekends. We may have to go into Bury, for example, to look at furniture. But like me, you clearly think it's good that he feels able to fall in love again.'

Edward smiled slowly. 'I most definitely do,' he said. He paused to let the waiter put a brandy snifter in front of each of them.

Jean's expression suddenly changed.

She looked at him in sudden nervous anxiety. 'But there was something you wanted to talk about, wasn't there? I seem to have taken over the conversation with Martin's news, so it's your turn now. What did you want to bring up?'

The eyes that stared at him were full of dread. Yes, dread was the right word, he thought in amusement.

'D'you know, I've quite forgotten,' he said, shaking his head. 'It can't have been important or I'd have remembered. If it comes to mind, I'll tell you. For now, though, why don't we have a brandy and toast Martin's success in finding the right person to walk at his side for the rest of his life?'

Her expression clearing, she picked up her glass. 'Oh, yes,' she said eagerly. 'Let's do that.' And she touched his glass with hers.

25

B*ury St Edmunds,*
The following Tuesday afternoon

STANLEY EMERGED from his small kitchen into the room behind Patterson's Antiques, a whisky in one hand and a gin and tonic in the other. He put the gin on the table in front of Gladys, sat down and put the whisky in front of himself.

'Cheers,' he said, raising his glass.

'This is very unlike you at such an early hour, Stan. I was expecting a cup of tea.'

'Tea doesn't revive you in the way that whisky does,' he said, and he took a deep drink of the whisky.

'Let me guess. Eric was in a particularly nasty mood,' she said drily.

'That's an understatement,' he said. 'He was in vile.'

She frowned. 'But why? You gave him the pax board, didn't you?'

'That's right. It's what he'd asked for. The trouble is,

when he saw it, he wasn't keen on making a replica. I hadn't realised that anything about it could pose a problem.'

'What sort of problem?'

'He said he would've expected simply to pour a silicon mould around the board and thereby make a perfect reproduction that was viable for casting. But there're a couple of things about that particular board that could make it tricky to reproduce it perfectly, he told me.'

'Such as?'

'Well, firstly, it has some damage around the edges, mainly to the top right-hand corner, which could be difficult to reproduce, and secondly it's very, very thin. He would've had to build up the back in order to create a reproduction. He said he could've done so, but it would've taken a huge amount of work, and for the money we'd agreed to pay him, it wouldn't be worth it.'

'Did you offer him more?'

Stanley glared at her. 'Of course I did, even though I didn't want to as we'd have risked being out of pocket.'

'Why? They're in demand aren't they, so you'd get a good price for it?'

'Not as much as they were. There seems to have been an influx of pax boards recently. Just in the last few weeks alone a number have come up for auction across the county. The same is true in Norfolk and Cambridgeshire. I suppose people who've bought a board hoping to sell it for profit, as opposed to your true collector, are trying to get what they can for it before the market's saturated. Even though I won't be auctioning it, it lowers the price I can ask.'

'Have you a buyer in mind?'

'I've got a customer who asked a while ago if there was any chance of me finding him one. He wants it for his collection. Fortunately, he's not one to frequent auctions so I doubt he knows how much the price has dropped. I'll be restrained in what I charge for it, though. But need you ask? You know I've always got a pretty good idea of where I'm going to sell any item that goes to Eric to be copied.'

Gladys nodded. 'I know you have. You're a master at what you do. And by the way, your plan for Tom and Lucy seems to be working, though not in the way you intended. Apparently, they've been seeing each other, and I heard her tell Violet how much she liked him. He was going to pick her up from work this afternoon, I believe, and take her to The Fox Inn this evening. You mark my words, she'll soon be changing her mind about working for him.'

'That's good to know. I must say, you, too, are pretty good at what you do, Gladys,' he said with an appreciative smile, 'and that calls for another drink.' He got up, went into the kitchen and returned with the bottle of whisky. When he'd refilled his glass, he put the bottle on the table in front of him.

'We talked a while ago,' he said, settling comfortably back on his chair, 'about you finding other ways in which to compromise Miss Hammond. Did your devious mind manage to think of anything?'

'Only one thing, I'm afraid, and it's a pretty obvious one. I haven't yet got round to doing it, though. I haven't had an opportunity.'

'Then you must create the opportunity, and do so soon,' he said steadily. 'So tell me, what's the plan?'

Lucy looked around the wood-panelled dining area in The Fox Inn and smiled across the dark wood table at Tom. She leaned slightly forward. 'It feels so historical,' she said in just above a whisper.

'Could that be because it was built in the fifteenth century?' he whispered back.

'You know what I mean,' she said at normal volume. She looked around her again. 'It's very kind of your mother to agree to cover the shop for such a long time,' she remarked. 'After all, we were at the museum for quite a while before we came here.'

'Yes, it is. But Mother could tell how much I enjoyed your company last week, and wanted to make it easier for me to meet you. That's mothers for you!'

'Mine's very kind, too,' she said.

'I'm sure she is. Her daughter's lovely, and she must have got that from somewhere.'

She went pink with pleasure.

'I don't want to ask too much of my mother, though,' he went on, 'as I know she wants to step back a bit, so I'm going to advertise for someone to help me in the shop.' Lucy's heart did a sudden lurch. 'But that's for the future,' he continued. 'What we're about to eat is in the present. Let's look at the menu.'

He picked up the menu next to him, and Lucy did the same. As she looked at it, to her distress, her vision blurred. She promptly blew her nose and surreptitiously wiped her eyes while he was studying the food on offer.

'It's a pretty good selection,' he said, 'given there's still some rationing, including meat,' he remarked, running his eye down the items on the menu. 'I think I'll have the grilled sausages. What about you?'

She cleared her throat. 'The same, please.'

'And I think I'll have a vodka tonic. What about you?'

'I'd love one, thank you.'

Mentally pulling herself together, she put the menu

back on the table. Tom did the same. The waiter came over and took their order, and then headed for the bar.

'It's a problem,' Tom began, sitting back and looking at her with visible amusement.

'What is?' she asked with a half-smile.

'I'd like to ask you how your week has been, if you've had an enjoyable week. That would be a normal thing to say. But I can't as you might think I'm subtly trying to get you to say you weren't happy and that I'd then pounce on you and suggest you change your mind about working for me after all. You see my dilemma?'

She adopted a serious expression.

'I do. But I can resolve it, I believe.' She paused to let the waiter put their drinks on the table.

'You can?' he asked. 'Do tell me how.'

'It's quite easy,' she said lightly. 'You won't need to ask me such a question as I'm about to launch into things to do with the museum, which, to almost quote you, would be a normal thing to do.'

'Fire away,' he said with a grin.

'Well, I enjoyed taking you round the museum today, including going downstairs. And it was fun to show you what we've earmarked for the active display. It's strange I couldn't find the pax board I told you about, the one with the dented right-hand corner, which depicted the passion of Christ, but it must've been put somewhere else. Probably by Gladys.'

'Why would she do that, d'you think?'

Lucy shrugged. 'I've no idea. But it isn't the first time I haven't been able to find what I was looking for. I think Gladys might be in the habit of going down to the basement, and if she believes we've put an item on the wrong shelf, moving it to where she thinks it ought to be. She must come in when the museum's closed or we'd have seen what she was doing. Though how she gets in I don't know.'

'Going into work when you don't have to, that's devotion to your job indeed.'

'I suppose it is.' She paused and bit her lip. 'But she does other peculiar things, too.'

She stopped talking, picked up her knife and fork and put them down again.

'Peculiar in what way?' he asked, frowning.

'It's hard to say. In fact, I shouldn't really say anything as you might think I'm a troublemaker. I wouldn't want you to see me in such a way and be glad I turned down your offer.'

'I'll never be glad you turned down my offer, Lucy, so that's not a consideration.' He paused. 'You can tell me.'

'All right. It might help if I said it aloud and was able to hear how silly I'm being.' She took a deep breath. 'There's something a little funny about some of the things that Gladys has done recently.'

'What sort of things?' he asked.

'You're going to think I'm mad,' she said with a self-disparaging laugh.

'I promise I won't. I think you're interesting, intelligent and perceptive, and that won't change. And I also think you're very lovely when you blush with embarrassment.'

'D'you really?' she asked, her heart beating fast.

He nodded. 'I do. And that's not going to change, either. You can safely tell me what's she's done that's worrying you, because you *are* worried, if I read you right.'

'They're just little things. First of all, after you came to the museum, she asked me what you'd been talking to me about, and I told her you'd asked me to work for you. She assumed I'd agreed, and was clearly disappointed when I told her I hadn't. Why would she want me to leave? They'd only have had to find someone to replace me and it might not be easy to do that. And it would be very difficult for Violet if I left.'

He frowned. 'I admit that does seem strange.'

'Also,' Lucy went on, 'when Stanley first came to the museum and met Violet, he indicated that he hadn't seen Gladys for ages, but I don't think that's true.'

Then she told him about how, some time later, Gladys had told them she had toothache and had left to go to the dentist, but she'd seen Gladys come out of Stanley's shop and it didn't look as if she'd been anywhere near the dentist. Furthermore, Gladys and Stanley had been very friendly with each other, which showed that what Stanley had implied wasn't true.

'What a nonsensical thing to lie about,' he mused.

'I wondered if they could be romantically involved,' she said with a laugh, 'even though both are quite old. But I suppose anything's possible.'

'That's true. But it doesn't explain why she wanted you to leave the museum,' he added after a minute or two. 'Nor why Stanley wanted you out of the museum, too.'

She sat up sharply. 'Stanley did?'

He nodded. 'That's right.' He told her about Stanley's visit to his shop earlier on the day that he'd met Lucy, and that it was Stanley who'd suggested he offer Lucy a job.

'Why would they both want me to go?' she wondered aloud.

They looked at each other, mystified.

'I've no idea,' he said at last. 'You could be right about them being romantically attached to each other and wanting to keep that a secret. Or it could just be a strong friendship. After all, they've obviously known each other for years. But I don't know where you fit into it.'

'Gladys said that Stanley sometimes advised them about good items to buy at forthcoming auctions. Maybe that's why they wouldn't want people to know they were friends. Gladys might worry about them suspecting her of passing on knowledge about the museum's finances, which Stanley could use to his benefit. That could be it, couldn't it?' She sat back, a hopeful expression on her face.

'I suppose so.' His tone was dubious. 'It'll do until we come up with something better.' He paused. 'Have you mentioned any of this to Violet?'

She shook her head. 'No, I haven't. I thought she had enough on her plate, being new and with so much to learn. Also, she's really busy at the moment. I wouldn't want her to waste her time worrying about something that might be nothing. In putting together a number of little things, I could be making two and two equal five.'

'That's a fair point. You're right—it's probably better not to say anything, unless, of course, something else happens which causes you real concern. Aha. Here comes the food! I suggest we both keep our eyes open and report back regularly to each other.'

'I don't know how long I'll be able to do that,' she said, picking up her knife and fork.

He paused in cutting his sausage and stared at her. 'Why not?'

'Well, if I started working for you after Christmas,' she said, her eyes on her plate, 'having seen Violet though the opening of her display and having helped with the first few classes in the museum, then I wouldn't be where I could carry on observing Gladys, would I?'

A slow smile spread across his face.

'If the offer's still open that is?' she asked, and she looked up at him.

'It most definitely is,' he said in obvious delight. 'But what made you change your mind?'

'It was when you said that you were going to look for someone to help you in the shop. I've really enjoyed the time I've spent with you and I knew in that moment that I couldn't bear the thought of anyone but me being with you all day, sharing your hopes for the shop and your plans for the future.'

She paused, and looked anxiously at him. 'I've been horribly forward, given we haven't known each other for long,' she said. 'If you'd rather not have me in the shop, considering what I've just more or less told you, I'd understand.'

'What are you doing next Saturday evening?' he asked with a grin. 'I've got some plans I'd like to tell you about. I've decided to build up my stock of furniture, and I could use your help. You could come and have dinner at my house. I know my mother would like to meet you, and we've known each other long enough for me to know that I very much want you to meet her.'

26

H*arton,*
The following afternoon

VIOLET STEPPED out of the museum into the late afternoon sun. She stood for a moment enjoying the slight breeze that was sending russet and golden leaves to the ground.

'It's certainly very autumnal now,' she heard Gladys say behind her. 'I'll lock the door, shall I?'

'That would be great, Gladys, thank you. It would save me getting my key out.'

The sound of the key being turned in the lock was followed by a flurry of air as Gladys came and stood at her side. 'This is my favourite month,' Gladys told her.

'It's certainly one of mine, too,' Violet said, and she started walking up the path to the road.

Gladys started walking at the same time, keeping pace with her.

'I've been meaning to ask how you're settling in,' Gladys

asked as they turned in the direction of Violet's house. 'It must be very different from living in London.'

'It most certainly is,' Violet said. 'It's a completely different pace of life.'

'Which do you prefer?'

'Oh, definitely living in Harton. I love the slower pace of life.'

'Of course, you're lucky enough to be able to have your cake and eat it, too, aren't you?' Gladys said. 'You live in Harton, and I hope you'll long continue to do so, but you can escape to London whenever you feel you're missing life in a large town.'

Violet nodded. 'I suppose that's true. So far, I've not been back to Kentish Town since moving here as I've been so busy, but I'll have to go back one Sunday soon. My parents have been here so it's my turn now to make the journey.'

She came to a stop in front of her house.

'At least you don't have far to go when you leave the museum,' Gladys said with a smile. 'I envy you. You'll have the kettle boiled and the tea made before I'm even across the marketplace.'

'I'm a pretty fast tea-maker, but not that fast,' Violet said with a laugh. Gladys didn't move. Violet hesitated. 'Would you like to come in for a cup of tea now? You can judge my tea-making speed if you do.'

Both laughed.

'That's very kind of you, Violet. I'd enjoy that. And it'll be interesting to see what you've done with the house. I knew it when it was being used for storage.'

'Come on in, then,' Violet said, and she led the way up the short garden path and into the house. 'Take a seat in there,' she said as they went through into the sitting room. 'I'll put the kettle on. I had a go at making shortbread at the weekend, so I don't know whether it's your lucky day or not that I've still got some left. I'm not the best of cooks.'

'I'm sure it'll be delicious,' Gladys said, and she took the armchair closest to the fireplace.

A moment later, Violet returned with a plate of shortbread and two serviettes, which she put on a small oak table standing next to the wall. She carried the table carefully across the room and placed it between the chair that Gladys was sitting on and the chair she'd be taking.

'Help yourself,' she said. 'The tea won't be a moment.'

A few minutes later, she returned with a tray on which there was a teapot covered with a knitted cosy, two cups and saucers, a milk jug and two small bowls, one for sugar and one for the tea strainer. She put everything on the table and sat down. 'We'll let the tea brew for a few minutes,' she said.

'I'm definitely impressed by your speed. When you visit me, which I hope you'll do one day before too long, you'll see that I'm very much slower than you.'

'In "Ode on a Grecian Urn", Keats seems to argue that the moment of anticipation is greater than the moment of receiving. If he's right, you're doing your guests a favour, and I'm doing the reverse,' she said brightly.

'That's a good way of looking at it,' Gladys said with a smile. 'So I won't attempt to force my old bones to move at a greater speed in future.'

She glanced towards the fireplace. 'Your flower display is most impressive,' she said. 'What a good idea to brighten the look of an empty grate in such a way. I like sedum enormously. They're such bold flowers, and the maroon colour they are at this time of year is most attractive.'

'I like them, too,' Violet said. 'Fortunately, they last quite long. But there won't be such a selection in winter, and I might have to resort to a display of twigs. Or give my parents a prod. They're having a tapestry fire screen made for me by one of the girls who works for them.'

'But surely you'll be burning coal or wood in winter, won't you? You won't need a screen or a display.' Gladys cocked her head questioningly.

Violet shook her head. 'I'm not going to use the fireplace for what it's intended. So much so that I haven't even had the chimney swept. This is only a small room and I think it'll be easy to keep it warm with the electric fire my parents have given me. I know from when I lived at home how much work a real fire is, and I don't fancy clearing out the ashes every morning when I get up. Also, soot could be a problem in a room this size.'

Gladys looked around. 'Yes, I see what you mean. I rarely use my fire for the same reason as you. But it does make a room look very welcoming when you come in on a cold day.'

'So, too, does a pot of tea. Let me pour you a cup.' She poured Gladys's tea and pushed the plate of shortbread closer to her. 'Would you excuse me a moment if I pop upstairs to the bathroom before I have my tea?'

'Please, do go right ahead.'

'I won't be a moment,' Violet said, and she left the room.

Gladys waited to hear her footsteps on the staircase and then moved fast.

Clutching her handbag, she knelt in front of the hearth and swiftly moved the floral display to the side of the fireplace. Leaning forward, being careful to avoid disturbing any soot, she felt for the small stone ledge she knew to be there. Finding it, she felt herself relax. She'd had occasion to take advantage of the ledge once or twice when the house was being used for storage, but it was still a relief to find that nothing had changed.

She put her hand in her bag and took out a small antique St John figurine.

Hearing Violet moving around upstairs, she hastily placed the figurine on the ledge, moved the display back into place, got up from her kneeling position, picked up her bag and had just sat down again in her chair when Violet came back into the room.

She looked up at Violet and smiled. 'I couldn't resist seeing if your sedum had the same lovely aroma as they have before they're cut,' she said, 'and I was pleased to see that it has, or it's almost as strong as when they're outside. But sit down and have your drink, dear. It'll be cold, which would be a shame when you make such a lovely pot of tea,' she added, and she put her cup to her lips.

WHAT WAS THAT ALL ABOUT, Violet thought as she washed up the items she'd used that afternoon. Never before had Gladys shown the slightest interest in having a cup of tea and a chat with her, and it was hard to see what she'd hoped to achieve that day by inviting herself there.

Wiping her hands dry, she moved to the sitting room doorway and stood staring around the room.

Nothing was out of place, and as far as she could tell, there was nothing missing. She didn't have many items on display that she didn't really need so she'd easily to see if anything had changed.

Could it be that Gladys had been feeling lonely and a bit left out, she wondered.

She and Lucy had been spending so much time together. The reception was getting closer all the time, and before that the active display had to be in place, all the accompanying labels written, and there should be samples of workbooks, too, if possible. She'd been so busy that she hadn't really been taking the time to tell Gladys what stage they were at.

She thought back to the huge interest Gladys had shown in the museum that afternoon when, for something to say, she'd mentioned how much the art teacher at the secondary school was doing to help with the display.

Yes, that was it, she thought with satisfaction. Her wanting to feel more involved would explain Gladys's surprising, and rather unwelcome, suggestion that perhaps Violet would go to her house one day and have a slice of the sponge cake she enjoyed making.

Gladys must definitely be lonely, she thought as she went across to the fireplace and bent down to return the display to its original angle in order to create a better balance in the arrangement of flowers.

In future she must keep Gladys more informed about what was going on and try to include her in her conversations with Lucy. First thing the following morning, she'd tell Lucy about Gladys's visit, and encourage Lucy, too, to include Gladys in anything they were discussing.

It couldn't have been easier, Gladys thought with satisfaction.

Firstly, Violet hadn't indicated in any way that she thought it strange that Gladys would want to come to tea when they saw each other every day and frequently had their lunch in the staffroom at the same time, after which they'd dredge up something to talk about while they had a cup of tea.

Secondly, there being an admirable lack of clutter in the

sitting room, she'd been able to place the figurine and get back to her seat much more easily than she'd anticipated.

Indeed, she hadn't even been sure that she would be able to hide the figurine that day with Violet's kitchen leading straight from the sitting room, affording Violet a view of anything that happened in the sitting room. Had Violet not gone upstairs it would have been impossible. Instead, it had all worked out very well.

Mentioning the scent of the flowers had been inspired. When she'd sat back down, she'd seen that the vase of flowers was at a slightly different angle from the way it had been before she'd moved it to one side. But if Violet noticed that, she'd assume that having made a comment about their aroma, Gladys had gone over to the flowers in her absence.

So that was done, and when she next spoke to Stan, she'd tell him which figurine she'd used.

If it proved unnecessary to reveal the figurine in order to establish beyond doubt Violet's guilt, Stan could always sell it and share the money with her. There'd be no need to give anything to Eric as they wouldn't require him to make a copy. The figurine would have been away from the museum for so long that it wouldn't be missed. And if it were missed, people would put that down to Violet.

Yes, a satisfactory afternoon's work indeed.

27

F*riday, one week later*

STANDING at one of the upstairs bedroom windows in the house for which he'd just put down a deposit, Martin looked at his watch. Jean was now an hour late. It was very unlike her, even when she was on duty.

Something serious must have happened that had held her up, and he decided to wait where he was, certain that she'd eventually come, just as she'd said she'd do.

Determined to stop thinking about Jean, and how she'd react when he told her that he'd effectively bought the house, he focused his attention on the view that would become his when the day came that the house was ready for him to move in.

With no house between him and the countryside to the north of the village, he'd be able to watch the changing hues of the trees in the small wood. At present they were a mass of dark green shot through with red and gold; in winter they'd become dark brown skeletal shapes lined with white; in spring and summer, they'd turn into a cluster of vibrant greens, broken up by the occasional copper beech, a home for numerous varieties of birds.

How he was going to enjoy watching the wood take on a different mantle with each new season!

Turning his head slightly, he looked from the wood to the patchwork of fields, some still green, some pale yellow from their sun-bleached stubble, all of them separated by hedgerows.

A narrow path ribboned into the distance and he followed the path with his eyes to a low, tree-crowned hill, at the foot of which cattle were grazing in the evening sun.

It was the sort of view he'd dreamed of having as a child. It had been a regret three years earlier that the house that he and Florence had chosen was lower in the village and that while it had a lovely garden front and back, it lacked the sweeping panoramic view that he would have liked.

He turned back into the room. He would now have that longed-for view, and he should be feeling elated.

So why wasn't he?

It wasn't that he didn't feel extremely happy with the choice he'd made for his future home, he mused as he crossed the room and went out on to the gallery landing, because he did. The house was everything he could want, and it had been made so much more special by the help that Jean had given him.

Everything about its location and the house itself was perfect, he thought as he went down the stairs to the spacious entrance hall. So why, when he'd entered the house that evening, had he looked around him and suddenly felt distraught?

He stopped abruptly in the centre of the hall. His hands flew to his head.

Oh, no, he inwardly cried, and he buried his face in his hands.

'What's the matter, Martin?' he heard Jean say, her voice full of concern.

He swiftly dropped his hands and looked up.

'I just realised that I forgot to do something I'd promised Edward I'd do,' he said.

Even to his ears, it sounded a little weak as an explanation for the anguish he was sure she would have seen on his face.

She came towards him, smiling. 'I'm sure Edward will understand, whatever it was. I'm afraid I'm late because he asked for my help. I'd just finished restocking my bag and was about to come up here when Edward rushed in and asked if I could go with him. He'd had an urgent call about the Carter baby. After a difficult birth, the baby had seemed to settle and had begun to feed well, but the mother was frantic as he'd started bringing up all his feeds.'

'I remember the birth. It was touch and go for a while, wasn't it?'

She nodded. 'It certainly was. When we got to the house, Edward examined baby Carter and found a small lump in his groin.'

'Was it a hernia?'

'That's right. It was a strangulated hernia. Neither of us had seen such a thing before in a baby that small. Fortunately, by applying hot compresses and gentle pressure, between us we persuaded it to go back. Hopefully, there won't be any further problems, but I'll visit the baby a couple of times a week for the next few weeks, just to make sure there's no sign of it happening again. If it did, the baby would urgently need an operation.'

'Well done, Jean. That must have been really distressing, seeing such a tiny baby so ill.'

Jean smiled happily. 'But the day ended well. Baby Carter looked waxen, but is responding, and I'm standing here in the house on what is a really lovely autumn evening.' She paused and looked around again. 'Have you decided whether to buy it?'

'I've bought it,' he said quietly. 'I put down the deposit this afternoon. I did it before you got here as I didn't want to put any responsibility on to your shoulders. If you'd influenced me to buy or otherwise, and things had gone wrong, you might've felt guilty. This way you won't.'

She clapped her hands in glee. 'Congratulations, Martin!' she cried, and she hugged him tightly. Then she pulled away and held him at arm's length. 'It's just like you to be so considerate. Does Edward know?'

'Not yet, but I'll tell him very soon.'

She tucked her arm into his. 'Shall we go and sit on the windowsill in the sitting room,' she said. 'It's wide enough to get comfortable there. In fact, you might like to have window seats made. Listen to me!' She tapped her wrist playfully in rebuke. 'I'm telling you again what to do in your house.'

'Keep telling me. I want to hear all your suggestions,' he said as they went into the sitting room and sat down on the windowsill.

Leaning back against the windowpane, Jean turned her head towards him. 'Now I want to hear the real reason why you looked in such despair when I arrived, and weren't dancing with joy.'

'I can't tell you,' he said, his eyes on the floor.

She straightened up and stared at him in surprise. 'Why not? I thought we were good enough friends to tell each other anything.'

He shook his head in despair. 'It's just that I've done something so stupid, Jean.'

'I find that hard to believe,' she said gently, and she took his hand. 'And even harder to believe that nothing can be done about it.'

'There's nothing to be done. I've let myself be really silly, and the only things that will get me over this are time and circumstances.'

'Dear Martin, I can't bear to see you looking like this. Do tell me what it is.'

'You'll hate me.'

She gave a little laugh. 'I couldn't hate you. You're my dearest friend. Tell me, what have you let yourself do that you shouldn't have done?'

He looked into her face. 'I've let myself fall in love with you. I've always told myself that my feelings for you were those of a close friend, and nothing more, even though deep down I knew I wasn't being truly honest with myself. How could they be more than that when you were engaged to Edward?'

'Oh, Martin,' she whispered.

'But when I walked into the house this evening and you weren't there, I knew how much I longed for you to be at my side. Not just today, but tomorrow, and the next day and forever. And you can't be, and I felt distraught. There's no other word. I love you with all my heart, and I shouldn't. I'm so sorry, Jean. I promise I'll never mention this again as I'd hate to lose your friendship.'

'If you don't mention it again, I shall be most disappointed,' she said, her voice shaking.

He looked at her with surprise. 'I don't understand.'

'I've loved every minute we've spent together. Every time we've separated, you to go back to the surgery, me to go home, I've felt utterly desolate. At some point, the friendship we've had since you moved into Harton has deepened into more than that. The Edward complication stopped me from seeing it. But I realise now that what I feel for Edward is a deep friendship, but nothing more. I know that because I can compare the way I feel about him with the way I feel about you.' Her voice caught.

'You really love me?' he asked in wonder.

'I do,' she said, her eyes filling with tears. 'So much. The more I'm with you, the more I want to be with you. And when we're not together, I can't stop thinking about you.'

'Oh, Jeannie.' He put his hands on her shoulders and pulled her gently to him.

She raised her face to his and he brushed his lips against hers. She caught hold of his face between her hands and for a long moment stared hard into his eyes. Then, reaching up, she pressed her lips against his.

His hands slid to the back of her head, and he pulled her closer to him and kissed her hard.

They finally drew apart, their breathing ragged as they sat side by side looking at each other, their eyes full of love.

'Will you marry me?' he asked when he could speak more easily again.

She put her hand to his cheek. 'Oh, yes,' she said with a sigh of happiness. 'I can't think of anything I want more than I want to be with you for the rest of my life.'

He put his arm around her, and they sat there, her cheek against his chest, his head resting on the top of her head.

'How soon can you tell Edward?' he asked after a while. 'And how soon after that can I speak to your parents?'

'I'll speak to Edward tomorrow,' she said, her voice muffled by his shirt. 'We're having dinner in town together. I can't see him suing for breach of contract.'

'Then, on Sunday morning, I'll visit your parents and ask for your hand in marriage. If they aren't too overwrought about having me as their son-in-law instead of Edward, we can arrange a wedding date there and then. I want to marry you as soon as possible.'

'And that's what I want, too,' she said, nestling closer to him. 'I don't know when I've ever felt as happy as I feel at this moment.'

She raised her eyes to look at him, and their lips met again.

28

B*ury St Edmunds, The Suffolk Hotel,*
Saturday, the following day

JEAN SAT down on the chair that Edward pulled out for her.

'I thought we'd have a change from the Brown Hare Inn,' he said, moving round the table to the seat on the other side and sitting down. 'We always seem to be going there.'

'It was a good idea to come here,' she said. 'I've not been for a while. It's a treat to have a change, and such a lovely change, too.'

'I wanted to thank you for your help with the Carter family yesterday,' he said. 'It was really kind of you to drop everything and come back out with me.'

Jean waved away his gratitude. 'I was glad to help. I do hope the baby thrives. The last thing that family needs is any more worry—the mother had such a hard time over the birth.'

'I dropped in on them today, and I'm happy to say that it looks good for the latest little Carter. We make a great team, don't we?' he said, and he smiled across the table.

She smiled back at him. 'I couldn't work for better doctors.' Then she glanced around the room at the walls. 'Is there a restaurant in the county that doesn't have a water-colour of a hunting scene?' she asked, deliberately changing the subject, hoping to delay ending their engagement till they'd had their meal. 'With all our beautiful scenery, it's a shame you see so little of it on the walls.'

'I've never actually thought about it,' Edward said, and he looked up at the painting at which she was staring. 'But you're right. It's not surprising, though, is it, as we're so close to Newmarket? Also, the red jackets worn by the huntsmen add a touch of colour to any scene, which must appeal to an artist.'

'That's true,' she said, nodding.

The waiter brought them a menu, and they each chose the roast chicken. Edward ordered a bottle of white wine, and asked the waiter to bring the wine at once.

As they sipped their wine while waiting for their food to be served, she tried desperately to think of some other delaying topics to talk about, but failed to come up with anything. All she could think about was Martin and his visit to her parents the following morning.

His visit to her father specifically.

Before he'd left her the day before, she'd said that such formality wasn't necessary. But Martin had insisted on doing everything the old-fashioned way, and he'd been sure that her parents would appreciate it. Nothing must stop her father from saying yes, he'd said, and he'd actually brought her hands to his lips and kissed the fingers on each of her hands.

'What have you been doing today?' Edward asked, breaking into her thoughts.

Her face lit up. 'You won't believe it, but I've been looking at china,' she said, and she laughed. 'It was much more exciting than it sounds. I went up to look at the house Martin's thinking of buying last night, and we got talking about dinner services. I ended up promising to go to Bury with him this morning. So this is my second visit to the town today. We went to T.H. Nice & Co in Abbeygate Street, and had a look at what they'd got. He didn't buy anything but he got some ideas. It was great fun. After that, we went and had a bite to eat. I didn't eat much as I knew I was eating out this evening.'

He sat back and stared at her. 'So Martin's definitely buying it, is he?'

'He'll soon tell you his plans himself, I'm sure,' she said hastily.

'It sounds as if I should start looking for someone else to live above the surgery,' he said.

'I'd wait till Martin's spoken to you. He'll obviously tell you if he's moving out, and if so, he'll give you an idea of when.'

'Then I'll take your advice and I won't do anything for the moment.' He paused. 'I imagine he's very grateful to you for all the help you've given him.'

She blushed. 'I suppose he is. But I've enjoyed it. Looking at houses is fun.'

They paused while the waiter put their food in front of them.

'You know, it's funny but it's a while since you've brought up the subject of wedding dates,' Edward remarked. 'I'd expected to be chastised for my tardiness this evening, and deservedly so.'

Her heart sank. She glanced up from her plate. To her amazement, he was regarding her with open amusement.

'Why are you looking at me like that?' she asked.

But as she said the words, she knew the answer, and she slowly smiled.

'When were you going to tell me, Jean?' he asked. 'Were you waiting till I had sufficient wine in me to be quite mellow when you told me that our engagement was off, or were you going to leave it to the end of the evening so you could say the words and duck straight into your house?'

'I was going to tell you as soon as we'd finished our chicken,' she said with a laugh. 'After that, we'd have a brief discussion over coffee, and then we'd leave. Waiting that long to tell you would have spoilt my enjoyment of my chicken, of course, as I was understandably nervous, but you'd have enjoyed yours, which I felt was more important as you were paying for the meal.' She paused and looked at him curiously. 'How did you know?'

'The recent change in your behaviour, for a start. You completely stopped asking me to fix a date. And I imagine you told Martin that you'd rather he didn't mention the wedding, either, as it's now a while since he's scolded me about my neglect of you.'

She put her hand to her mouth and giggled. 'He's never done that, has he?'

'I'm afraid he has,' he said solemnly, 'and more than once. It was like being chastised by Nanny.'

'And is that the only thing that made you suspect I'd changed my mind?'

'Well, there's also the fact that you've started putting your head down as you reach my house and cycling furiously past it on your way home. Had I wanted to ask you to stop for a cup of tea, I would've had to rush out from the house like a bat out of hell and scream my invitation after you. It wouldn't have been very elegant.'

Both of them laughed.

'But the last reason,' he said, his face suddenly serious, 'is that I realised you no longer felt about me as a woman should feel about the man she's going to marry.'

'I'm sorry, Edward, really I am.'

He laughed. 'You're not sorry at all, Jean, you're radiant. I've not seen you this happy for so long.'

'And you don't mind? You're not going to sue me for breach of promise?'

'Of course I'm not. I'm delighted for you. You and I will always be the best of friends, but we've both realised we'll only be friends—not husband and wife. I think my reluctance to fix a date stems from a growing feeling that perhaps we were not as suited as we'd thought.'

'Now it's my turn to correct you, Edward. The reason for your reluctance to fix a date is quite simple. It takes the shape of a pretty young woman with huge dark eyes and an abundance of imagination, a woman who shares your love of history and of the museum. That's the source of your reluctance, dear Edward. Now you can pursue her with all you've got, and I wish you the very best of luck.'

'And you wouldn't mind?'

'Of course not. You're a free man now. I couldn't be happier for you than I am.'

'Thank you, Jean, my dear, dear friend.'

He stood up, walked round the table and took her hand. She felt her eyes fill with tears as she stood up. They smiled warmly at each other, and then he put his arms around her and hugged her to him.

'You'll always be very special to me,' he said.

She nodded. 'And you will to me, my lovely friend.'

With a final hug, they drew apart and sat down again.

'Instead of coffee, I think we ought to toast our future,' he said. 'We'll always be the closest of friends, no matter the paths we take, so our toast should be to friendship.' And he turned to catch the waiter's eye.

29

H*arton,*
Sunday morning

JEAN'S MOTHER opened the door to Martin. Jean appeared at her mother's elbow, and Martin could see that she looked happy, excited and nervous, all at the same time.

Rather like the way he felt, he thought.

'Good gracious, Doctor!' her mother exclaimed. 'What a lovely surprise! Do come in. I do hope no one's ill,' she remarked in sudden anxiety as he went into the oak-panelled hall.

'I don't believe they are,' he said with a smile. 'It's a pleasure to see you again, Mrs Forbes. But as I'm off duty, Martin would be fine.' He went up to Jean. 'Hello, Jean. How are you since yesterday?'

She smiled up at him.

'Would you care to come into the drawing room,

Martin?' Mrs Forbes asked, and she indicated a door across the hall.

He hesitated. 'Actually, I was hoping to have a word with Mr Forbes. Would that be possible?'

Her mother glanced quickly at Jean. A question hovered over her lips.

'Of course,' she said, turning back to Martin. 'My husband's in the library. I'll see if it's convenient now. One moment, please.'

She went across to a door on the opposite side of the hall from the drawing room, knocked and went into the room.

'I gather you didn't say anything to your parents,' he remarked. 'Your mother looked extremely surprised to see me.'

'I just told them that Edward and I had decided not to marry, but will always be good friends.' She moved closer to him and said quietly, 'I warned Cook that there might be an extra person at lunch. I hope you'll lunch with us.'

'If your father doesn't boot me out in disgust, I certainly will. I don't want to be apart from you for a minute longer than I have to. You've no idea how much I love you, Jean.'

'I have,' she whispered, and she kissed him on his cheek. 'Because I feel the same about you.'

Their eyes lingered on each other.

'Dennis said to go in,' they heard Jean's mother say.

Both turned sharply towards her. She stood in the doorway to the library, holding open the door. 'He's looking forward to seeing you again, Martin,' she added. Her gaze moved to Jean, and she shook her head in puzzlement.

As he went into the library, he heard the door close behind him.

. . .

DENNIS FORBES WAS SITTING in one of the leather armchairs in the library, his pipe and a tin of Three Nuns tobacco on the mahogany occasional table next to him. He half rose as Martin came in. Then, sitting back down, he indicated that Martin should take the armchair opposite his.

Wincing as the armchair creaked as he sat on it, Martin perched himself on the edge.

'As I'm sure my wife remarked, Doctor, it's a pleasure to see you again.'

'Please call me Martin, Mr Forbes. This is not about anyone's health,' Martin told him. 'It's purely social.'

Dennis Forbes inclined his head. 'Of course.' He picked up his pipe and tobacco tin, opened the tin, took out a wad of tobacco and then promptly put the tobacco back in the tin, closed the tin and replaced both tin and pipe on the side table. 'Edna and Jean both want me to give this up,' he said in a sorrowful tone of voice, indicating the pipe. 'If I want any peace in my own home, I'm going to have to listen to them, I'm afraid.'

'I'm not surprised they're anxious about you smoking,' Martin said. 'They'll want you to remain in good health. The signs have long been there that smoking can be harmful, but this year a major study has proved for the first time that smoking can, indeed, cause serious damage to one's health. Cigarettes are worse than a pipe, I believe, but if you can avoid both, so much the better.'

'You're as bad as Edna and Jean,' Dennis said drily. 'So what can I do for you, Martin?' he asked.

Martin cleared his throat. 'As you know, my wife Florence died three years ago. I took a long time to get over my grief as I'd loved her deeply. But though I shall always love Florence, I know now that I'm able to love again, and to do so just as strongly as I did before. I know this because I know what I've come to feel for Jean.'

'For Jean?' Dennis exclaimed. He reached for his pipe. 'Well, that's a surprise!'

'Yes, sir. For some time now, I've greatly admired Jean. No, that's wrong,' he said apologetically. 'I've adored her. But I've had to keep a check on my emotions because of her engagement to Edward. Recently, though, circumstances have taken a strange turn, and I'm now able to tell her how much I love her. I'm the luckiest man alive as she reciprocates my feelings.'

Dennis grunted.

'I should like to ask you, therefore, sir, for Jean's hand in marriage. I've a secure job and a house of my own, one of the newly built houses in the village, and I'm confident that I can support Jean in the manner to which she deserves. I love her, sir, and I can't think of anything more wonderful than marrying her. I would do everything in my power to make her happy for the rest of her life. I hope you will agree to this.'

He fell silent, drew in a deep breath and held it.

Dennis rose to his feet, and Martin swiftly did the same. Then Dennis stepped forward and held out his hand. 'This is the second time I've welcomed a young man into this family,' he said with a wry smile. 'I do hope there won't be a third.'

'I can assure you, sir, there won't be,' Martin said, enthusiastically shaking Dennis's hand.

'In that case, welcome, Martin,' he said.

Martin felt himself relax, and he let himself breathe out.

'From what you've said, I believe that you appreciate what a wonderful young woman Jean is,' Dennis said. 'She deserves to be happy, and a few months ago, her mother and

I began to feel anxious that she wasn't. Just recently, though, she's changed and become the old Jean again. This must be because you were in her life. When you marry, it'll be with my blessing,' Dennis went on. He glanced towards his cocktail cabinet. 'I think we should toast this, don't you?'

Martin smiled broadly. 'Indeed I do.'

'You'll stay to lunch of course,' Dennis said as he went over to the cabinet on which there were two cut glass decanters and a set of four crystal glasses.

'But we'd better be quick with our toast,' he added. 'I've no doubt my wife and daughter are busy brushing the dust from their knees after taking up residence at the keyhole for the duration of our discussion, and I wouldn't want them to burst in and exclaim in horror at the earliness of the hour for brandy. Or for you to remember a report that claims that brandy is bad for you, for that matter.'

The door swung open and Jean rushed in ahead of her mother. She stopped abruptly, her eyes shining, and stared at Martin.

He gave her the broadest of smiles and made a move towards her. At the same moment, she flung herself forward and threw herself into his waiting arms.

In the distant wood, an owl hooted as Jean cycled down the hill.

Martin had left an hour or so before, having stayed for lunch and also for tea. Her parents, having got over their initial surprise at the rapid replacement in their lives of Edward by Martin, had increasingly shown their delight at seeing their daughter far happier than they'd seen her for months, and they'd showered Martin with warmth.

When it was time for him to leave, he'd just stared down

at her, love pouring from his eyes, overwhelmed by the joy he felt, unable to speak. She, too, had felt the same, and had moved closer to him.

He had put his arms around her and together they'd stood there, no words necessary.

But there were some words she had to say before she went to bed that night.

She reached Edward's house, got down from her bicycle and knocked at the door.

The door opened and Edward stood there.

'Well, this is a surprise!' he exclaimed. 'It's so late that tea would be inappropriate. How about a brandy?' he asked, and he held the door wider open.

'That would be lovely,' she said, and went into the hall. 'I can't stay long, though. As you say, it's already quite late.'

'Come on into the sitting room and I'll pour the drinks.'

She went in, glanced at the sofa, but walked past it to the armchair. Soon after, he came across with snifters of brandy. He put one on the small table next to her chair, and sat down on the sofa, with the other in his hand.

'Am I right that a toast is called for?' he asked, raising his glass.

'A toast?' she echoed in surprise.

'You're right, it should be champagne, not brandy. But we'll wait till Martin is with us to have that champagne.'

'Martin?' she repeated.

'He should be with us, of course, when we toast your engagement to him.'

Her heart leapt. 'You know,' she cried. 'But how?'

'My dear Jean, I've seen your face recently. Every time you've mentioned Martin your eyes have lit up. I was amazed that the restaurant didn't go up in flames yesterday, you were burning so brightly. And I didn't think a china dinner service could've had such a profound effect on you, nor even a stylish dining room table on which to set it.'

She laughed with relief. 'Oh, Edward,' she said. 'And you don't mind?'

'Mind you being happy? Of course I don't. On the contrary, I'm delighted that you are. We're the closest of friends, remember? And a true friend always wants what's best for the other. Martin's a good man. He's a loyal friend and an excellent doctor. It's time he fell in love again, and I'm delighted that the person he's fallen in love with is you.'

'Thank you, Edward. You've no idea what it means to me to hear you say that.'

'Let's have that toast, then.' He held up his glass.

'We're going to toast not only my future, but yours, too,' she said. 'I've a feeling that your story will soon have a happy ending, too.'

30

T*he following morning*

EDWARD GLANCED at the clock on the wall in his surgery. It was twenty minutes before his morning surgery was due to begin—just enough time for him to catch a glimpse of Violet if he moved fast. As there could be no better way to start the week, and as he'd already finished preparing for his surgery, that's what he'd do, he decided.

He got up and hurried out into the hall.

'Back in a minute,' he told the surprised receptionist as he rushed past her, and with a brief nod towards an elderly man waiting to be seen, he hurried out of the building, turned left and rushed the short distance down Church Road to the village hall.

He stopped at the foot of the village hall drive, which was carpeted by the red and gold leaves that had been blown from the ash, sycamore and horse chestnut trees in the garden. Caught by the early morning breeze, the leaves had fluttered along the drive to the curve in the road and gathered there in a heap of gold.

He stood still and stared down High Street to the house where Violet lived, and then to the museum not far beyond it. A milky-white mist was gradually rising from the lower part of the hill, revealing roofs and gables that sparkled in the early morning light, and both buildings could be clearly seen.

He took a step forward. It must be about the time that Violet left her house each day to go to the museum. If he wasn't too late, he'd see her.

Admittedly she'd be in the distance and he'd see only her back. Unaware that he'd be standing there desperately hoping for a glimpse of her, she'd have no reason to turn and look up to the village hall, but seeing no more than her back would be better than nothing. At least he'd have had the pleasure of seeing her at the start of his day.

And what a way to begin his first day as a free man!

But hopefully, before too long, he'd be seeing her every day, and for more than just a few seconds in the morning. What he really longed for was to see her sitting across from him at the breakfast table every morning, and across the dining table every evening. And he wanted her face to be the last thing he saw before he gave in to sleep, and the first thing he saw when he woke up.

Quite simply, he loved Violet and he wanted her to be a part of his every morning, afternoon and evening until forever.

He couldn't wait for her to know that he was no longer engaged to Jean because only then could he seriously begin to court her. Ideally, it would be better if she didn't know that his engagement was over until after the display had been opened, but with Jean and Martin likely to be shouting their news from the rooftops, she was bound to hear about it before too long.

Unfortunately, though, this wouldn't be the best of times to start courting Violet.

It was only just over a week to the unveiling of her active display and the reception, so unsurprisingly she was the busiest she'd been since she'd started at the museum.

When he'd stopped by at the museum a few days earlier with the confirmation from Wendy Ives of their order, he'd seen some of the screens in the staffroom that would be fitted into the back of the tall glass-fronted display cabinets, and some of the scenery which was gradually being dropped off and for which they'd had to find a temporary home.

Violet hadn't been able to restrain her pleasure at how amazingly well the art teacher had painted a realistic scenery. Indeed, she'd been close to tears when she'd told him how grateful she was to the teacher, who'd done much of the painting in her free time.

As well as the scenery, he'd seen the mannequins that her father had delivered to her, and the garments that her mother had made for the mannequins to wear. Violet's excitement had been palpable.

She'd told him that Gladys had been helping them to remove the exhibits from Gallery Five and take them down to the basement, where they were being carefully stored.

Also, they were being inundated daily with the RSVP replies to their invitations to the reception. These had to be sorted out, and then the number of those attending had to be given to Wendy.

This certainly wasn't the time to distract Violet by declaring his love for her. The last thing she needed at such a time was someone she'd so far known only in the context of work making an obvious attempt to woo her. Difficult though it was going to be to hold back, he'd just have to be patient until the reception was over.

And then, when he did start taking her out, he would take things very slowly. They needed to spend time together now that he was unattached in order for them to get to know each other in a way that had so far been impossible.

Delaying his pursuit of her was going to be one of the hardest things he'd ever done, but if he could see her for even a moment or two each morning, and perhaps find an occasional work-related reason to drop in on her at the museum after his surgery, it would keep him going until he could start inviting her out.

He stared down the hill. Please come out now, Violet, he inwardly pleaded, knowing he'd soon have to return to the surgery.

And then he saw her.

A slender figure in sage green, she reached the end of her short path, her arms full of papers, turned and went quickly towards the museum.

He smiled at her retreating back.

At the entrance to the museum, she paused.

His heart stood still.

Then she turned round and gazed up towards the village hall.

She was looking in the direction of the surgery, he thought, where she knew he would be. She must have wanted to see him.

He drew in a deep breath and took a step forward.

Across the distance, their eyes met.

As he felt the warmth that was flowing towards him, he knew that she, too, was smiling.

. . .

What on earth had made her turn at that moment, she wondered as she went into the museum. But wherever the impulse had come from, she was very grateful she had. Had she not glanced round, she wouldn't have seen Edward standing in front of the village noticeboard.

What luck that at the very moment that she'd glanced up the road, he must have been turning to go back to the surgery after looking at the notices. It meant that she'd been able to see his face.

She realised that the light played strange tricks, and even more so when there was an early mist, as there was that morning, nevertheless it had looked to her as if he'd been smiling, so she'd smiled back.

She shook her head as she went into the museum. She was probably imagining that he'd smiled at her because she so wanted it to be true.

She crossed the hall to her office, went in, closed the door behind her and stood still.

She'd done it again, she scolded herself.

She'd let herself think about Edward in a way she shouldn't. He was an engaged man, so they could never be anything more than work colleagues. People didn't think about their work colleagues every minute of every day, and she mustn't do so either.

Sadly, it wasn't the first time she'd resolved to put him out of her mind, but this time she really must succeed. It was a Monday, a good day on which to make a resolution, and this time she was going to stick to it.

The only contact she'd have with Edward must be about work. That was the way it had to be. And with the board of trustees' very pleasing response to her September report, and the plans for the reception well under way, there was no reason for her to see him as much as she'd been doing, which should make it easier to get over him.

She sat down and pulled a pile of RSVPs towards her. Next to it, she placed her list of those who'd already accepted their invitation, and then she started to go through the replies that had arrived the previous Friday.

The light was draining out of the day when Violet closed the door to her office, left the museum and went to lock the front door. Gladys and Lucy had already gone, both of them remarking on how the days had shortened.

Hearing footsteps on the path behind her, she turned.

'Hello, Lucy,' she said, surprised to see Lucy back at the museum. 'I'm about to lock up for the night. Did you forget something?'

Lucy shook her head. 'No, it's that I heard something interesting and couldn't wait to tell you! Two women at the bus stop were talking, and I couldn't help overhearing what they were saying. Even though I thought I'd heard correctly, I asked them for confirmation just in case. Yes, I know, it was a bit of a cheek,' she added with a giggle.

Violet looked at her questioningly. 'What did they say?'

'That Jean, the Jean who's our district nurse and who's engaged to Edward, is going to marry Dr Lloyd! Not Edward. Even though she and Edward have been engaged forever.' Lucy nodded. 'You may well look surprised. I certainly was. I couldn't wait to tell you.'

Her heart beating fast, Violet finished locking the door and started walking up the path from the museum with Lucy at her side.

'I'm glad you told me, Lucy,' she said, hoping her voice

sounded more normal to Lucy than it sounded to her. 'I'd have hated to put my foot in it with Edward. I wonder how he's taken it? I wonder if it was a surprise? I'll congratulate Jean and Martin when I next see them. As for Edward, I'll decide what to say to him when we next meet. I'll take my lead from what he says and how he seems.'

'Me, too,' Lucy said. 'Ah, good, the women are still at the bus stop. The bus must be a bit late this evening. If I hurry I might learn something else.' She started to run. 'Have a lovely evening,' she called back over her shoulder, and gave her a little wave.

THE LIGHT of day had given way to dusk, and a thickening gloom was slowly shrouding the furniture in the sitting room.

The table lamp was within reach, but Violet sat there in darkness, motionless.

Why was she sitting there, waiting for someone who was obviously not going to come that evening, she berated herself, someone who could have come at any point earlier in the day if he'd wanted?

Because she was so stupid, she told herself.

No matter how hard she'd tried to convince herself otherwise, she'd come to believe that deep down she and Edward had made a connection that was nothing to do with work. If that was so, he'd surely want her to be one of the first to know that he was no longer engaged.

But as he hadn't called on her that day, she'd obviously got everything very wrong.

Or had she?

The ending of Edward's engagement was something that could have only just happened. In a small village, news travelled like wildfire, and she would surely have heard it sooner had the break-up happened an appreciable time before that day.

There could be any number of reasons why he hadn't yet been to see her. His failure to do so didn't necessarily mean she'd been completely wrong about them feeling something special for each other, something that neither had been able to put into words because of his engagement to Jean, and she'd be unwise to let the fact that he hadn't yet called upon her weigh her down.

She switched on the lamp and stood up.

She'd get herself something to eat, and then she'd do her best to have a good night's sleep. Edward would probably drop in at the museum tomorrow to see her, or he might even turn up at her house the following evening. Whichever it was, she wanted to be at her freshest for when she saw him. After all, it would be the first time she'd spoken with him now he wasn't engaged.

She hugged herself in growing excitement. She couldn't wait for the following day.

31

T*he following day*

IT HAD FELT A VERY long day, Violet thought wearily.

When she'd reached the museum that morning, she'd paused outside the entrance and glanced hopefully up at the village hall, just in case he was there again, but this time she'd had an unobstructed view of the noticeboard, and disappointed, she'd gone into the museum.

Throughout the day, whenever she'd heard footsteps outside her office, her spirits had soared in hope and excitement. Minutes later though, when her door had opened and it had been either Lucy or Gladys standing there, her spirits had plummeted like a ton of bricks.

So he hadn't stopped by that day after all, she thought as she despondently packed her bag to go home. And he was unlikely to be calling on her that evening, she'd realised at some point during the day.

Despite her fervent hopes of the evening before that if he didn't come to the museum during the day he'd stop by at her house that evening, common sense had intervened, bringing with it a reminder of what would be considered acceptable behaviour.

A different set of rules applied now that he was no longer engaged, she'd suddenly realised, and with great reluctance she'd had to accept that it was very unlikely he'd put her in a compromising position by calling at the house of an unmarried woman who was living on her own.

Even though the war had finally put an end to the need for a well-bred unmarried woman to be chaperoned whenever she was with a man, at least until she'd reached an age where she was unlikely to marry, a requirement that had been in decline from the moment women took on men's jobs during the war and when they started riding bicycles, which precluded a chaperone, it was better to be overcautious about behaviour, especially when living in a small village where people talked and reputations were important.

For Edward to visit her in the house where she lived alone would be unwise, and he'd know that. It would be a feast for gossipmongers.

He'd realise that the only place they could legitimately meet was in the museum. In choosing not to call in there on one of the first few days after his broken engagement, he was making a strong statement.

A statement for her alone.

A statement intended to destroy any expectation that could have arisen from the occasions they'd recently met.

How could she have been so wrong about his feelings for her?

But she must have been.

She must have imagined that there was something

between them that could grow if nurtured because now that he was free to nurture it, he had chosen not to. His absence from the museum was telling her that, and by telling her in such a way, he was revealing something unpleasant about his character, something which greatly surprised her.

He was showing himself to be a coward.

He should have had the gumption to come and tell her to her face that he wanted to restrict their relationship to one based on work. He had apologised before for an impression he might have given. On this occasion above all, he should have had the guts to make his feelings for her clear.

Knowing that he was a coward would help her to get over him. He didn't deserve the feelings she'd developed for him, so he was doing her a favour by keeping away.

She picked up her bag and looked down at her desk where everything was in neat piles. Fortunately, she'd got a lot of work to do when she got home that evening and she wouldn't have time to think about him.

HE ONLY HOPED that Violet realised what a tremendous effort it had been for him to keep away from her that day, Edward thought, staring despondently at the four walls of his surgery.

The day had seemed never-ending, despite the fact that a large number of people had turned up for both his morning and afternoon surgeries, and both surgeries had gone on for longer than they usually did.

He'd welcomed the extra length of his working day, and had been quite disappointed that there'd been no requests for any house calls that evening, as they would have filled some of his outside-surgery time. But Jean was doing the only two calls that had come in. She was going to dress an arm cut on broken glass and check the breathing and pulse rate of an elderly, disabled female patient with asthma, neither of which necessitated his presence.

Jean would be relieved not to have any more house calls than those two, he was sure. She'd almost certainly want to spend as much time as possible with Martin. Perhaps they'd go up to the house that Martin had told him that morning that he'd bought. She'd make it into a lovely home for them both, he was sure.

Sitting back, he wondered why he hadn't seen how well suited Jean and Martin were, and why it had taken Jean's visible enjoyment of Martin's company to show him that. He wondered also why, after repeatedly putting off fixing a date for his marriage to Jean, it had taken him so long to question his reluctance to do so.

Looking back, he could see the reason so clearly now.

If he lived in a society where women and men entered into arranged marriages, a strong friendship would be an excellent basis upon which to build a marriage. But he lived in a society where men and women chose the person they wanted to marry, and without him being conscious of it, a feeling had been growing within him that he wanted more than just friendship, strong though it was. It was only that, for a long time, he hadn't realised it.

It had taken Violet's arrival to open his eyes.

If only he had examined his feelings sooner. At the very least, it would have been fairer to Jean. He had got it wrong with Jean, but he wouldn't do so with Violet.

Having given a lot of thought as to the best way to tell Violet how much he adored her, he was sure that holding back until after the reception was the right approach. But how he was going to manage to keep away from her, he didn't know.

As for his plan of catching a secret glimpse of her whenever he could, he wasn't sure if it was making his pain worse or better. He glanced at his clock. It was about the time she'd be going home now. If he went down to the curve in the road, he might see her going back to her house. Even if it worsened his pain, it'd be worth it.

He swiftly got up, hung his white coat on a hook behind his door, went out into the hall, and out of the surgery. Then he reached the village hall, he stopped and looked down the road to her house. There was a light in her window. He felt a sharp stab of disappointment. He was too late to see her do the short walk from the museum to her house.

If only he could be sitting in her house with her!

It would require no more than a few steps to bring him to her doorstep. He went one pace forward, and stopped.

It was too soon.

He would embarrass her, and it would be wrong, arriving out of the blue on her doorstep, expecting to go inside with her, an unattached man alone with a single woman. No, he must do everything by the book. She mustn't be made to feel uncomfortable.

But when the reception was over!

His face lighting up at the thought, he turned round, walked back into the building and shut the front door firmly behind him.

32

B*ury St Edmunds,*
The following Friday

Gladys and Stanley faced each other across the table in Stanley's small back room.

'Eric's impatient to know why you haven't dealt with Violet yet,' Stan told her tetchily. 'He can't see what the hold-up is. Nor can I for that matter. It's now more than two weeks since you planted the figurine in Violet's house. Like Eric, I'm beginning to wonder if you're ever going to try to discredit her.'

'You know I wanted to wait till after the reception. It's only a week away, after all,' she said sharply. 'Just think about it. People are in and out of the museum all the time, dealing with things related to either the display or the reception. It's a hive of activity, which is not, in my opinion, the best time to go to the police.'

'I would've thought the reverse,' Stanley said.

'That's because you've not thought it through,' Gladys snapped. 'With artefacts being legitimately moved from downstairs to upstairs and vice versa, it'd be easy for Violet to dismiss the figurine in her fireplace by saying she'd run out of time that day and had hidden it there overnight for safety. And that's assuming the police would take an anonymous claim seriously enough to make a search.'

'Surely it's worth a try,' Stanley said sulkily.

'Use your head, will you? If they found the figurine, the police might insist on a complete check of the artefacts against the inventory to see if anything was missing. It wouldn't take long before they discovered that not all the items from Gallery Five had made their way downstairs. I was the person who'd organised the transfer of location, and I did most of the removing, so I'd be a suspect, more so than Violet. If I was dismissed, or even worse, I wouldn't have achieved anything, but I'd be out of a job which offers us a lucrative sideline.'

'So why bother to put it in the chimney if it can be so easily explained away?'

'Because it wouldn't be so easily to explain it away once the reception was over. The museum will return to normal, with the addition of a few school parties, I expect, and Violet would no longer be able to blame lack of time for doing something so reprehensible.'

'I suppose you're right,' he said grudgingly.

'Also,' Gladys went on, 'whatever the disagreement between Edward and Violet, it could have intensified by then. For the past couple of days, he's been in and out a few times but never once has he made any attempt to speak to Violet. It's clear they're no longer as friendly as they used to be. I imagine that now he's got rid of Jean, he wants to look further afield for a replacement. It means he could be quite keen on seeing Violet go.'

'I take my hat off to you, Gladys,' Stanley said, shaking his head. 'You certainly seem to have thought it through.' He paused. 'And what about the money she's supposed to have been putting regularly into the bank?'

'Don't worry, I've been dropping sums of money into the new account, courtesy of the night safe so that there's no connection to me. There won't be many more drops as I'll be making my move as soon as things quieten down.'

He looked at her and frowned. 'We've never actually talked about how to bring this to a close. Have you any idea what you'll do? You can't really walk into the police station and say that someone's stealing from the museum, but that someone isn't you. Dense the police may be, but even they would require some proof. And they're certainly not going to turn Lucy and Violet's homes upside down on the basis of a single statement.'

She frowned. 'I want Lucy left out of this.'

'You never cease to amaze me, Gladys!' Stanley exclaimed in wonder. 'Not so long ago, we were trying to get the girl out of the museum and into Tom Bradley's shop, but now you want her to stay where she is.'

'That's not exactly so.' She gave him a dry smile. 'She'll be getting into Tom's shop all right. And that's not the only thing she'll be getting into. His bed's another, unless I'm very much mistaken. She's clearly seeing Tom, so your intervention had the desired effect, just in a different way. Knowing their closeness to each other, I wouldn't want to risk Tom flying into a hot-blooded defence of Lucy, as that could raise some doubts in the minds of the police.'

'That sounds very wise. If Tom's anything like his father,

he'd not take a slur on someone in his family without putting up a good fight.'

She nodded. 'So that's another reason not to rush things. I'm guessing that Lucy will start working for Tom soon after the reception. She won't go before as she won't want to leave Violet in the lurch. And when she's gone, which won't be too far from now, I'm sure, the guilty party will be more clearly visible to the police.'

'So what's the plan for exposing Violet?' he asked.

'As soon as Lucy's out of the picture, I'll go to the police station in Bury in tears. I'll claim that a favourite artefact has disappeared from the museum. I'll say that recently I'd wondered about some other pieces that just seemed to have vanished, but this time I know for certain the artefact was there, and I think someone must be stealing from the museum. They're bound to search Violet's house, and they'll find the figurine.'

'What would you use as that favourite piece?'

Gladys gave a slight shrug. 'Probably the hanging vessel in which they burned incense to the household gods. You know the one—it was dug from the floor of that small Roman building a few miles away. There're very few of them and it would command a good price. When the police investigation is over, and Violet long gone, you can sell it and we'll divide the proceeds. And we wouldn't have to give anything to Eric,' she added with satisfaction.

He thought for a moment. 'So how will you expose the account you set up to take her regular payments?'

'Just before I go to the police, I'll get the statements the bank has sent, which I've been removing before she sees the post, and put them into the filing cabinet in her office. I imagine they'll search her office before anywhere else. When they find the statements, it'll encourage them to search her house. And if they aren't bright enough to think of doing so, I'll steer them in the right direction.'

He sat back. 'Well, you obviously know what you're doing, Gladys. I'll pass that on to Eric.'

'Well, before you pass that to Eric, you can pass me something—a glass with some gin in it,' she said a trifle acidly. 'After Eric's relayed criticism, it's exactly what I need before I return to Harton.'

33

Harton,

The evening of the reception

WHAT AN EVENING IT HAD BEEN, Violet thought.

As the last of the invited guests left Gallery Five, she walked slowly around the room and came to a stop in front of the large wooden-framed glass structures in which the active displays were housed. For a few minutes she stood there, remembering the swell of interest and excitement they had generated that evening.

The characters in the display that captured a scene of the Angles and Saxons at war with the Britons had been so lifelike that some of the guests had been quite startled, and had then fulsomely praised the way in which the purpose and use for items such as the ninth-century scramaseax, a single-edged weapon intended for combat, had been depicted.

There was vocal appreciation also for the way in which

items such as an engraved helmet were shown to be both decorative pieces of metalwork and also functional pieces of armour.

The scene that captured Anglo-Saxon life indoors had also been greatly admired.

The headmistress of the local school was congratulated by many on the way in which the art teacher had set the scene, both with the backcloth and by helping Violet to construct a sloping thatched roof out of leftover thatch given to her by a local roofer. They'd positioned the roof inside the top of the glass cabinet, thereby creating the effect that visitors were being given a glimpse of real life inside the house.

Many of the guests remarked that the barley and bean stew looked as if it was actually simmering in the tenth-century metal pot that hung above the fire, and that the hearth cakes appeared to be cooking on live embers.

The labels that she and Lucy had fixed to the diagrams of the two displays, each fixed on the wall next to the relevant glass unit, had been highly praised for their interesting content, and for the way in which they were so easy to understand.

Ringing in her ears over and over again were the expressions of approval from everyone there and their hearty congratulations.

She looked again at the two large structures, the visualisation of her ideas and hard work, and the hard work of the museum staff and the school's art teacher, and of her parents, whose help had been invaluable.

The mannequin figures her father had found, and their Anglo-Saxon clothes made by her mother, had brought the display alive in the way that she'd so much wanted, but had feared for a time she'd be unable to achieve.

Edward, too, had given her an enormous amount of help. What a team they'd made, she thought. And Lucy's help and support had been invaluable.

When it had been time for her to make a short speech, which she'd been dreading ever since Gladys had pointed out a couple of weeks earlier that she would be expected to say a few words, she'd praised all the people who had helped to bring her ideas to fruition.

The first person she'd credited was her sister, Iris, whose inspired displays in their father's haberdashery shops during the war years had given her the germ of an idea which she'd developed.

She'd seen the look of pleasure on her parents' faces when they'd heard her mention Iris, and then when they heard themselves thanked in front of everyone for what they'd done.

Throughout the evening, their happiness had shone out.

She'd noticed, too, that Edward had spoken to them at length, for which she was grateful.

Because people were continuously coming up to talk to her, it had proved impossible to say more than a few words to her parents, and she'd been anxious about them as they didn't know anyone there. They'd met Edward when they'd come to lunch that Sunday, of course, but that had been fleeting, and they didn't really know him. They would never have gone up and spoken to him, but must have been delighted when he made a point of going across to them.

Whatever they'd found to say to each other, it had been a conversation of some length, which must have contributed to their enjoyment of the evening, and when they'd left to go back to the Angel Hotel where they were staying the night, they felt extremely proud and happy, they told her.

She'd suggested that she have breakfast with them the

following morning, but they were sure she would have things to do at the museum, and said they'd be perfectly happy having a short walk in the vicinity of the hotel before going home.

Smiling to herself, she moved across to the three tables set out at the side of the room. In the centre of each was a small glass jar filled with wild anemones and asters. A number of guests had commented on the attractiveness of such a natural table display.

But the tables would soon have a different use, she thought happily. She intended that groups of pupils should sit around them while answering questions relating to the displays in their workbooks. When there were no school parties, two of the tables would hold a number of large, colourful history books, and be comfortable places for the children to sit and browse through the books. The third table would have crayons and pastels and sheets of paper, each with a different activity.

Looking beneath the tables, she saw boxes in which the empty plates, serving dishes, cups and saucers and glasses had been carefully stacked, ready for the caterers to take them away early the following morning. Wendy and her helpers had taken the two tea urns home with them that evening.

It was hard to believe, she thought, but as recently as two hours ago, three of the serving dishes had been filled with tiny sandwiches piled on top of a white paper doily, their crusts removed, and each plate fronted with a small label indicating the filling, and there were also two plates of small oval-shaped bridge rolls topped with egg and cress. The table next to it had been home to a variety of plates containing small scones, triangles of shortbread and squares of seed cake and gingerbread.

At the start of the evening, Wendy Ives had stood in the corner of the room, talking to three young girls who were going to hand round the plates of food. Each of the girls had worn a white blouse and black skirt, and had one of Wendy's aprons tied around their waist. Wendy had taught them well, she realised as the reception progressed and she'd seen them move unobtrusively among the guests with trays of food.

Jean, who'd looked radiant, had helped Wendy's girls hand out some of the dishes. She and Martin had moved around the gallery looking blissfully happy. To her amazement, Gladys, too, had helped with serving the food.

The third table had been covered with cups and saucers for tea, and glasses for the orange squash. Two urns stood at the end of the table, manned by Wendy and a middle-aged woman.

Her role had been to circulate throughout the evening, meeting the councillors and officials from Bury St Edmunds, including representatives from the police, the heads of the schools in Bury, and representatives from St Edmundsbury Cathedral, St Mary's Church and the Moyse's Hall Museum, as well as prominent people in Harton, and guests from outside the village, such as Stanley Patterson and Tom Bradley. She hadn't realised that Tom and Stanley knew each other, so it had been a surprise when she'd seen them chatting together.

She couldn't really remember any particular conversation with anyone, but she'd felt herself bathed in the warm glow of their appreciation and enthusiasm for what she'd done, and the evening had sped by in a glorious haze.

For the two hours of the reception, she'd almost forgotten about Edward.

In the last few days, she'd been increasingly nervous

about seeing him again, as she'd done no more than glimpse him since the end of his engagement. On the few occasions he'd popped into the museum to hand over things such as an extra batch of leaflets, she'd kept out of his way and they hadn't spoken.

She'd also noticed, though the others might not have done, that he'd chosen to give whatever he'd brought with him to Lucy or Gladys, and hadn't made any attempt to see her. If she'd been around when he arrived, he'd nodded politely, but no more than that.

As he couldn't have made it clearer that he lacked any interest in her, she wasn't in any hurry to have a conversation with him. Not while there was a risk of her giving away the fact that she still had feelings for him. It was a source of great annoyance to her that she hadn't yet managed to get him completely out of her system.

She took a final look around. It was time for her to leave. The following morning she'd be coming in to check that everything was all right, but for the rest of that evening she'd go home and do nothing. She felt utterly exhausted, but very happy.

At the sound of footsteps behind her, she turned. 'Lucy!' she exclaimed with delight. 'I thought you'd have left by now. You've had a very long day, and when I saw Tom leave, I assumed you'd be off, too.'

'He's waiting for me outside. I couldn't go without saying goodbye, and telling you how amazing the evening's been. I'll never forget it.'

'I'm sure you'll have other wonderful evenings, too,' she said, and paused slightly, 'when you're working with Tom,' she added, a smile in her voice.

'How did you know?' Lucy exclaimed. 'I haven't told anyone I'm leaving. Except Tom, of course. And his mother knows, too, and so do my parents. I was waiting till after this evening to tell you. I thought I'd leave in a month.'

'I didn't know—I guessed. For some time now, the sparkle in your eye was telling me you had a romantic interest, and I thought it must be Tom. You can thank Gladys for that. She told me that Tom had asked you to go and work for him but that you'd turned him down, and she mentioned how good-looking he was.'

'She's so nosy! She cross-examined me after Tom had offered me the job. She wanted to know exactly why I'd turned him down, which was none of her business. Fancy her telling you about the offer and not leaving it to me to decide whether or not I wanted you to know.'

Violet nodded. 'I thought the same thing. But from what she said, she was anxious I didn't let you into too many secrets of the museum in case you left taking them with you.'

Lucy giggled. 'What secrets?'

Violet laughed. 'Your guess is as good as mine.'

'Gladys is very strange as well as nosy,' Lucy said slowly. 'I couldn't help noticing that she and Stanley Patterson didn't talk to each other at all this evening, yet I know they're good friends. You would've thought that at some point in the evening they'd have said a few words to each other.'

Violet frowned. 'How d'you know they're good friends? I've never seen any sign of it.'

'That's what I mean!' Lucy exclaimed. 'On the few occasions I've seen them together, you'd think they were strangers. But I saw Gladys come out of his shop a few weeks ago, and the way they were with each other showed they were really close. I even wondered if they could be romantically attached.'

They stared at each other, and then burst out laughing.

'Maybe not,' Lucy said.

'But leaving Gladys aside, when I met Tom this evening, and saw how charming he was, and how much he adored you'—Lucy beamed at her—'it wasn't hard to predict your departure.'

'I've told you before, you should be a detective,' Lucy said happily. 'And you're not angry with me or disappointed?'

Violet shook her head. 'Not at all. I'm happy for you, and very grateful to you for staying long enough to get me through the display and reception. It's one thing to have ideas, but it's only when you start to put those ideas into effect that you see difficulties you could never have predicted, and discover issues to be considered. You helped me iron out those difficulties and deal with those issues, and I'll always be grateful to you for that.'

'Thank you,' Lucy said tremulously. 'I hate leaving as I've been so happy here, but I'm very much looking forward to working with Tom. He says I have to say I'm working with him, not for him. He wants us to build up the shop together.'

'That sounds interesting. In what way?'

'He's ended up with far more bits of china than genuine antiques. He's now got hardly any cabinets or tables and chairs, for example, and he wants to develop the antiques side of the business, which is how it used to be when his father was alive. With me there, he can go to more auctions. He's going to one tomorrow, in fact, the first he's been to for ages. His mother's so pleased he's taking on help that she's volunteered to cover the shop.'

'That'll be exciting,' Violet said.

Lucy nodded vigorously. 'We're going to change the shop

layout so there are two distinct areas, one for china figurines, plates and so on, and the other for antiques.'

'It sounds fantastic, and something you'd really enjoy doing.'

'I know.' Lucy paused. 'Tom's really lovely. I'm so happy I met him.'

'I look forward to getting to know him better,' Violet said. 'And I'm sure I'll have many opportunities to do,' she added in amusement. 'I'm glad you've such a lovely future, and even more so that you won't be moving so far from here that we can't visit each other. At least, I imagine you'll be changing your place of residence before too long.'

Lucy blushed. 'Maybe. I hope so.'

'Anyway, you'd better get off now. I'll walk downstairs with you, get my bag and then I'll go home, too.'

Together they left Gallery Five and started down the staircase.

'Oh, look, it's Dr Russell!' Lucy exclaimed in surprise. 'I thought he'd already left.'

Violet's stomach gave a dull thud.

She glanced down to the hall and saw Edward standing at the foot of the stairs, staring up at her.

She stood where she was.

'You get off home, Lucy, and I'll find out what he wants,' she said. 'Don't forget we're closed tomorrow and Sunday. I'll see you on Monday.'

Lucy ran down the stairs. 'Goodbye again, Dr Russell,' she said as she hurried past him and disappeared out of the building.

Edward moved closer to the bottom stair. 'Are you going to come down to me?' he called up to her. 'Or should I come up to you?'

Her heart beating fast, she resumed walking down the stairs.

When she reached the bottom, she faced him and took a deep breath. 'Thank you, Edward,' she said, struggling to keep her voice steady, 'for everything you did to help with tonight, both before and during the evening. Thank you, also, for circulating in the way you did, and for your kindness in taking the time to talk to my parents. They won't have found it easy to mix, given this is very different from their haberdashery world, and you obviously put them at their ease.'

'I like your parents, and I enjoyed our conversation, so there's no need to thank me, not for that nor for anything else. I'm the one who should be thanking you. I know I've said this before, but I can't say it too often. Thank you for the ideas you had, and for putting in the hours necessary to bring them to fruition. Tonight was a triumph. And it was your triumph.'

'It was the triumph of everyone who helped. I didn't do it by myself. But I'm tired now,' she said shortly, 'as you must be. I'm ready to go home, so if you'll excuse me, I'll get my bag and leave.'

She turned towards her office.

'Have I offended you in some way?' he asked quietly.

She stopped walking, looked to the floor, and stayed silent.

'It's just I'd thought you might like to go to Harry's and talk over the evening,' he said. 'But the message I'm getting is that you want to get away from me as fast as you can.'

'Are you surprised?' she retorted, spinning round.

She took a step towards him. 'From the moment Jean broke your engagement, you've done everything you could to avoid seeing me. I'm not stupid, Edward. It's obvious you regret behaving in a way that suggested you felt some affection for me. Well, I've got the message. Now, please leave. I can't lock up till you've gone.'

'I'll go because you've asked me to,' he said steadily, 'not because I want to. I can see you're tired and this is no time to talk. You'll need to rest tomorrow so I promise not to trouble you, but I'd like to see you on Sunday morning. From what you've just said, there are some misconceptions that need clearing up. Shall we say ten thirty? I'll pick you up and we'll go for a walk. Good night, Violet.'

Without waiting for a reply, he turned and left the building.

Numb inside, she stared after him.

Then she went into her office and slammed the door firmly behind her.

34

Sunday morning

After two sleepless nights, Violet lay back in her bed on the Sunday morning and stared at the ceiling. She'd thought that after all the work she'd done in recent weeks she would have slept soundly on both Friday and Saturday night.

But not so.

Her mind was still too active and each night she'd found herself reliving the short conversation she'd had with Edward on Friday evening, at the end of which he'd informed her that he'd be calling on her on the Sunday morning. He hadn't even waited for her to reply. Had he done so, she would have told him she didn't want to go anywhere with him, and she'd have asked him not to visit.

Or would she?

She'd asked herself that question several times in the night.

Yes, he'd behaved in a cowardly manner by avoiding her in the way he had, but a part of her wanted to hear how he'd explain his behaviour, even if there could be no good reason for him to have shunned her.

And also, she couldn't erase from her mind the expression in his eyes on Friday when she'd told him to leave. He'd looked so disappointed. More than that, he had also looked hurt.

But why? She wanted to know that.

After all, she'd been the person who'd been let down, not him, and there was nothing he could say to change that.

In the wee small hours of Sunday morning, she accepted that she wasn't going to be able to sleep until she'd heard the excuse he made.

And to her intense frustration she realised as she lay in bed, waiting for daylight to break through the dark of night, that deep within her, lying alongside her disappointment with him, was her excitement at the thought of seeing him again.

He really ought to get up, Edward told himself. He'd been lying in bed, wide awake, for hours on end, longing for it to be time to get up, but now that the time had come, he couldn't bring himself to move.

It was fear, he thought.

Fear was keeping him where he was, fear that something he'd inadvertently done had destroyed the affection he'd been so sure that Violet felt for him. There was no other way to account for her antagonism towards him at the end of the reception.

But was it just after the reception that she'd seemed to withdraw from him?

He rolled over on to a narrow patch of cold sheet.

Thinking back, he'd been into the museum two or three times since his broken engagement, and once or twice she'd been in the hall at the same time as he'd been there. He hadn't asked to speak to her, knowing how busy she must be and not wanting to divert her from her work, but she could have come over and spoken to him. Yet she didn't.

It wouldn't have needed to be a lengthy conversation. A few words would have sufficed. But they would have shown friendship, and perhaps a degree of sympathy for him at his separation from Jean. For all she knew, he might have been hurt by Jean falling in love with Martin.

Was it that he was free, he thought with a sudden sharp stab.

Could that be the reason for her loss of affection for him?

Had he been attractive to her because, being engaged to someone else, he was unattainable? And now, did the fact that, with neither attached to anyone else, it was all suddenly very real?

More real than she liked.

It wouldn't be surprising if she didn't want any romantic involvement with him. After all, she was ten years younger than he was.

And his career, too, might be a possible deterrent. He was out on house calls for much of the time that he wasn't in his surgery.

Furthermore, as a man who'd been engaged for a long time, but no longer was, he could be seen as having been rejected. Did that in some way demean him in her eyes?

He threw back the bedcover. This wasn't getting him

anywhere. Instead of lying in bed, working out all the possible permutations of the situation, he'd do well to get up, have breakfast and get ready to call on her. At just after ten thirty he would know the truth.

His stomach clenched, he went across his bedroom and out on to the landing.

HEARING EDWARD'S KNOCK, Violet opened the door, stepped outside and closed the door behind her.

'Where are we going?' she asked.

'As it's a lovely day, I thought we'd head for the area north of Harry's,' he said. 'There are some pleasant walks up there. Sometimes it's easier to talk when you're on the move.'

'That sounds fine.'

But neither spoke as they went up Museum Road to the marketplace, crossed over the marketplace, walked past the road leading to the school and came out near Harry's.

'If you want, we can stop for a bite to eat on the way back,' he said as they skirted the inn.

She nodded, and they continued in silence to the fields that stretched out behind Harry's.

Edward glanced towards the woods in the distance on their right.

'I love the autumn colours,' he said, 'when the trees are a mass of gold and bronze and crimson. And green also, of course. Not all of the leaves are down yet. The few elderberries left in the hedgerow bushes add touches of colour, too. They'll keep blackbirds and thrushes going throughout the winter months.'

'I see,' she said.

A few minutes later, the path opened out on to a view of

the fields and the woods. Edward stopped walking, and she, too, stood still.

'There's a bench,' he said, glancing to his right. 'I know I said it might be easier to talk while we're on the move but we haven't exactly said much yet, so we might as well sit down. I think we've some catching up to do.'

'All right.' She went across to the bench and sat down.

He sat next to her.

For a moment neither spoke.

'Who's going to begin?' he asked, breaking the silence. 'Shall we observe the ladies first rule?'

'If you want.' She turned to him. 'When we used to talk or go anywhere together, I always had a vague feeling that if circumstances had been otherwise, things might've been different between us. And I thought you'd felt that, too.'

He nodded. 'I did.'

'So why didn't you come to me after your engagement had ended,' she continued, 'and tell me openly that you and I would never be more than friends? Instead, you told me that in a sneaky way. Why your engagement ended is none of my business, but the way you behaved towards me afterwards is.'

He turned to her, frowning. 'I've no idea what you mean. In what way was I sneaky?'

'Instead of being honest with me about your feelings, or lack of them, from the moment you were free, you deliberately kept your distance. You didn't call on me, and never once did you try to speak to me when you came into the museum. You couldn't have made your lack of interest clearer. The way you did that was sneaky.'

'You're wrong, completely wrong!' he exclaimed. 'I was doing you a favour.'

'A favour?' she echoed in disbelief. 'By making me feel unwanted?'

He shook his head vigorously. 'You were never unwanted. If anyone felt unwanted it was me as you deliberately avoided me in the museum. I thought the fact that I was no longer engaged had made you realise that you didn't want us to be anything more than friends. If so, you're completely mistaken. I love you deeply, Violet.'

'Then why didn't you say so?' she asked, bewildered.

'Because you were busy preparing for the reception. I didn't want to crowd you at such a time, or burden you with the knowledge that I wanted to court you. I thought I'd keep out of your way till the reception was over.' He paused. 'But why didn't you come over when you saw me in the museum?'

'I thought your silence was telling me that you didn't want me in your life. I wanted you to know that I'd got the message.'

They stared at each other, then he smiled slowly. 'I think we've shown that we don't yet know each other very well, but we know that we feel something for each other nevertheless. I suggest I start to take you out, not for matters to do with work, but solely for pleasure. That way we'll begin to get to know each other.'

Her face broke into a radiant smile. 'I think that's a very good idea. We can call this a first date. Being older, you'll be more experienced than I am so we won't make any mistakes. You'll know, for example, how long to leave it before you kiss me, and I kiss you back. You'll have to let me know when sufficient time has passed for us to embark upon that stage.'

'I certainly will. In fact,' he said, looking at his watch, 'the time's now up.'

His put his arms around her and pulled her closer to him. 'Oh, Violet,' he said, looking deep into her eyes. 'I'm so looking forward to getting to know you.'

Smiling, she leaned forward at the same moment as he did, and their lips met.

35

L*ater that day*

SITTING on one of the wooden benches in Abbey Gardens at the side of the large circular lawn that housed a multitude of colourful island beds filled with cyclamens, winter pansies and asters, Lucy tucked her arm into Tom's and moved closer to him.

'I can't believe it, Tom,' she said, her face ashen. 'Are you sure it came from our museum?'

'As sure as I can be. You'd described it so clearly. The pax board up for auction was damaged in exactly the same corner and in the same way, and it depicted the passion of Christ, just like the Harton pax board. And if you remember, you couldn't find the board when we went to your museum and you wanted to show it to me. It's too much of a coincidence.'

'It does sound like ours.' She looked at him with alarm.

'That means someone must've come in and stolen it. Though how would they have known where it was and then got to it? It was in the butler's room in the basement. They couldn't have used the back door as it's always kept locked.' She bit her lip. 'It's quite frightening to think about it.'

Tom put his arm round her shoulders.

'There's something else, Tom. I wasn't sure I was right, so I've never mentioned it before—not to Violet or anyone. But just occasionally I've thought an artefact looked a bit different from the way it used to look. Just some really little thing. So little I thought I might be imagining it. Not the stone artefacts, which are often very roughly finished, but some of the metal and antique pitchers, for example.'

'So you think it possible someone's making copies,' Tom said, 'and you could have some replicas in the museum.'

'When you put it like that, I don't know,' she said, a tremor in her voice. 'What did the auction house say when you told them you thought the board was stolen?'

'Nothing much at first—they weren't particularly interested. They told me they'd followed all the correct procedures for establishing that the vendor had the right to sell the item, and that they'd got a proper consignment agreement between him and them.'

'Didn't they try to make sure that it wasn't stolen before they accepted the board?' Lucy asked indignantly.

'They said they did some research, but it was mainly to help them know how to describe it for the catalogue, and to know what reserve to set and give an estimate. They claimed they had to take the vendor's word to some extent as there were far too many lots up for auction to allow them time to investigate each.'

'And what did you say to that?'

'I told them I intended to go to the police at Bury St

Edmunds this morning and was going to tell them I thought the auctioneers could be selling stolen goods. They pulled the board from the auction the minute I mentioned the police.'

'What did the police say they'll do?' she asked.

'At first, it didn't look as if they were going to do much. They didn't show any more interest than the auction house. It was only when I told them that I wouldn't be surprised if an organised ring was targeting museums in the area, and it would be to their credit if they smashed the ring, that they took it seriously and asked for the catalogue. Amazingly, from what you just told me, it sounds as if my wild statement might actually have some substance to it, and I'll pass on to them what you said about differences in the artefacts, which should make them much more interested.'

'Did you see the pax board in the catalogue before you went to the auction?'

He shook his head. 'Unfortunately, no. I was only interested in furniture and didn't look at anything else.'

'When d'you think we'll hear from them?'

'Certainly not for a few days or even longer. It'll take some time to look into this,' he told her. 'They're bound to go to the auction house and examine all the papers relating to the sale, and possibly the paperwork for all the lots they've recently sold, just to check that everything's being done correctly. One thing that could be fortunate is that from what the auction house said, it didn't sound as if the vendor was using an agent.'

'So at least they'll know who he is,' she said. 'That must help.'

'Not as much as one would hope,' he said drily. 'They'll interview the vendor after they've finished with the auctioneers, but I doubt they'll get very far. He'll have spoken to the auction house before the end of yesterday as he'll have wanted to know how much they'd got for the board. By the time the police get round to interviewing him, he'll have bought the board from a stranger he met in a pub, who was in such dire financial straits that he was having to sell the items left to him by his grandfather. Or some such story. The vendor will insist he bought it in good faith. Without any evidence to show that he knew it was stolen, it's hard to see that the police could charge him with anything.'

She thought for a moment. 'That's what he'd say, but that's obviously not what happened. The board will have been stolen from the museum, so who stole it? Could it have been the vendor?'

'It's not impossible, but it's unlikely, considering that the board wasn't visible in the museum. Also, a thief would distance himself from the item he'd stolen, I would've thought.'

'So who could it be?'

He glanced at her. 'Once the police have spoken to the auction house and the vendor, they're certain to look at the people who work in the museum.'

She straightened up and stared at him. 'Do you mean us? Surely they wouldn't think any of us would steal from the museum?'

'I hate to say it, Lucy, but it's very likely they would. No one could have a better opportunity to do so, or to know what could be removed without attracting attention. And when I tell the police that a number of items could be replicas, it makes it even more likely that the thief is someone from inside the museum.'

She stared at him, disbelieving.

'Well, it isn't me,' she said at last. 'And I'm certain neither Violet nor Dr Russell would do such a thing. And it couldn't be Gladys. She's strange, I know, but she's worked in the museum for years. Also, if she did steal something, she's not the sort of person to know what to do with it. No, Gladys wouldn't steal from the museum any more than I would. It's more likely one of the cleaners, or the school caretaker. Or even the experts who did the evaluation. Though I can't really believe it'd be any of them.'

'The police may uncover something we haven't thought of.'

She looked at him with alarm. 'Shall I tell Violet? What d'you think?'

He thought for a moment. 'I'm inclined to think... no. I don't think she's a thief any more than you do, but I think it's wiser to keep this to ourselves. At present, you and I are the only ones who know what's happened, plus the auctioneers and the vendor, and I think we should leave it at that.'

'And the person who sold the pax board to the vendor,' Lucy added. 'Unless the vendor stole it himself. If he bought it from someone, he's very likely to have contacted the person and asked for his money back.'

Tom nodded. 'Yes, him, too. So five of us know, maybe six. For a week or two, anyway. Then it'll be more of us as the police will be knocking on the door of the museum to search the premises and possibly the homes of the staff.' He paused. 'The thief will already know that suspicions were raised about the board. Hopefully, whoever it is will think the police are unlikely to be involved, and decide to sit tight and do nothing.'

'D'you think that's likely?' she asked.

He shook his head. 'I don't know.'

They stared at each other in deep concern.

36

T*hat day, Sunday evening*

AT THE SOUND of someone knocking on her door, Gladys got up and opened the front door.

'There's whisky waiting for you and a gin for me, Stan,' she said as she ushered him into her sitting room. 'From the unusualness of you coming here, I'm guessing we'll be in need of something stronger than tea.'

'Good thinking, Gladys,' he said sitting down.

She went across to her sideboard, picked up the tray of drinks and carried it across to where he was sitting. She put the glass of whisky next to him, and the gin on the table next to her armchair. She returned the tray to the sideboard. 'So what's the urgency?' she asked sitting down.

'The idiot customer who bought the pax board telephoned me at lunchtime, just before I rang you,' he told her.

'He was in quite a state.' And he relayed the conversation to her.

She sat very still.

'How can he have been so stupid?' he fumed as he came to the end of the conversation. 'He'd told me he was adding it to his collection. The man never puts anything into an auction!'

'Well, he clearly did so this time,' Gladys retorted. 'It didn't walk into the auction house by itself.'

His eyes narrowed. 'I'll bet someone offered him a different pax board, one in a better condition. Yes, that's what it'll be. So he ditched the one he'd got from me. Honestly, Gladys, knowing how many there are in circulation at the moment, you should never've taken the damn thing.'

'*You* knew the market was flooded with them,' she said icily, ' but I didn't. Not till I'd given it to you. And there was nothing to stop you from giving it back to me. I could've easily returned it. So don't blame me.'

'Well Eric will certainly be looking for someone to blame. Even though he had nothing to do with the board, we'll have to tell him what's happened. I'm sure he'll think as I do—we must play it safe in the next few weeks and not take anything else from the museum till the dust has died down.'

'Maybe there won't be any dust,' she said. 'The auction house might not do anything about it. Numerous lots pass through their hands and this won't be the first time that someone has claimed an item was stolen. Checking ownership is difficult to do and time-consuming. If I were the auctioneers, I'd tell the person making the complaint that I'd investigate, but I wouldn't do a thing.'

'Which is exactly what I told my lunatic customer. "The

auction house might not," he told me snippily, "but the police will".'

'The police!' she exclaimed, and straightened up.

'That's right,' Stanley said grimly. 'Apparently, the auction house said that the young man who'd made the complaint told them he was going to the police. I'll bet it's Tom Bradley. He told me at the reception that he was off to an auction to build up his stock of furniture. If he's not reported it today, he will tomorrow. He won't want to give the auction house time to falsify their documents. I'm assuming my customer signed a valid consignment agreement, but you never know. I hope so, as he'll be the first person the police visit.'

Gladys's face went white. 'Will he say it came from you?'

'Not likely! He'll want to come across as a buyer who bought in good faith. Buying an artefact like that from an antique dealer like me would shriek out that it was stolen.'

'Don't tell me, he's going to say he bought it from an unknown man in a pub, isn't he?' she said with a sneer. 'That would be even more suspect. The police must've heard that story a million times by now, and they'll know just how much credit to give it.'

He grinned knowingly. 'Of course he won't. He bought it from a pretty young woman with chestnut-coloured hair, didn't he. He'd seen her walking along, clutching a box in her arms, and he'd noticed she was crying.'

'I wonder who that could be?' she remarked wryly.

He laughed. 'Like a good Samaritan, he'd stopped and asked what was wrong. She'd told him that she badly needed money so was trying to sell something her grandfather had left her, but the antiques shops weren't interested in it. You can take it from there. I suggested he hold up his hand to giving her less than he knew he could get for it, but say that he was guilty of nothing else.'

She frowned anxiously. 'So they might turn up at the museum tomorrow or Tuesday.'

He held up his hand to stop her. 'I very much doubt it! You're crediting them with moving at speed, when their customary pace is the opposite of that. And you're assuming they'll instantly discover the identity of the woman and link her with Harton Museum. No, I think it's more likely that it'll be a couple of weeks or so before they roll up at your Georgian door.'

'I certainly hope you're right,' she said. 'So what d'you suggest I do till then?'

'Put Violet's bank statements in a folder at the back of her filing cabinet. Put it where she'd be unlikely to come across it, but where anyone searching the cabinet for evidence would find it. The police are bound to search the museum before they ransack the houses of the staff. When they do search the houses, they'll find the figurine in Violet's chimney, and that will seal her guilt. So apart from putting the statements in the cabinet, there's nothing for you to do. Just behave as you normally would at the museum. Whatever you do, don't go around looking furtive or guilty.'

'I hope it'll be as easy as you say.'

'I'm sure it will,' he said reassuringly. 'If I'm correct in that the person who spotted the pax board was Tom, it means that Lucy will have seen it in the museum. She must've told Tom about its damaged corner or may have even shown it to him, otherwise there'd have been nothing to make him suspicious as a number of pax boards have come up for auction recently. When questioned, Lucy will tell the police she'd seen it in the museum.'

'And what will I say when they ask me?'

'That you, too, saw it in the basement. You'll say a bit more than that, though. Looking very worried, you'll tell the police that you'd wondered recently if some of the items in the basement hadn't been disappearing. You didn't say anything to anyone as you thought you must've been mistaken—so few of you work there and no one was likely to be stealing from the museum.'

'I can easily manage that,' she said.

'You might also casually slip in that you wondered at Violet choosing to work in such a small out of the way museum when she had such a good teaching qualification. But you'd add that you were extremely grateful that someone of her calibre had decided that this was what she wanted to do. That could also get the police thinking.'

Gladys nodded slowly. 'It could work. I think you've covered just about everything. So after they've taken her away, all we'll have to do is lay low for a while, and then resume our activities.'

He nodded. 'With you in charge, of course. I can't see the trustees allowing Edward to choose the replacement for the thieving Violet. They'll want someone they trust implicitly. And who else could that be but you? And you will be the one to choose the replacement for Lucy, who's sure to leave, distraught at the revelations about her heroine Violet. You'll choose someone unlikely to poke their nose where it doesn't belong.'

'It all sounds very good to me, Stan. I think we can have that drink now.' She held up her glass, waiting for him to do likewise.

37

M*onday morning*

The early morning rain had passed and a watery sunshine was emerging by the time the bus from Bury St Edmunds stopped in Harton and Lucy stepped down from it. As the bus drove off, she went slowly towards the museum, then paused.

Standing still on the path, she stared at the entrance to the museum, her face deathly white.

How was she going to be able to behave in a normal way when she knew that the police had already started an investigation that would eventually bring them to the museum? She'd been worrying about that since she'd said goodbye to Tom the day before.

When she'd woken up that morning, she'd been so tempted to stay at home for a day or two, just until she'd adjusted to the situation, but that would have been doing something out of the ordinary, and it was vital, she'd realised instinctively, that she carry on as usual.

Whoever at the museum was responsible for the theft must be made to feel safe from discovery so that they didn't attempt to cover their tracks. Even if they already knew that the pax board had been withdrawn from the auction, which they probably did, they wouldn't know that Tom was the person who'd spotted it, so they'd have no reason to think it would lead back to Harton.

But feeling as worried as she did, summoning up a cheerful manner was going to be extremely difficult.

She took a deep breath. She really must pull herself together. After all, the thief must be one of the cleaners. It couldn't be anyone else. And as she hardly ever saw the cleaners, she was needlessly getting herself into a state. There was no reason for her not to relax.

But suppose she was wrong about the cleaners?

It would've helped if she'd been able to run through everything again with someone other than Tom. Although she and Tom had repeatedly gone through every aspect the previous evening before he'd set off for home, someone else might have picked up something that they'd missed.

She'd glanced at her parents after the Sunday evening meal, wondering whether to lighten her load by sharing it with them. But her mother had been contentedly knitting a scarf for her father, and her father had fallen asleep in the armchair, and she knew that she'd hate herself if she told them something that was certain to cause them anxiety.

Also, neither of her parents was the person with whom she really wanted to talk.

That person was Violet.

But Violet was one of the people who mustn't be told what had happened.

As she stood in front of the museum, tears trickled down her cheeks.

The sound of a bicycle coming closer broke into her consciousness, followed by the sound of feet on the ground.

Hastily wiping her eyes, she turned to see who it was and saw Jean wheeling her bicycle over to her.

'Why Lucy!' Jean exclaimed. 'I came over to say hello, but I can see that something's the matter. Whatever is it?'

Lucy shook her head. 'It's nothing. I was just being silly.'

'It doesn't look like nothing to me. Is it anything I can help you with?' Jean asked.

At the kindness in Jean's voice, Lucy's tears started to fall again. 'No, there's nothing really. I'm fine, thank you.' She gave a loud sob.

Jean gave her a sympathetic smile. 'If you don't mind me saying so, you don't look fine. Won't you let me help?'

Lucy stared at Jean and felt a momentary hope. Jean wasn't one of the people who could be the thief, so she could talk to Jean. Relief shot through her, and she nodded.

With a smile, Jean held out her bicycle to Lucy. 'Hold this a moment, will you?' she said.

Lucy took hold of the bicycle, and Jean went down the path to the museum, pushed open the front door and went into the hall.

'I bumped into Lucy outside,' she heard Jean say. 'She's got such a bad headache that she feels nauseous. I'm going to take her to my surgery and give her something for it. Can you manage without her this morning, do you think?'

'Poor Lucy. Of course we can. Give her our best wishes.' It was Gladys who'd answered Jean.

Jean emerged from the museum, closed the door and came back up the path. She took her bicycle from Lucy.

'Now, let's go to the surgery,' she said cheerfully, 'and see what I can do for you. It's fortunate I was going past. I'd just been to see how our newest villager is getting on. He's only two days old and came down with laryngitis yesterday. His mother was panicking as he's still not making any sound, so I made her my first call of the day.'

'Was he all right?' Lucy asked.

'Happily, yes. He looks a healthy little chap. I told her the laryngitis might last another day or so, but then he'll get his voice back. If it returns at two in the morning, as happened with one of my mothers, she'll be wishing it had lasted longer,' she added with a laugh.

Lucy managed a faint smile.

They walked the rest of the way in silence. When they reached the surgery, Jean propped her bicycle against the wall, lifted her Gladstone bag out of the front basket, opened the door, went in and held it open for Lucy to follow.

Jean said good morning to the receptionist as they crossed the hall to her surgery and went in. Jean put down her bag, took off her navy cloak and uniform hat, and hung them up. 'You sit down,' she told Lucy, 'and I'll pop into the kitchen and make us a cup of tea.'

'Don't you have any patients to see?' Lucy asked.

'I've some house calls to make, but there's nothing that won't keep till later. Something's clearly bothering you, Lucy, and I want to help. And help is better given along with a cup of tea. I'll be back in a minute.'

Before long, she returned with two cups of tea and a plate of rich tea biscuits. 'Help yourself,' she said, putting the plate on her desk and pushing it towards Lucy.

She pulled the chair from behind her desk, put it close to Lucy's and sat down.

'I know something's worrying you, Lucy,' she said gently.

'That's obvious. There isn't a thing you can't tell me. I promise that whatever you say will be in confidence.'

Lucy burst into tears.

Jean moved closer to Lucy, put her arms around her shoulders and gave her a quick hug. 'Nothing's so bad that you can't tell me.'

'I'm not having a baby, if that's what you think,' Lucy sobbed.

'Well, that's one possibility out of the way. So what is it?'

Lucy stared at her. 'I'm not supposed to tell anyone,' she said weakly.

Jean thought for a moment. 'Are you not supposed to tell anyone who's part of the problem, or anyone at all, regardless?'

Lucy frowned. 'Who's part of the problem, I suppose.'

'And could I be part of the problem?'

Lucy shook her head. 'Definitely not.'

'So you can tell me. I promise, it'll go no further than me.'

Feeling a huge weight begin to lift off her shoulders, Lucy told Jean about Tom's discovery of the pax board that belonged to the museum.

She told her how she'd described it to Tom so he'd recognised it at once, and had spoken to the auction house and then the police. 'They know it came from the museum so at some point they'll turn up and try to find who took it. The others don't know this and it's going to be hard to act as if nothing's going on when I know that it is.'

'Do you have any idea who took it?' Jean asked.

'I suppose it could be one of the cleaners. Though on the few occasions I've seen them, they seemed very nice and didn't look like thieves.'

'I imagine that the best thieves don't look like thieves,'

Jean said with a wry smile. 'They wouldn't be very successful if they did, would they?'

There was a hesitant knock at the door.

Jean got up and opened it. 'I thought that was your knock, Martin,' she said.

'Are you with a patient?' he asked. 'I wondered if you wanted to go out to dinner tonight.'

'Lucy and I are having a chat,' she told him. She glanced at Lucy. 'I think it might be an idea to ask for Martin's help, Lucy, don't you? Like me, he isn't in any way involved in this.'

'All right,' Lucy said, and Jean opened the door wider so that Martin could enter the room.

'Are you sure you want to include me in what you're discussing, Lucy?' he asked. 'I won't be offended if you'd prefer me to leave.'

'I want you to stay,' she said quickly. 'I feel so much better since telling Jean, and if you know, too, I'll feel doubly better.'

'Well then.' He smiled, pulled up a chair and sat down.

'While I make a fresh pot of tea and bring a cup for Martin, you can be telling him what you told me, Lucy.'

By the time Jean returned with a pot of tea, Lucy had told Martin what she'd told Jean.

Jean filled a cup for Martin and refreshed her cup and Lucy's. 'What do you advise, Martin?' she asked as she put the tea strainer back on its bowl. 'Lucy wants to carry on as if nothing's happened but will obviously find that quite difficult. Can you suggest anything else?'

'This needs thinking through. I don't want to be an alarmist, but if someone's stolen an item from the museum—'

'I think several things might have gone missing from the

museum,' Lucy cut in. 'Not just the pax board. And some of the items might be replicas,' she added.

'Before Violet came or after?'

Her brow creased. 'I can't really say. I only started regularly going to the basement after Violet arrived. Most of the missing things were stored in the basement, I think, although one or two items in display cabinets in the galleries looked a bit different.'

'So we can't rule Violet out.'

Lucy gave an audible gasp. 'You don't think she could be the thief, do you? Surely not. I'd never believe that.'

Martin smiled. 'I don't either, but we can't rule anyone out on the basis of instinct or liking for a person.' He paused. 'What about Edward? D'you think he could be the guilty party?'

Lucy shook her head vehemently. 'Definitely not.'

'And I don't, either,' Martin said. 'And not just because he's a friend, but because he's far too smart to steal and sell anything that could come back to the museum. If he wanted to steal anything, he'd have done so in such a way that the item couldn't be linked to him or the museum. He need not have passed every donation through the museum's books, for example. So we can be sure that Edward's innocent.'

'Does that mean I should tell him about this?' Lucy asked.

Martin nodded. 'I think so. Especially as you think other things might've been stolen, too. If someone's got a lucrative business going, they're bound to want to see it continue. They'll know by now that the pax board was spotted, and they'll be doing all they can to cover their tracks. Edward's sure to have some ideas about what to do. He's not at the surgery yet. I'll telephone him and let him know you're on the way, and that he should stay where he is. I'll do his surgery as well as mine.'

Jean and Lucy both stood up.

'Violet and Gladys are in the museum, you say,' Martin added, 'so no one who's possibly involved is likely to see you go to Edward's. Nevertheless, it would be better if you went separately. You go first, Lucy. Jean can follow in a few minutes. That way it won't look as if you're together should anyone see you. You can tell me later what Edward's advised.'

38

A *few minutes later*

HAVING TAKEN his guests into his sitting room, and asked Mavis to bring in some coffee, Edward sat down in the armchair opposite the sofa where Jean and Lucy were sitting.

'Well,' he said, 'this is a surprise, as was Martin's telephone call.' He paused. 'But judging by your expressions, and the fact that when each of you arrived you were looking worriedly over your shoulders, the reason that's brought you here isn't a pleasant one.'

He glanced at Jean and raised his eyebrows.

'Detective skills like that could come in very handy,' Jean said with a slight smile. 'But I'm going to leave it to Lucy to tell you why we're here.'

'Mavis will be back with our coffees in a minute. Why don't we wait till then?' he suggested.

As he spoke, the door opened, and Mavis came in with a tray from which a strong aroma of coffee arose. When they all had a coffee on the table next to them, and Mavis had gone out again, Edward glanced at Lucy. 'Right, Lucy. Why don't you tell me now what the problem is? At least, I'm assuming it *is* a problem.'

'I suppose that's as good a word as any,' she said, and she told him exactly what she'd told Jean and Martin. When she'd finished talking, she sat back.

'It's very lucky for us that you'd told Tom about the pax board and had described it so well,' he said slowly. 'If you hadn't, he'd never have realised it came from here.' He thought for a moment. 'I think if I'd been you, when Tom told me about finding an artefact that had obviously been stolen from the museum, we would've talked about who we thought the guilty party might be. Did you do that?'

She nodded.

'And did you come to any conclusion?' he asked.

She shook her head. 'Not really. We just felt it couldn't be you, Violet or Gladys, so it must be the cleaners. They're in the museum on their own and could easily go down to the basement and remove an item.'

'How would they know what they could sell?' he asked.

'Perhaps someone told them the sort of thing to take?' she said hopefully.

'While it's possible, it's not very likely, not if you consider the jumble of uncatalogued items there were in the basement. Before Violet started sorting everything out, it would've been difficult for the cleaners to identify what they'd been asked to find.' He paused. 'And you think things had been going missing before Violet started at the museum and that some had been copied?'

'I told Jean they might have been, but to be honest, I'm

not really sure. It's just that some of the items didn't look exactly the same as they used to, and I think that predates Violet.'

'Which makes it even more likely that it's the cleaners, then,' Jean said.

'I'm not ruling them out,' Edward said. 'It's just that we've used the same two cleaners for a number of years. They're local women. Neither seems the sort of person to mastermind thefts like this.'

'It doesn't sound very likely when you put it like that,' Lucy said. 'There's always the caretaker, but I can't see it being him.'

'Nor can I,' Edward said. 'Most of his time is spent in the school, anyway. There's never been the slightest suggestion of wrongdoing on his part over the many years he's worked at the school and also done a bit for us.'

'If we rule out the cleaners,' Lucy said, 'that leaves us with Violet and Gladys and me, of course.'

'And me,' Edward said.

'We've already decided it couldn't be you,' Jean told him with a smile.

'Thank you for that,' he said. 'And I think we can safely rule you out, Lucy.' He paused. The colour slowly drained from his face.

Jean leaned slightly forward. 'I'll say what it'd hurt you to say, Edward dear. We're going to have to consider that Violet could be guilty.'

'She isn't!' Lucy exclaimed. 'I'll never believe she is. And if you think about it, it's thanks to Violet this has been discovered. If she was stealing things, she'd never have opened up the basement in the way she's done. And she'd have kept me as far away from there as possible. And she'd never have tried to get more people to come to the museum. The less activity the better, she'd think.'

'And another point,' Jean said. 'How would she find a dishonest person who'd buy stolen items from her in the short amount of time she's been here? And it'd have to be a person who knew someone who could forge artefacts. Potential fences of stolen goods don't walk around with a placard advertising their nefarious activity. Unless, of course, we think she could have been recruited while training to be a teacher and planted here. As I think that's highly unlikely, I'm with Lucy on ruling Violet out.'

Edward swallowed hard and nodded. 'Thank you, Lucy, Jean. I, too, could never believe that Violet would do such a thing. Every instinct tells me she's scrupulously honest, and now that both of you have added reasoned arguments to my instinct, I'm happy to say that we believe Violet to be completely innocent.'

'Which leaves Gladys,' Lucy said quietly. Then she sat up sharply. 'Of course it's Gladys!' she exclaimed.

They stared at her with surprise.

'It makes sense of several strange things she's done recently,' Lucy said, her words tumbling over each other. 'I told Tom about them. We thought them a little peculiar, but not sinister, so I didn't say anything. And I certainly didn't connect them to the thefts till just now. It didn't even occur to me when Tom and I were talking yesterday—we just dismissed the idea of Gladys being guilty as she always seems so to have the museum's welfare at heart. But her being the thief explains why she wanted me out of the museum, and why Stanley Patterson did, too.'

Edward frowned. 'Stanley Patterson! How does he fit into this? Why would he and Gladys want you out of the museum?'

'Because I was helping Violet so much!' Lucy exclaimed triumphantly. 'I was either with Violet in the basement, or covering her slot on the rota so she could work downstairs for longer. It meant that Violet was getting through everything much more quickly than she would've done if I hadn't been there.'

'But they'd have had to replace you,' Jean said.

'If Gladys was involved in the interviews, which I'm sure she would've been, she would've persuaded Violet to appoint the person least likely to interest herself in the items in the museum.'

'I think you'd better tell us everything you know about Gladys, Lucy,' Edward said.

'All right, but I'm warning you,' she said, 'it'll sound like a lot of little things, but I think they might add up to something big.'

She took a deep breath and began to go through all of the occasions when Gladys had done something that had surprised her.

'I think the lie about her toothache, and the closeness I saw between her and Stanley when they didn't know they were being watched,' Lucy said, 'which was the reverse of how they act when others are around, makes a strong case for Gladys being the thief. She passes the stolen items to Stanley Patterson, who either sells them or has them copied. It all fits.'

'That sounds very convincing,' Jean said. 'So what are we going to do about it, Edward?'

Lucy looked at her in surprise. 'Surely we must go to the police?'

'It'd be our word against theirs,' Edward said. 'If you think about it, there's nothing to link Gladys and Stanley to the stolen item, so nothing to prove they were involved. It's all superficial. And there could be another way of linking everything, but we can't see it.'

'But the auction house will contact the person who put the item up for auction. He might admit he got it from Stanley, mightn't he?' Lucy suggested. 'Then it'd be more than just conjecture on our part.'

Edward shook his head. 'I very much doubt he'd mention Stanley. To buy such an item from an antiques dealer suggests it was stolen.'

Lucy frowned. 'I don't understand.'

'It's to do with the price. The antiques dealer would know the true value of the item but being unable to sell a stolen item in the normal way, he'd charge a lot less to get rid of it. The vendor would guess the reason for the low price. The same vendor could buy the same item from an ordinary person at a very low price because the ordinary person could be presumed not to know its true value.'

'I see,' she said.

'The last thing the vendor would want is for the police to think he would knowingly buy stolen goods.'

'D'you think he'd make up a seller, then?'

'I do.' He paused. 'We know that the police will come here when they and the auction house have completed their enquiries about the vendor. And we can assume that the vendor has told Stanley about what happened. Almost certainly, Stanley's told Gladys by now.'

'Of course,' she said slowly 'That hadn't occurred to me.'

'The question is, what will happen when the police get here? If we're right in what were assuming, Gladys will have talked with Stanley and will have a story ready,' Edward mused.

'There'll have to be a guilty party who isn't Gladys,' Jean said, 'so they're bound to put the blame on someone else.

On either Lucy or Violet, I suspect. Perhaps on Lucy as they were keen to get rid of her before.'

Edward shook his head. 'I don't think it'd be Lucy. The damage they'd wanted to prevent by sending Lucy to Tom's has already been done. I think they'll put the blame on Violet. If Violet is sacked from the museum, Gladys and Stanley can allow a period of calm, and then resume their activities. Violet's the one they'll want to see go.'

'But there isn't any evidence pointing to Violet, is there?' Jean said.

'There might be,' he said quietly. 'If I were them, I'd have been preparing for such an emergency for a while now, and I'd have some physical evidence against Violet.'

'How can they? She's done nothing wrong!' Jean exclaimed.

'They'll manufacture it,' he said bluntly. 'If they hadn't already done so before the weekend, there'll be something in place by now. They'll guess that Tom will have told Lucy about his find, but they don't know what Lucy will do. They'll be hoping she keeps quiet as she knows the police are investigating, but they're unlikely to bank on it and they'll be ready for anything that might happen.'

'What could they possibly manufacture?'

'I don't know. I can only guess that there might be something Violet unwittingly did that could be used against her.' He turned to Jean. 'I think it's best that Lucy goes home and writes up everything she told us about Gladys. The police will need a full account at some point. Could you call in at the museum and say that Lucy's unwell and has just got the bus home?'

Jean nodded. 'Of course.'

'Go straight home, Lucy,' he told her, 'and don't go out until you go to work tomorrow.'

She nodded. 'I'll do that.'

'I wouldn't be surprised if Gladys visited you later today,' he added. 'If I were Gladys, in the light of what's happened, I'd be curious to know if you really were ill.'

'I'll be prepared,' Lucy told him.

Jean looked at her wristwatch. 'There'll be a bus quite soon. You'll be able to get that. But what will we do about Violet, Edward?'

'We need to hear what she has to say, but that'll have to wait till after my afternoon surgery. We don't want any change to Violet's working day, or mine. It could make Gladys suspicious.'

Jean nodded. 'That makes sense.'

'I suggest that I pop down to the museum as soon as the morning surgery's over—they won't know that Martin's been doing it for me,' Edward went on. 'I'll fulsomely thank both Gladys and Violet for all for their hard work over the display and the reception, and give them each the souvenir pin I ordered as a thank you. I'll make a point of catching Violet on her own and ask her to come to my house this evening at about seven. I'd be grateful if you were here, too, Jean, and also Martin, if possible. If you could fill Martin in beforehand, it'd be a help.'

'I'll be here, and I'm sure Martin will, too,' Jean said. 'Off you go, Lucy. As soon as you're on the bus, I'll go to the museum.'

He glanced at them both. 'If you can come in earlier than usual tomorrow, Lucy, Violet will let you know the plan.' He gave them a wry smile. 'I suspect it's going to feel a very long day for us all, and a difficult one.'

39

T*hat evening*

'HOW VERY CLOAK AND DAGGER!' Violet said, laughing as she handed her jacket to Edward. Giving her a quick smile, he hung the jacket on the coat stand in the hall and led the way into the sitting room.

Martin and Jean stood up as she entered.

She stopped short at the sight of them, glanced at Edward in surprise, and then looked back at Jean and Martin.

'Hello, you two,' she said slowly. 'Edward didn't say you'd be here, too. Come to think of it, Edward didn't say anything.' She gave him a half-smile. 'You just put a piece of paper in front of me while you were clipping the souvenir pin to my lapel, whispered to me to destroy it when I'd read it, and hurried out.' She looked back at Martin and Jean. 'It was all very mysterious.'

'I'm afraid I wouldn't make much of a spy,' Edward said ruefully. 'But it was the only way I could think of getting you here without Gladys knowing.'

Her brow creased, and she stared at him in puzzlement. 'Why didn't you want Gladys to know I was coming here?'

'All will become clear. But do sit down. Firstly, would anyone like a drink?'

Martin shook his head. 'We're fine,' Jean said.

'So am I, thank you.' Violet glanced from one to the other. 'You all seem very serious. Is something the matter?' She looked anxiously at Edward.

'I'm afraid there is,' Edward said, sitting down. 'It's something Lucy told us, and thank heavens she did. She can't tell you it herself as she's at home now.'

'I was sorry to hear she was ill,' Violet said. 'I hope she didn't overdo it with all the hard work she's been doing recently.'

Jean leaned forward. 'Don't worry, Violet, she's perfectly all right. Just very worried, as we all are.'

'I don't understand,' Violet said, her voice shaking.

Jean glanced at Edward. 'Shall I tell Violet what Lucy told me? After all, I've now heard the story twice. If you think I've left something out, you can jump in at any time and tell me.'

Edward nodded. 'Good idea. Go ahead.'

So Jean told Violet everything that Lucy had relayed to them from the moment that Tom had come across the pax board, and finishing with their suspicions about Gladys. When she came to the end, Violet stared at her in disbelief.

'I can't believe it,' she said at last. 'Gladys of all people. She's done so much for the museum over the years. To be so dishonest. Are you sure there isn't any other explanation?'

'I wish there were,' Edward said. 'But having gone

through everything we know, we think it must be Gladys. In effect it's only speculation, but as far as we can see, there's nothing else that fits all the facts. We'll have to assume it's her, and ask ourselves what we do next.'

'What we do next?' Violet echoed.

'The police will assume the guilty party works in the museum. Gladys and Stanley will know that, which means they'll be sure to point them away from Gladys. The person it's to their advantage to frame is you, Violet. I'm afraid to say that we think they'll plant something that makes you look guilty, and we have to do our best to work out what it is.'

The blood drained from Violet's face.

'I suppose there's my cupboard in the staffroom,' she said. 'Maybe she'll put a stolen item into that to make it look as if I was planning to take it home? Oh, but surely not.'

'I thought of that,' Edward said, 'but it would be too risky for Gladys. As she doesn't know what day the police will finish their preliminary investigations and turn up at the museum, there's no time when she could be confident of you not finding the planted artefact before they did.'

'That makes sense.' She paused. 'Perhaps she won't do anything?' she suggested hopefully.

'She'll have done something, I'm certain. She'll have heard over the weekend that the police were involved, so there's certain to be some evidence against you by now. She's had all weekend to think about this. As it won't be in your cupboard, we have to decide what it might be and where she'd put it,' Edward said, failing in his attempt to hide his anxiety. 'Your office is the other obvious place.'

Violet clasped her hands tightly in her lap. 'What d'you think it could be?' she asked, a tremor in her voice. 'I can't think of anything. My mind's a blank.'

Martin moved over to the chair next to hers. 'Would it help if I asked you some questions?'

Violet nodded gratefully. 'It might.'

'As you trained to be a teacher,' he began, 'is it fair to say that working in a museum rather than a classroom was quite a challenge?'

'It definitely was,' she told him. 'But everyone was so helpful that it made it relatively easy for me.'

'Was Lucy one of the people who helped you?' he asked.

She thought for a moment. 'Not in the way I think you mean. She helped by taking over some of my slots on the rota so that I could get on top of the office work, it all being very new. And she helped me enormously with the display and reception. But not with the administration side of things.'

'Who helped you with that?' he asked.

'Mainly Gladys. She used to run the museum by herself when Edward was very busy so she knew exactly what had to be done. It wasn't just the accounts she helped with, but she gave me some good ideas, too, such as including a pictorial representation of my display as part of my report for the trustees. It was an excellent idea.'

Edward and Martin exchanged glances.

Edward moved closer to the edge of his seat. 'To come back to the accounts you mentioned, Violet,' he said. 'Can you tell us in what way Gladys helped?'

'She explained what an operating budget is, and said I'd need a project budget for my display and she helped me set it up. Also, she told me about keeping the balance sheet up to date so that anyone could see on any specific date the financial position of the museum—any deposits made into the bank account, for example. And she gave me all the documents you'd signed, which I had to sign, too, in order to change the authorising signature from yours to mine.'

'And how did you go about changing the signature?' Edward asked. 'Did she take you to Lloyds and introduce you to Mr Armstrong, the manager?'

She nodded. 'That's right. I signed the documents and then we went to the bank together. We went—'

A sudden fear clutched at her, and she stopped abruptly. Her hands flew to her face.

'Oh,' she cried out. With panic in her eyes, she stared through her fingers at the others.

'What've you remembered?' Martin asked quietly.

She dropped her hands. Tears sprang to her eyes. 'I did something very stupid,' she whispered. 'I signed the documents she gave me without reading them. My father had always warned me never to do that, but it had been an incredibly long, very busy day, and reading all the bank jargon would've taken an age. I remember thinking the following day,' she went on, 'when I was going through what I'd done, and was berating myself for my stupidity, that she should've left the signing for another day. It wouldn't have mattered.'

'She won't have wanted you to read the forms. The timing will have been deliberate,' Jean said. 'What did she do with the signed documents?'

'Put them into my filing cabinet. I checked them the following morning but there was nothing I wouldn't have signed had I read it first.'

'There wouldn't have been,' Edward said. 'There was probably one signed document that Gladys didn't file with the others. My guess is that it'll have enabled deposits to be put into an account purporting to be on behalf of the museum but that was in your name. It'll seem as if you were stealing from the museum. It must've looked authentic as Brian Armstrong didn't question it when he went through the forms with you.'

Tears trickled down her cheeks.

'He didn't go through them with us,' she said, her voice trembling. 'He said he'd do so later. It was almost closing time when we got there, and he was in a hurry. Gladys told me afterwards that she'd chosen that time as she'd known he had a meeting to go to. She said she'd wanted to spare us the tedium of him going through everything.'

'If I'd had any doubts about the guilty party being Gladys, that would have erased them,' Edward said.

'But the monthly statements would be sent to the museum, wouldn't they?' Martin said.

Edward glanced at Violet. 'Martin's right.'

Violet shook her head miserably. 'Gladys told me she always used to handle the post for you.'

Edward nodded. 'That's true.'

'She said she used to pass on anything for you, and file the rest or throw it away. She suggested she carry on doing it, so I'd have one thing less to worry about at a time when I had so much to learn.'

'So Gladys will have intercepted each one,' Edward said. 'If we're right about this, they'll have been covering themselves since you started here. They won't have thought it necessary to do so before then as no one was taking such a keen interest in the exhibits, both upstairs and downstairs.'

'What do you think they'll do with the statements?' Jean asked.

'They'll be where they implicate Violet, which means in her office,' Edward said. 'I imagine they're now probably in the filing cabinet where Violet wouldn't notice them. They might be in a file relating to museum acquisitions, for example, which Violet would have no need to access, but which the police would be sure to find. We need to remove them as soon as possible.'

'Couldn't we leave them there and just tell the police what she's done?' Violet asked, wiping her eyes.

'If they find them in your office, it could make them feel they must investigate you, which could take time. And it'd only be your word that you didn't put them there. I'd rather they kept their focus on Gladys. We can give them the bank statements after they've arrested her. When they examine the signatures on the paying-in slips, they'll see that your signature on each slip is a forgery.'

'I could remove the statements every morning when I got to the museum,' Violet said, 'and replace them in the evening, but what if Gladys came into my office during the day when I wasn't there? If she did, she'd find them gone and know we were on to her.'

'You're right,' Edward said. 'So we'll have to make sure the police come to the museum soon after we've removed the incriminating statements. Make sure you know where they are before you leave work tomorrow evening—I'm assuming they'll be in your filing cabinet, but they could be somewhere else in your office. Then you can remove them first thing on Wednesday morning.'

'Will you be going to the police on Wednesday morning, or tomorrow evening?' Martin asked.

'I thought we'd telephone them tomorrow evening and tell them we know who the thief is, and that if they come to the museum early on Wednesday morning, they'll apprehend her and I can give them evidence. That'll be the bank statements with Violet's forged signature. I don't want to go into Bury as I know that Gladys might go there to visit Lucy, and I wouldn't want to risk her or Stanley seeing me.'

'Why don't you go there on Wednesday morning to make sure they come early in the day?' Martin asked.

'Because I was rather hoping you'd telephone them early on Wednesday morning and remind them to go at once to the museum, where they'd find evidence and can arrest the thief.'

'I don't mind doing that at all,' Martin said, 'but why don't you telephone them yourself?'

'From the moment that Violet's removed the files, I must stay in her office so that Gladys can't check the cabinet. If Violet was in there alone and Gladys suddenly felt suspicious and tried to get Violet out of the office, it'd be difficult for Violet to refuse. It's better that I keep Gladys in your office, Violet, working on something with me.'

'But what could you work on that wouldn't make her suspicious?' she asked. 'You don't run the museum now.'

'Before you took over, I was approached by a large property company near Ipswich who offered to make a very generous donation to the museum if I associated their name with an exhibition I'd been thinking about putting on. The unspoken reason behind the offer was that they wanted to buy a site of historical interest and develop it, a deal the trustees were opposing, and they were hoping that their donation would soften the trustees. Gladys had been in favour of accepting the money, and I could tell her that they've been hounding me about the matter, and I wanted to have another look with her at their proposal again.'

Martin nodded. 'That sounds genuine.'

'I'll try to get to the museum at the same time as you, Violet,' Edward went on. 'We can remove the bank statements and I'll put them into my briefcase. I'll settle myself in the office, and you'll send Gladys to me as soon as she's left her things in the staffroom. If for any reason we can't find the statements, we'll hold off contacting the police.'

'It's a shame we can't plant an artefact in Gladys's staffroom cupboard, as that would've been ideal,' Jean cut in. 'But she'd be sure to find it. Or better still, plant something in her house. But alas, we'd never be able to get inside her house.'

'She invited me there for a cup of tea after work one day,' Violet said. 'I could take her up on that tomorrow.'

Edward shook his head. 'It's too suspicious. She'll be alert to anything unusual. If you'd taken the offer up sooner, it might have worked, but not now. And you don't know what her house is like inside so you wouldn't know where to hide anything in the short amount of time you'd have.'

'When did she invite you to tea, Violet?' Martin asked.

'When she'd virtually forced me to invite her for tea one day after work. Just before she left my house, she said I must have tea with her one afternoon.'

'I wonder,' Martin said thoughtfully. 'Although the bank statements would compromise Violet, they're not the strongest of evidence. And they wouldn't necessarily prove that Gladys was guilty.'

'What're you saying?' Jean asked.

'He's saying that Gladys and Stanley might have wanted some further evidence against Violet,' Edward said quietly. 'They might've wanted the police to catch her with an artefact she intended to sell. What better place to put it than in Violet's home? Did you leave Gladys alone at any point, Violet?'

'Only when I went to make the tea. I left her in the sitting room, but the kitchen's just off the sitting room, and the door between the rooms was open. It would've been impossible for her to hide anything while I was in the kitchen.'

'And that was the only time she was alone?' Edward asked.

Violet nodded. 'Yes. Well, and for the few minutes it took me to go up to the bathroom,' she added.

'That could have been enough,' he said, sitting back in satisfaction. 'Gladys knows the house very well as the museum used to use it for storage. I'll bet there's something hidden in your house, Violet.'

Her brow furrowed as she thought back to Gladys's visit. Then her face cleared.

'I know where it must be!' she exclaimed. 'It'll be in my fireplace! After she left, I moved the flower display front of the empty grate back into the right position. She'd commented on the aroma of the sedum so I just thought she'd knocked the vase out of place when she'd bent over the flowers to smell them. But she could've deliberately moved it.'

'There's a ledge inside the chimneys of houses like yours,' Edward said. 'I'll be amazed if you don't find something there. But even if we find it, we'll search the room in case she's hidden something else in there as well. Whatever it is, it won't be large as she won't have wanted you to see her carrying it in, so it should easily fit into her staffroom cupboard, as that's where we'll put it.'

'Will both those things incriminate Stanley Patterson, too?' Violet asked. 'I don't like the idea that he could still be around after Gladys has been arrested. He might want his revenge for the fact that his business has come to an end.'

'Anything against him will be more circumstantial,' Edward said. 'Of course, Gladys might turn on him, hoping to get a lighter sentence. And the man who bought the pax board from Stanley might be persuaded to testify against him in return for lenient treatment if the police decided to charge him with receiving stolen goods. The police would be able to link the pax board from Gladys to Stanley, and thence to the man who put it up for auction.'

'I hope that's what happens,' Violet said. 'I'd feel safer if he was behind bars.'

'I'm sure Stanley won't have been the person who made the forgeries, though, but I doubt we'll find out who that is. He wouldn't be any threat to you, though, Violet, as he knows you don't know who he is. Or even if it's a man.'

'Did you say we'd put the item that Gladys hid in my house in her staffroom cupboard?' Violet asked.

'That's right,' Edward said. 'On Wednesday, once Gladys is safely in the office with me, you can put it in the cupboard. I've obviously got a spare key for everyone's cupboard, and I'll give you her key before you leave. Make sure you check for those bank statements as soon as you get to the museum tomorrow, won't you?'

'I won't forget,' she said firmly.

He glanced at Martin. 'We'll need the police to be here early on Wednesday morning, Martin. Lucy can bring us a coffee to save us leaving the office to get one, but I won't be able to keep Gladys from going into the staffroom once it gets to the lunch hour as she'll have to get her food from the cupboard.'

'Suppose they don't get there till after lunch?' Jean asked. 'Or Gladys asks to go to the toilet? You can't really stop her.'

'Good point.' Edward thought for a moment. 'As a precaution, Lucy had better sit in the staffroom all morning. She can tell Gladys she's still feeling a little weak, and that you've given her some work to do in the staffroom. If it gets too close to lunchtime, she'll have to remove the artefact and replace it when Gladys returns to the office. When you've put the item in Gladys's cupboard, Violet, give the key to Lucy.'

'She can work on some more ideas for the pupils' workbooks,' Violet suggested.

Edward nodded. 'As I say, let Lucy know the plan as soon as she arrives on Wednesday.'

'I think I ought to get back now,' Violet said, standing up, followed by Martin and Jean. 'I'm impatient to start searching the sitting room.' She paused. 'Thank you, all of you, for believing in me,' she added, her voice breaking, 'and for trying to help me to stay out of prison.'

'And it's a huge thank you from me, Martin and Jean,' Edward said fervently. 'You've been an enormous help. We couldn't have worked this out without you. I know that most of it is speculation and guesswork, but it all fits together and it's hard to see that there could be a different explanation for what's happened.'

When Martin and Jean had left, and he'd given Violet the key to Gladys's cupboard, he put his arm round her shoulders. 'I'll walk you home,' he said.

Stepping out of the house with her, he pulled the door shut behind him.

'It's a lovely night,' she said, looking up at the night sky, which was alive with stars and a crescent moon. 'And it's not exactly far,' she added in amusement. 'I think I can walk back the very short distance on my own.'

'I'm coming with you as I'm going to help you search. I'm sure Gladys isn't watching us, but just in case she is, we must make it look as if we've been having a romantic evening, and that it's going to be carried on inside your house.' He pulled her gently to him and kissed her lightly on her lips. 'Like that,' he said. 'Now rest your head on my shoulder, we must make this look realistic.'

Laughing, she moved into the crook of his arm, slid her arm around his back and nestled up to him as they started walking down Church Road, so close together that anyone watching might have thought they were but one person.

40

W*ednesday morning*

VIOLET STARED for a moment at the fourteenth century figurine that she and Edward had found in no time at all on the Monday evening. Then she wrapped it in the same paper as she used for her sandwiches, put it into her handbag next to her lunch, checked that she had the key to Gladys's cupboard, shut her bag and opened the front door.

Pausing on the doorstep, she looked back into her sitting room.

On the Monday evening, they'd closed the curtains as soon as they'd got inside the house, switched on the light and begun their search. Edward had instantly found the figurine, which had been in the chimney where he'd expected to find it.

After they'd found it, they'd thoroughly searched the rest of the sitting room but there'd been nothing else.

Neither had been surprised about that as all it would take to prove Violet a thief was one stolen artefact that was clearly destined to be privately sold by her.

Feeling it wise to leave everything as it had been before their search, Edward had returned the figurine to its hiding place in the chimney breast for one more day, telling her to bring it to the museum on the Wednesday morning. He suggested that they both aim to be there at eight o'clock as Gladys was seldom there quite that early, and that the first thing they'd do would be to remove the bank statements from Violet's filing cabinet.

They'd also be able to fill Lucy in when she arrived.

Violet had nodded, expecting he would then leave and go back to his home, but he had stayed where he was.

She'd glanced up at his face as he'd stood in the centre of her sitting room. She saw that he was looking down at her, and the expression in his eyes had taken her breath away.

Neither had moved.

In the still of the night, embraced by the shadows, just him and her, they lingered there, each drinking in the sight of the other, the eyes of both heavy with longing.

'After Wednesday,' he said at last, his voice thick with emotion, 'all this unpleasantness will be behind us, and ahead of us will be a future with nothing to mar it. I'm forcing myself not to think about that future until after Wednesday. But when this is over... I can't wait for that moment.'

'Nor me,' she said.

Their hearts full, not needing to say more, they'd slowly smiled at each other. Then he'd turned away and gone home.

. . .

And now Wednesday had arrived, she thought, pulling her front door closed behind her and turning towards the museum.

This was the day that would bring to an end to Gladys and Stanley's dishonest activities, and if all went according to plan, it would mark the beginning of a wonderful future for her and Edward.

She took a deep breath, and holding her handbag tightly, she started to walk towards the museum.

Edward caught her up as she was making her way down the path to the entrance.

Giving him a quick smile tinged with nervousness, she unlocked the front door and together they went into the entrance hall and straight across to her office.

He quickly closed the office door behind them as she went up to the filing cabinet, pulled open the lowest drawer and took out the folder containing the bank statements.

'This is it,' she told him. Pushing the drawer closed, she gave him the folder and he swiftly put it into his briefcase. Then he took a black file from his briefcase, sat down in her chair and opened it.

She picked up a cardboard box full of workbooks from the floor next to the filing cabinet and started to carry it over to the door. Seeing what she was doing, he hastily stood up and took the box from her. His hands brushed against hers, and for a long moment, neither moved. Then he carried the box out of the office and into the staffroom, after which he hastily returned to her office.

A few minutes later, she'd left her handbag and sandwiches in her cupboard and was arranging the workbooks on one of the staffroom tables as Lucy came into the room.

She had time to tell Lucy very quickly that, claiming she was still feeling weak, she was to sit in the staffroom all day to see that Gladys didn't find the figurine that Violet would be placing in Gladys's cupboard once Gladys was safely ensconced in the office with Edward.

Just before lunchtime, she continued, if the police hadn't yet arrived, Lucy should remove the figurine and put it back again after lunch. As she finished speaking, they heard the museum's front door click shut.

'How are you feeling, Lucy?' she asked, looking pointedly towards the staffroom door.

Lucy indicated that she knew what Violet was telling her.

'Much better, thank you,' Lucy said. 'I'm not quite right, but I'm almost there.'

'I thought that would be the case,' Violet said, making sure she sounded sympathetic. 'As I want you to have an easy morning, I thought you could sit in here and see if you can improve on the workbooks we've done so far. Would that be all right?'

'Well, yes. But it sounds a little unfair on you and Gladys to have to do all the work. Gladys kindly came to see me last night,' Lucy added. A flicker of amusement brushed across her face.

'How very thoughtful of her,' Violet said, her voice exaggerating her approval.

'I was in bed so she didn't stay long, but I thought it very nice of her. So did my parents.'

'Ah, here you both are!' Gladys exclaimed, coming into the staffroom.

'Gosh, you made me jump, Gladys,' Violet said with a laugh. 'In fact, we were just talking about you. Lucy said you called to see her last night. That was thoughtful of you.'

'Not at all,' Gladys said, looking gratified. 'Lucy's so seldom ill that I wanted to check that all was well. And it was. Although she did look a little pale. And indeed, you still do, my dear. Don't you think you should be at home today?'

'Mother suggested I stay at home, but I felt well enough to come in.'

'I agree with you, Gladys,' Violet said. 'I don't think Lucy looks her usual healthy self, and I've given her something that she can sit and do in here.' She turned to Lucy. 'If you don't feel completely well by lunchtime, Lucy, you must go home. I'll cover the reception desk this morning. Edward's in my office now, Gladys, and would like your help. It's not quite the time we start work, though, so do have a coffee first if you want.'

'Help with what?' Gladys asked, her sudden sense of unease palpable.

Violet shrugged. 'I'm not really sure as it was something that came up before my time. He mentioned a property company wanting to sponsor us. Does that mean anything to you?'

Her relief visible, Gladys smiled. 'It does. I do hope this means that he's going to take up their offer,' she said. 'I'll go and see what I can do to help.'

Having put her bag into her cupboard and locked the door, Gladys went swiftly out of the staffroom. A moment later, they heard her knock on the door to Violet's office, and then they heard the door close behind her.

They went and sat at the table with the workbooks for a few moments, discussing the tasks they'd set, just in case Gladys returned for something she'd forgotten. But she didn't, and Violet finally stood up, took the key to Gladys's cupboard from her pocket, unlocked the cupboard, took the figurine from her handbag and put it into the cupboard, and locked the door again.

'And now we wait,' she said, handing the key to Lucy.

LESS THAN AN HOUR after the museum's official opening time, Violet heard the sound of cars pulling up outside the museum.

As she rose to her feet, the front door opened and four male police officers filed in, three of them wearing dark blue tunics with polished silver buttons and trousers in a matching colour with a sewn-in truncheon pocket, and one in an everyday suit. He must be a detective, she thought.

Through the open door behind them she glimpsed two black Wolseley cars.

The non-uniformed detective stepped forward, identified himself and asked to speak to Dr Russell.

'I'll take you to him,' she said.

Seeing Lucy open the staffroom door, she gestured to her to stay where she was. One of the uniformed policemen walked across to the staffroom and stood in the open doorway where he could see inside the room.

Glancing over her shoulder as she led the way to her office, she saw that the detective and one of the uniformed officers were following her, but the third uniformed policeman had remained near the front door.

Reaching her office, she knocked on the door.

'Come in,' she heard Edward call, and she opened the door.

'Sorry, miss,' the detective said, and he pushed past her into the room.

Gladys jumped up from her chair. Violet saw panic sweep across her face.

'Excuse me,' Gladys said, collecting herself. 'I'll leave

you to your visitors, Edward, and return later.' She moved towards the door.

The detective put up his hand to stop her. 'Everyone must go to the staffroom, apart from you, Dr Russell. You'll be able to assist us with the museum's accounts.' He looked at Gladys and Violet. 'Both of you must go straight to the staffroom. Don't attempt to leave the building.' He turned to the uniformed policeman. 'I'll take the filing cabinet, you can start searching the rest of the office.'

Violet saw a hint of triumph on Gladys's lips as they went into the staffroom and sat down at the same table as Lucy.

The uniformed policeman moved from the doorway into the staffroom and explained that the police were investigating possible thefts from the museum. He mentioned the pax board, but they felt that the board might be only the tip of the iceberg. The policeman and detective in the office, he told them, were used to conducting searches of administrative files and office paraphernalia, and if there was anything to be found, they'd find it.

After reminding them that there was a police officer at the front door, he went on to say that he was going to search the staffroom, and he asked them to give him the key to their cupboards. All three readily handed over their key.

Lucy's cupboard was the first they searched.

The policeman had his back to them, but they saw him take out her cardigan and shake it, remove a book and flick through the pages, and then open her box of sandwiches. He felt around the cupboard, and then put the box, cardigan and book back inside.

Next he searched Violet's cupboard, opened up her pack of sandwiches, and then returned it to the cupboard.

When he reached Gladys's cupboard, he took out a

package wrapped in brown paper, opened it, made an audible exclamation, turned and held up the figurine for them all to see.

Gladys jumped up. "That's not mine!' she screeched, her face contorted with fear. 'They did it. They're trying to frame me.' She rounded on Violet. 'You put it there,' she spat.

Frantically pointing at Violet, she yelled at the officer, 'She was the one who took it, not me. She planted it there to make me look guilty. She's the one who's going to sell it and pocket the money. You can check and see if I'm telling the truth,' she raged uncontrollably. 'She's got bank statements in her filing cabinet that prove she's been stealing from the museum. Just look in the cabinet and see.' She stopped, panting heavily, her face wild.

The policeman went calmly to the staffroom door and called to his colleague in the office, asking if anything untoward had been found in the office files.

'They've not found any such bank statements,' he told them as he turned back into the room.

'Are they blind?' Gladys shouted, her voice shrill. 'Have they looked through the whole of her cabinet, including the bottom drawer? Go and look,' she yelled, waving her arms angrily towards the office.

'Is that where you hid them, then? In the bottom drawer?' the plain clothes detective asked, coming into the staffroom. 'Is it, Miss Wilson?' he repeated. 'If it is, haven't you rather condemned yourself by knowing that?'

She stood there, her breathing ragged, her mouth hanging open.

'I'd like the key to your house,' he said.

'What for?' she gasped.

'There may be some other stolen items there. Or perhaps the pen and ink you used to forge Miss Hammond's signature on the paying-in slips that will have accompanied each deposit. Our experts will find that the signatures were forged, you know.'

'I thought you said you didn't find anything in her cabinet?' she said, her face a sneer.

'We didn't. Dr Russell handed over the file.'

Violet saw the fight go out of Gladys, who visibly shrank before her eyes.

He held out his hand. 'Your house key, please, Miss Wilson, and then you'll be taken to the station where you'll be formally arrested and charged.'

STANDING in front of the reception desk, Edward, Violet and Lucy watched the uniformed policemen make for the front door, one in front of Gladys, one on either side of her, and the detective behind her.

Holding the figurine that he'd been asked to take to the station the following day, Edward stepped forward and indicated that he'd like them to stop a moment.

'Why do it, Gladys?' he asked quietly.

She turned to him, her face a mask of hatred. 'You don't have to worry what'll happen to you when you're too old to work. Your family left you with plenty. But not everyone's so lucky. The museum should've paid me more. I'm worth it. I was only taking what I'm due. After years of hard work, my pay's just enough to live on, but not enough to provide me with a comfortable future. Not that someone like you would understand the fear felt by someone like me,' she said bitterly.

'You don't know me very well, Gladys, if you think I'd have let you be destitute. The museum would have given you a pension when you retired.'

'Having to rely on scraps thrown from your table?' she sneered. 'I don't think so.'

One of the policemen indicated they must move, and Edward stepped back as Gladys went out through the front door, followed by the uniformed policemen and the detective.

'So she's lost her freedom for nothing,' Violet remarked a few minutes later when they heard the police cars drive away. 'How very sad.'

Edward stared at the figurine in his hand. 'When I said she didn't know me very well, that wasn't true. She did. And she knew she'd always be provided for. Whatever her motive, it wasn't that. I suspect that it was a touch of excitement in a lonely life, but I doubt we'll ever know the truth for sure.'

He glanced down into Violet's face and gave an exclamation. 'You're crying,' he said. 'But it's over now.'

She gazed up at him. 'I know,' she sobbed, laughing through her tears. 'But I can't stop. I think it's relief that it's all behind us and that it's turned out so well. And a part of me can't help being sorry for Gladys.'

He took his handkerchief from his pocket and with his free hand he gently wiped her face. Then he put his arm around her shoulders and drew her to him.

Her tears ceased.

'I'll leave you now,' they heard Lucy say.

Giving them a delighted smile as she passed them, Lucy opened the front door, turned the sign on the door to "Closed", went out and shut the door behind her.

41

The moon was large and glittering in the black velvet sky that lay high above Harry's Inn.

Far below the velvet canopy of night, Edward and Violet strolled hand in hand past Harry's and out to the distant dew-encrusted fields that were sheened with silver in the light of the moon.

'It's all so beautiful,' Violet said with a sigh. 'How I love it here.'

Edward stopped walking and turned to look down at her.

'Enough to stay here forever,' he asked, 'despite what's happened?'

She nodded. 'All that's in the past now. There's nothing that could make me want to leave. I love working in the museum, and I've so many ideas about what else we can do. The last thing I want is to go anywhere else.'

'Good,' he said.

They started walking again in companionable silence.

'Is it only the museum that makes you want to stay here?' he asked. And again he stopped walking.

'And I've come to love Harton, too,' she said, assuming an expression of gravity. 'If I went somewhere else, I'd have to leave the friends I've made, and that would be very sad.'

'Yes, it would,' he agreed, and they started walking again.

He stopped abruptly.

'I was hoping that I might be one of the reasons why you wanted to stay,' he said awkwardly. He took her hands in his. 'I know we decided to go slowly, giving us time to get to know each other. But I find I can't. '

'I see,' she murmured.

He took a deep breath. 'I must seem to you like someone who's always focused on work and is very serious, and very teacher-like at times. And to be honest, I *am* quite serious as a person and I'm serious about my work. But I love life, too. You've not yet seen that side of me because I was engaged to Jean for a lot of the time we've known each other. It means I've never been able to show you my lighter side. But there is one.'

He stopped talking and stared hopefully at her.

'And?' she asked quietly, trying to keep from smiling with happiness.

'And I'm trying to tell you how much I love you. That from the moment I met you, you're all I've been able to think about. That I couldn't bear it if you moved away. That I desperately want to marry you.'

Her face broke out into a radiant smile. 'And I want to marry you. I love you so much, Edward. I've so done since the day we met. For weeks I've been ordering myself not to think about you every single minute of every day, but I could never get myself to obey. I love you so much that there's nothing I want more than I want to marry you.'

'Oh, Violet!' he exclaimed in sheer delight. He turned to face the sparkling fields. 'Can you hear that, Harry?' he yelled into the distance. 'The most wonderful girl in the world loves me, and I love her. Oh, how I love her.'

He turned back to Violet. 'I love you with all my heart, Violet Hammond, and I always will.'

Cupping her upturned face in his hands, he bent his head to her waiting lips and kissed her long and hard.

IF YOU ENJOYED THE WOVEN LIE ...

... it would be very kind if you could take a few minutes to leave a review of the book.

Reviews give welcome feedback to the author, and they help to make the novel visible to other readers.

In addition, reviews help authors promote their books as a number of promotional platforms now require a minimum number of reviews.

Your words, therefore, really do matter.

Thank you!

LIZ'S NEWSLETTER

You might like to sign up for Liz's newsletter. Liz sends out a monthly newsletter with updates on her writing life, where she's been travelling, and an interesting fact she's learned. Subscribers also hear of promotions and offers.

Liz would never pass on your email address to anyone else, and if you write to Liz, which you can do through her website, you will always get a reply.

As a thank you for signing up for Liz's newsletter, you'll receive a free novel.

To sign up and get a free book, go to Liz's website:

https://lizharrisauthor.com

INTRODUCING: DARJEELING INHERITANCE

The Woven Lie completes the trilogy Three Sisters, which began with *The Loose Thread* and *The Silken Knot*.

You might not be familiar with my series, The Colonials, however, which comprises four novels set in Asia in the 1930s, the time of the British Raj - *Darjeeling Inheritance*, *Cochin Fall*, *Hanoi Spring* and *Simla Mist*. Each is a stand-alone that is complete within itself.

A fifth novel, set in Jaipur, India, will be published in autumn/fall 2025.

If you haven't yet read *Darjeeling Inheritance*, the first book in the series set in Asia, you might be interested in reading its Prologue, which you will find in the next few pages.

DARJEELING INHERITANCE: THE PROLOGUE

In the foothills of the Himalayas,
Darjeeling, April, 1919

The early spring sun beat down on the back of the seven-year old girl as she struggled to keep up with the man in a worn safari suit who was striding ahead of her up the steep path. Every so often, the girl slipped and fell on the red earth, picked herself up, brushed the dirt from her dress and hurried more quickly after the man.

But Charles Edwin Lawrence, lines of grief etched deep into his sun-browned face, neither turned to his daughter nor paused to wait for her. His eyes fixed in front of him, he continued resolutely up the narrow path that led between the tiered rows of tea bushes, the tender young leaves of which shone brilliant green in the light of the sun.

When he arrived at the summit, he stood in the cool breeze and stared down at the neat rows of terraces that fell away beneath his feet.

His vision blurred with unshed tears, he turned to face the mass of dark green forested slopes that rose in layers beneath the clear blue sky, and the range of mountains behind them, their gold-tipped peaks linked in a chain of gold above the snow-covered slopes, as if suspended in nothingness.

The girl reached the place where her father stood, slid her arm round his leg and put her thumb in her mouth.

He glanced down at her, bent slightly and gently pushed her thumb away from her mouth. 'Only babies do that, Charlie. You're not a baby any longer.'

'I'm seven now.'

He nodded. 'That's right. So you're not a baby any longer, are you? You're a big girl, who'll soon be off to school.'

Biting her lower lip, she stared at the ground and nodded.

She sensed him smile his approval.

Glancing up, she saw tears on his cheeks, and she frowned. 'You're crying. You've got a wet face.'

He shrugged his shoulders dismissively. 'It'll just be perspiration. I suggest you look at the view instead of looking at me.'

Picking her up under her arms, he swung her high up above his head, and slid her on to his shoulders. Her legs hung down in front of him on either side of his face, and he took hold of each foot.

Clutching his forehead with one hand, she ran her other hand down the side of his cheek.

'You *are* crying, Papa,' she said, her voice accusing, and she wiped her wet hand on the skirt of her dress. She pulled the *topi* from his head, let it fall to the ground, wrapped her arms around his chin, leaned forward, and rested her cheek against the back of his head. 'Is Eddie ill again? I haven't seen him today.'

She felt him tighten. He pulled one of her feet closer to the other so that he could hold them both with one hand, and she wobbled as he swiftly ran his free hand across his face. Then once more, he held a foot in each hand.

'Yes, he's been ill again,' he said after a short pause.

Her forehead wrinkled with puzzlement at the strange note she heard in his voice. She inclined herself sideways in an attempt to see his face.

'But not any longer,' he added quietly. 'He's gone to join your brothers.'

She straightened up and let out a wail of misery. 'I don't want him to go. I want him to play with me.' A sob rose in her throat, and she screwed up her face, ready to cry.

'You're not going to cry, are you, Charlie? Remember what we said about you being a big girl. Well, I need you to be big. Kick your foot against me if you're going to be big.'

She swallowed her sob, and with his hand still tightly holding her leg, kicked his chest with her right foot.

'Good girl,' he said. 'You see, it's just you and me now. And all of this.' Slowly he turned in a full circle, with Charlie sitting high on his shoulders. 'Just look at it all. Sundar is Hindi for beautiful. You can see why my father called it Sundar. We love it here; it's where we want to be. My grandfather and father both loved Sundar, and so do we, you and me. Isn't that so?'

She nodded.

'Say it, Charlie. Say, It's where I want to be.'

'It's where I want to be,' she echoed.

'Good girl. Look around you. I bet you've never noticed that tea bushes don't grow all year round—they're asleep from late November to early March. They won't wake up and start growing again until the first rains of spring have fallen and the sun has warmed the air. But then they'll grow so quickly that they'll need to be plucked every four to five days. Did you know that?'

She shifted her position.

'Hold tight,' he said, 'and I'll get you down.' He raised his arms, lifted her up over his head and stood her on the ground next to him.

Then he knelt down beside her and stared into her face. 'There's only you left now, Charlie. There won't be any more.'

She felt a momentary fear at his serious expression, and put her thumb back into her mouth. 'But I know that Sundar's in your heart, just as it's in mine, and when the time comes I'll do my very best to make sure you have a husband who'll be able to run the garden when I've gone, and who'll continue to grow the very best tea that Darjeeling can produce. There'll always be a Lawrence at Sundar. That's what we both want, isn't it?'

She could tell that he wanted her to nod, so she did.

He gave a dry laugh, and stood up. 'You've no idea what I'm talking about, have you?' he said, his voice relaxing. 'But one day you will.' He gave a playful tug on the long auburn hair that hung from under her *topi*.

She stared up at his face, and saw that his eyes were red and he still looked sad, even though his mouth was shaped into a smile.

'It's where I want to be,' she repeated.

His smiled broadened, and this time his eyes smiled, too, and she felt a glow of happiness spread through her.

She was very sad that Eddie had gone to join the two older brothers she'd never met. She'd loved Eddie and had been looking forward to him being old enough to play with her, and now she was left with only the servants' children to play with and her *ayah*. But she was happy that her father thought that she and he were alike. She wouldn't have wanted to be like her mother, who always seemed angry.

'I want to grow tea, too, Papa,' she said.

Her father laughed. 'Like I said, you're a Lawrence through and through, Charlie.' He leaned down and hugged her. Then he straightened up and stared again at the terraces that lay below them and on either side.

His gaze drifted across the verdant bushes to the house where the last of his sons lay, silent ever more, and his smile faded.

ACKNOWLEDGEMENTS

Yet again, I have to thank my brilliant cover designer, Jane Dixon-Smith, for another striking cover that perfectly captures the tone of the novel, and my excellent editor Richard Sheehan for his sterling work.

A huge thank you also to my Friend in the North, Stella. Stella is always the first person to see my completed manuscript and she's never failed, in all the years I've been writing, to give me constructive criticism. I value her input more than I can say.

Before I began to write *The Woven Lie*, I went to stay in Bury St Edmunds for research purposes. I had never been there before and it surpassed my expectations. It's a really lovely graceful little town. One of the things I did when staying there was look for an area just outside the town where I could locate the fictional village of Harton. Armed with a map of Suffolk in the 1940s, which showed me the roads that had been built by that time, I found exactly what I was looking for.

As always when writing a novel, I drew upon a number of books for information. To name but a few: *Suffolk Summer*, by John T. Appleby; *The NHS 1948-2020*, by Susan Cohen; *Nurse on Call*, by Edith Cotterill; *The NHS - beginning, middle and end*, the autobiography of Dr John Marks, and *Bury St Edmunds History Tour*, by Martyn Taylor.

If there are any mistakes in what I've written, the fault will be mine alone.

Finally, once again I'd like to thank my husband, Richard, for all the support I receive from him. It would be much harder to write my books if I weren't able to close my study door and live in my fictional world for so much of the day.

ABOUT THE AUTHOR

Born in London, Liz Harris graduated from university with a Law degree, and then moved to California, where she led a varied life, from waitressing on Sunset Strip to working as secretary to the CEO of a large Japanese trading company.

Six years later, she returned to London and completed a degree in English, after which she taught secondary school pupils, first in Berkshire, and then in Cheshire.

In addition to the nineteen novels she's had published, she's had several short stories in anthologies and magazines.

Liz now lives in Berkshire. An active member of the Romantic Novelists' Association and the Historical Novel Society, her interests are travel, the theatre, reading and cryptic crosswords. To find out more about Liz, visit her website at:

https://lizharrisauthor.com

ALSO BY LIZ HARRIS

Historical novels

The Colonials

Darjeeling Inheritance

Cochin Fall

Hanoi Spring

Simla Mist

The Linford Series

A sweeping saga set between the wars

The Dark Horizon

The Flame Within

The Lengthening Shadow

Distant Places

The Road Back

In a Far Place

The Heart of the West

A Bargain Struck

Golden Tiger (formerly The Lost Girl)

A Western Heart (to be published December 2024)

Three Sisters

The Loose Thread

The Silken Knot

The Woven Lie

Contemporary novels

The Best Friend

Evie Undercover

The Art of Deception

Word Perfect

Translations into German

Eine Erbschaft in Darjeeling

(Darjeeling Inheritance)

Liebe und Verrat in Cochin

(Cochin Fall)

Am Tagesende

(The Dark Horizon)

Die Wiederkehr

(The Flame Within)

Im Dämmerlicht

(The Lengthening Shadow)

Am seidenen Faden

(The Loose Thread)

Printed in Great Britain
by Amazon

62870365R00201